THE
WRECKED SERIES

Beneath
the
Wreckage

CATHERINE
COWLES

Editor: Susan Barnes
Copy Editor: Chelle Olson
Proofreading: Julie Deaton and Janice Owen
Paperback Formatting: Stacey Blake, Champagne Book Design
Cover Design: Hang Le

Beneath the Wreckage

Prologue

Piper

PAST

"WHAT DO YOU THINK?" JENN SPUN IN FRONT OF the skinny mirror on the inside of the closet.

"It's perfect." I flicked one of the small little rhinestone buttons in the shape of a flower. It was sophisticated, and the pale pink was beautiful against Jenn's summer-tanned skin. "I didn't think there was any way you'd need a sweater while we were here but I should've known better."

"Doesn't matter that it's summer; it's always freezing at night."

I should've remembered. Our families had been making our yearly trip to Anchor Island for as long as I could remember.

"Okay, finishing touches." Jenn motioned me forward so I stood in front of her. "Look down."

My gaze caught on the half of a heart around her neck that read: *Friends*. My fingers sought out my half, rubbing circles on it as Jenn swept something across my eyelids.

"Okay, finished. You can look." Jenn stepped behind me,

her hands on my shoulders. "My bestie is a stunner. Those high school boys won't know what hit them."

Facing the mirror, I rolled my eyes. "I just hope no one shoves me into a locker on the first day of class." The high school we were attending in the fall was so much larger than the middle school we'd gone to, and I wasn't exactly looking forward to the new experience.

She hooked an arm through mine, so we were looking at each other through the mirror. We were polar opposites. Jenn with her blond hair and long, sinewy form. Me with my dark hair and petite stature. But fourteen years of being hitched to each other's sides had made us more like sisters than friends, even if we looked nothing alike.

"We'll handle it like we do everything—"

"Together," I finished.

She grinned into the mirror. "I have a surprise…"

The mischievous glint in Jenn's blue eyes had my stomach dropping. "What?"

She stuck out her tongue at me in the mirror. "Don't be like that. It's a good one."

Jenn's *good* surprises could be anything from: I scored us some double fudge brownie ice cream, to we're going to toilet paper our pre-algebra teacher's house. "All right, spill."

"I ran into Ethan earlier, and he and his friends invited us to a party. They're having a bonfire up on the cliffs." She did a little running-man dance and let out a squeal.

That dropping sensation in my stomach turned to cramps. I should've known when Jenn had said she wanted to give us both a makeover that something was up. "I don't know." I wandered out into the main room of the cabin, Jenn on my heels.

"Come on, Piper. Pleeeeeease? It'll be fun, I promise."

I slid into a chair at the table, studying the drawing we'd been working on every night since we'd arrived at Whispering Falls a week ago. "You know my uncles wouldn't like it. Neither would your parents."

She leaned a hip against the table, looking down at me with that same mischievous smile. "What they don't know won't hurt them. And don't you want to start high school having gone to one party?"

I didn't. If I could avoid parties for the foreseeable future, that would be just fine with me. But that was something changing between Jenn and me. I was happy with how we usually spent our yearly vacation here—excursions with our families during the day, whale watching, hiking, shopping in town. And our nights working on our plans for when we'd buy the Falls one day, while our favorite movies played in the background.

"Come on," Jenn pleaded. "I really want to see Ethan again. And don't you want to hang out with Nick? You'll like it. He said they tell ghost stories at the bonfire. You're super into all of that."

No number of ghost stories could get me out of this cabin tonight. I had never lied to Nathan and Vic. Okay, I had never lied to them *after* I'd told them that a fox had kicked the soccer ball and broken the window when I was nine. I was pretty sure there were no foxes in Seattle, and the guilty look on my face had given me away. My uncles trusted me, and I didn't want to ruin that. "It's a stupid idea. I bet those guys don't even know you're fourteen. They wouldn't have invited you if they did." They must be at least sixteen—too old to be interested in an incoming freshman.

Jenn stiffened. "I told them I was in high school."

"But not a freshman," I challenged.

"It doesn't matter. What's going on with you? Are you scared or something?"

"I'm not scared. I just think that party's going to be lame, and as soon as they figure out how old you are, they're going to kick you out anyway. Why waste time?"

Jenn straightened from her perch against the table. "Well, I don't want to watch another lame old movie and doodle on those stupid plans. I want to have some fun. Live a little."

"Fine. Go without me, then." The words were out before I could stop them.

"I will." With that, she took off, slamming the door against the wall as she went.

Tears stung my eyes as I stared down at the map we'd been working on all week. The sketches of the buildings and the swimming pool blurred.

"What's going on? Jenn tore out of here like the cabin was on fire," Nathan asked as he entered, Vic in tow.

Concern laced Vic's features as he crossed to me. "What are these tears, Munchkin?"

I let him fold me into a hug, the familiar scents of cedar and something just a bit floral wrapping me in comfort. "It's nothing."

"Doesn't look like nothing to me," Nathan said, a bit of extra gruffness to his tone as he sat across from Vic and me.

I gave my head a little shake. "Just a fight. I think high school is going to be different…" I let my words trail off. I didn't know how to explain it. Everything felt as if it were changing, and all I wanted was for things to stay the same.

Nathan and Vic shared a look, and then Vic turned to face me. "Friends aren't always forever. Sometimes, they're just for a season. Others might fall away, only to come back when you least expect it. I have a feeling you and Jenn will find your way."

"Maybe." I couldn't imagine my life without her. We'd been friends for so long, she felt more like another limb. I took a shuddering breath. I could take it back, apologize tomorrow. Or maybe she'd have a horrible time at the party and realize that a movie night was better.

Nathan stood from the table. "Why don't I make sundaes, and we can pile onto the couch and watch that awful movie for the millionth time?"

Vic pressed his lips together to hide his chuckle, but he wasn't very successful. "You love *Troop Beverly Hills*. It's why you decided to lead Piper's Girl Scout troop."

Nathan leveled Vic with a glare. "Don't remind me of those dark days."

"The moms loved you, though," I offered.

"I thought I knew what being competitive meant, but I had no idea until we had to sell those damned cookies. I swear those moms would've sold a kidney to win one of those cookie prizes."

"Language," Vic chided.

I rolled my eyes. "I think I've heard the word *damn* before."

Vic pulled me into a tight hug and then covered my ears. "Let me keep you young and innocent forever."

I immediately went for his sides, where I knew he was ticklish. "What was that?"

Vic's hands flew off my ears with a shriek. "Uncalled for, young lady!"

Nathan just shook his head at the two of us.

Eventually, we settled onto the couch with bowls of ice cream in hand—extra whipped cream on mine, no peanuts, just the way I liked it. I burrowed into the couch cushions between the men who always had my back, no matter what life threw my way. But the ice cream sat heavily in my stomach, and I couldn't help but imagine where Jenn was. Wondered if she was having so much fun, she hadn't thought about me.

By the time the movie had ended, I was a walking zombie, brushing my teeth on autopilot and falling into bed. I pulled back the curtain to peek out the window. I saw no light on in Jenn's room at her cabin. My stomach twisted. Clearly, she was having way more fun than I'd thought she would. I lay back on my pillow and stared at the ceiling. It was a while before sleep finally came, and when it did, it was fitful. Dreams of being stuffed into a high school locker, kids laughing and pointing.

When an arm shook me awake, I thought it was because I'd screamed in my sleep. Nathan's face filled my vision. "Did you hear from Jenn last night?"

I blinked the sleep out of my eyes. "No." Cell phones barely worked on this end of the island. You had to stand in one of three spots to get service.

Nathan's jaw tightened. "Do you know where she was going? The truth, Piper."

My heartbeat fluttered, wings beating against my rib cage. "Sh-she wanted to go to a bonfire. With some high school kids. What's going on?"

He eased down onto the bed. "The Brantons can't find her. She wasn't in her bed this morning."

"What?" I croaked. Jenn might stay out late, but all night? Never.

Nathan took my hand. "No one's seen her. She's missing."

Chapter One

Piper

PRESENT

MY SUV JOLTED AS I GUIDED IT OFF THE FERRY RAMP and onto the streets of Anchor. Rolling down my window, I took in the scents of salt air and a hint of pine. The smell was the same, even ten years later. My heart gave a stutter step as I took in The General Store. We'd always stopped here directly off the ferry to stock up for our few weeks on the island, Jenn and I trying to sneak extra candy and cookies into the carts.

I let out a slow breath, trying to balance the healthy doses of nerves and excitement that flooded me. "We've got this. Right, Bruno?" I glanced in the rearview mirror as if my one-hundred-and-fifty-pound dog might answer me. Instead, his tongue simply lolled out of his mouth. "I'm taking that as a yes."

I guided my vehicle onto Main Street, following the steady stream of cars. It wasn't high season yet, but late spring brought a healthy dose of tourists to the small island. From what my realtor had told me, at the height of summer, the thirty-mile island could swell to over two thousand people. I just hoped some of those tourists stayed at Whispering Falls once I got her up and running.

I rolled down the back window so Bruno could feel the wind on his face. As soon as a crack appeared, he attempted to shove his massive head through the space. "Don't hurt yourself," I muttered.

Traffic moved slowly through town, a combination of too many vehicles and vacationers not knowing their way around yet. I didn't mind. It gave me a chance to take things in. The central street in town was mostly the same—the buildings, at least: a picturesque mix of Victorian, Craftsman, and raw brick. But many of the shops and restaurants had changed hands. Or maybe I'd simply forgotten in all my years away.

I smiled as I caught sight of The Catch Bar & Grill. Their BLTs and Shirley Temples had been my favorites, and I knew that Nathan and Vic would be thrilled to hear that the place was still in business. I saw an Italian restaurant I didn't remember from years past that looked promising. The ice cream shop and The Mad Baker bakery were still around. Farther down the street, an antiques and furniture shop called Second Chances looked new and had me wanting to pull over for a closer look.

"Tomorrow," I said to Bruno. "We'll come into town and check everything out." He lifted his head into the breeze as if to say that he liked the idea.

Traffic fell away as we drove out of town. The island had always been a mixture of historic neighborhoods, farmland, and protected nature preserves. I was relieved to see that none of that had changed. Glancing ahead, I took in Mount Orcas to the northeast. I couldn't wait to spend some time hiking her again, but I had a feeling I wouldn't be getting that wish anytime soon.

The road bent and curved, taking me away from the neighborhoods and through farmland. A handful of cows raised their heads as I drove by, and Bruno let out a bark. "You're not a city dog anymore. You're going to have to learn to make friends with creatures other than fellow dogs." I quickly glanced back at him in the rearview mirror. God, I hoped he didn't get into a tussle with some wild animal, thinking he was protecting me.

The paved road turned to gravel, and I was suddenly thankful that Nathan had insisted I trade in my sedan for an SUV. A pothole jarred my spine, further cementing my gratitude. After a few minutes of bouncing along, I came to a stop at the entrance to the property. The resort sign I remembered had clearly seen better days. The wooden posts holding up the sign were crooked, and *Whispering Falls Lodge & Resort* had faded to the point where it was barely readable.

It would be the first thing I fixed, I decided on the spot. And it wouldn't be hard. The posts themselves seemed to be in good shape; they simply needed to be secured better. A little paint and the sign would shine again.

I slowly took my foot off the brake and switched it to the accelerator. As the resort came into view, my chest constricted. Cabins dotted the hillside, leading up to the cliffs, and the lodge stood proud and majestic with a view of the sea, the old barn peeking out in the distance. Memories slammed into me, one after another, a slideshow of the good and bad. But no matter which kind passed, they left an ache in my heart that I wasn't sure would ever go away. Because I had come back without Jenn.

An SUV door slammed across the drive, jarring me free of my memories. I pulled into a spot near the other vehicle. As I climbed out, the woman waved.

"Welcome home," she beamed.

My lungs seemed to shake as I inhaled. *Home.* Thanks to foreclosure and the inheritance my grandparents had left behind—plus a healthy dose of insanity that made me think I could make this work.

Nathan and Vic certainly thought I was crazy. Even with degrees in hospitality and interior design, almost ten years helping with their restoration business, and two years working for a premier hotel in Seattle, they still worried. Maybe I was a little overly ambitious to tackle this alone, but I couldn't wait.

Losing Jenn had taught me that life was fleeting. When an opportunity presented itself to chase your dreams, you didn't let it slip through your fingers.

I gave my head a little shake and returned my realtor's smile. "Thank you. Are you okay with dogs? He's very well behaved."

Corrie's eyes widened a fraction as she took in Bruno's head, sticking out of my SUV's window. "Love them." I opened the back door, and Bruno immediately hopped out and went to meet the new person. Corrie stuck out a hand for him to sniff and then rubbed his head. "Aren't you a beauty?"

"He knows it, too."

Corrie chuckled, continuing to give Bruno scratches. "As he should." She looked up and met my gaze. "How was the trip?"

"Not bad at all. I'd forgotten how gorgeous the view is coming in on the ferry."

"Can't beat it." She stopped her petting, much to Bruno's dismay, and riffled through her purse, coming up with a set of keys that looked as if they should belong to a janitor. "The place is officially yours."

The ring of metal sat heavily on my palm—the weight of risking everything for a dream I'd never been able to let go of. "Thank you for all you did to make this possible." I hadn't been able to make it out to the island to see the place in person before I bought it, but I'd had my memories. And Corrie had sent me at least a hundred photos and had gotten the property assessed for me.

"It's more common than you'd think, people not being able to make it in from the city. Properties fly off the market faster than you can blink. This one, though…" Her words hung in the air as she pressed her lips together.

I chuckled. "Let's be honest. Someone would have to be a little crazy to buy this place."

"You said it, not me. Were you able to get in touch with Hardy Construction?"

I kept an eye on Bruno as he explored the property around us, seemingly following some invisible scent trail. "I did. The owner's coming out next week to finalize everything, and I think they'll be able to start a few weeks after that."

What I needed was someone to start yesterday, but quality work was better than quick work. And in the meantime, I'd just have to be patient and do what I could to get the place in shape. Thankfully, I still worked the occasional weekend on one of Nathan and Vic's sites. The knowledge and practice I'd gained there should give me a bit of a head start.

Corrie slid a tablet out of her purse. "That's wonderful. I've got three summer-long rentals already booked for you. The details and copies of the leases have been sent to your email. And I've got a few more maybes."

"That's perfect." I would need to fill as many usable cabins as possible to help cover the renovation costs. "And your assessor said those cabins are workable?"

"He did. And I did a second walkthrough of the ten on the north side. They're going to need a good cleaning, but everything works."

Cleaning, I could handle. I had a couple of weeks before anyone would arrive, and the summer-long rentals didn't include meals or a maid service unless it was specifically requested. Which meant I had some breathing room.

"Thank you for everything, Corrie. You've gone above and beyond."

"I'm happy to help." Her gaze swept the property around us.

"I'm glad someone's going to bring this place back. It's been empty for far too long."

My hand moved to the necklace that dipped under my shirt—the little half of a broken heart with *Best* on the front and *Piper* on the back. I hoped I was up to the challenge. Because if I could bring Whispering Falls back to life, then maybe I'd be able to keep a piece of Jenn with me always.

⟜⊙

I pulled open the door to the coat closet, and the doorknob fell off in my hand. I stared at it as a cloud of dust plumed around me. I let out a series of violent sneezes, each one worse than the one before as if some sort of allergy demon had possessed my body. Sinking to the floor, I rubbed at my eyes. "This is bad," I muttered to Bruno.

I wished the doorknob was the first thing to break off in my hand, but it wasn't. The pulls on more than one kitchen drawer had suffered the same fate. The handle to my shower door. And last but not least, the pull chain on one of the antique toilets. I wasn't even going to try to fix that one.

Bruno looked at me with judgmental eyes from his bed in the corner, silently asking why the hell I had yanked him from his sleek loft in downtown Seattle and brought him to this rundown lodge in the middle of nowhere. The call of nature and the new smells had lost their appeal when he took in where he'd be sleeping.

"Don't give me that look. It's going to be great." I wasn't sure if I was talking more to Bruno or myself. Neither was a good sign. But I'd give myself a pep talk daily if that's what it took.

I glanced around the large room. It wasn't that bad. More than anything, it needed a thorough cleaning, just as Corrie had said. Once I did that, I'd be able to see what I was dealing with. And maybe the lodge I remembered from all the summers I'd spent here would start to reappear.

I sighed and pushed to my feet. "You want to go for a ride?" The little traitor perked right up at that and bounded to my side. "Sure, now you like me." I headed outside and towards my SUV. Pulling open the back door, Bruno hopped up. He likely hoped I was taking him back to Seattle and away from this falling-down nightmare covered in dust and grime.

I climbed into the SUV and started the engine, taking a moment to soak in everything around me. Yes, the cabins that dotted the hillside needed a little work, as did the landscaping, but none of that detracted from the pristine beauty surrounding us. I rolled down my window and took a deep breath, the familiar scents easing the panic that had a firm hold on my body.

The land extended as far as the eye could see and was all mine. And I would make it sing again. From the cliffs that dropped off to the sea to the rocky beaches and the dock below, to the forest and the rolling hills. I could picture all the families and friends who would come through here, filling the Craftsman-style bungalows and log cabins. One day, there would be weddings and family reunions.

I'd expand and build a spa and more cabins. We'd have guides to take the guests out on fishing and whale-watching trips. I'd bring in glamping tents and install hot tubs at some of the cabins, just like Jenn had wanted.

I rubbed at the space between my breasts that always burned when a memory of her hit—the spot where my necklace lay. "One day," I promised myself. "But first, I need to clean." I'd used the last of my wipes and dusters while cleaning the bedroom and bath I was using at the lodge. I needed supplies, and it would take a lot of them.

The resort was on the farthest northern point of Anchor, the quaint downtown area a good twenty minutes away. It meant that cell service, internet, and power were iffy, to say the least.

But it also gave the feeling of being removed from the rest of the world, and that was precisely what vacationers wanted.

It was something I realized I needed, as well. Quiet and peace. It was so easy to get caught up in Seattle. Working too many hours, agreeing to too many dinners out, squeezing in time with my uncles. My life was full, but I rarely had time to just…be. To slow down and appreciate my surroundings—not that they were as beautiful as this. My new life on Anchor would force me to be more present, and I wasn't mad about it.

I guided my SUV down the bumpy gravel road and sighed in relief when I hit pavement. A smile stretched across my face as I drove through downtown. I couldn't wait to really explore. I wanted to frequent as many shops and restaurants as possible so I could give guests catered suggestions of where to visit and eat.

I turned left and headed just a few blocks away from Main Street, pulling into the local hardware store's parking lot. I needed heavy-duty cleaning supplies and not the stuff I would find at the grocery store. I also needed at least a hundred shop rags. Probably more. Buckets and a mop instead of the little disposable doodads I'd been using up to this point were also on the list. Heck, a hazmat suit probably wouldn't be a bad idea either.

A wave of anxiety swept through me as I pictured just how much work needed to be done. Seeing the photos was one thing. Seeing it live and in person as the dust set off an allergic reaction, and my muscles were already weeping from cleaning a single room, was another. I pulled in a long and steadying breath. Just one step at a time.

As I backed into my parking spot, my phone buzzed in the cupholder. I glanced down at the screen.

Vic: *You getting settled okay?*

Before I could type out a reply, another message popped up in our group chat.

Nathan: *Make sure you have your pepper spray and get emergency supplies as soon as possible. You shouldn't drive in a storm on that island.*

Me: *Don't worry. I've picked up a few hitchhikers to keep me company and took lots of candy from strangers on the ferry, so I should be good.*

Nathan: *Not funny.*

I grinned down at my phone. I could practically hear Nathan's growl.

Me: *I'm fine. Just getting to the hardware store to pick up supplies. Pepper spray is in my purse, and I've got enough bottled water to get me through an apocalypse. Love you both. Stop worrying.*

Vic: *It'll never happen. Worrying is our job.*

I sent a few heart emojis in return and climbed out of my SUV, leaving the window cracked for Bruno. Heading into the store, I picked up one of the jumbo carts. I would need it. I winced, thinking about how much this shopping trip would cost. But it was unavoidable. Renters wanted clean cabins, and I didn't think my allergies would survive a week living in a dust tunnel. I mentally added a mask to my list. That might help.

I took my time, slowly weaving my way up one aisle and down the other. Wandering in a store with no real hurry was one of the simple pleasures in life. But as I passed each section, my anxiety ratcheted up a level. Each display of tools and supplies reminded me of something that needed to be done at the Falls.

I stopped in front of a display of industrial cleaners and supplies. "One step at a time," I whispered to myself. "And the first one is a clean surface so I can evaluate."

"Are you okay?"

My head snapped up at the question. I'd been lost in my frantic struggle to escape the downward spiral of my thoughts and hadn't noticed the blonde next to me. I couldn't help the slightly hysterical laugh that escaped. "No. I'm really not. I bought a resort, and I'm in so over my head, it's not even funny. Things are falling apart left and right. There's enough dust in the buildings that I'm going to become a permanent asthmatic. And I'll have to get extremely creative if I have a prayer of bringing the place back to life."

The woman let out a full and uninhibited laugh and then held out a hand. "I'm Bell Kipton. And you must be Piper."

Heat hit my cheeks. "I'm not sure I even want to know how you know my name after I just unloaded like that."

Bell waved a hand in front of her face. "Please. We all have days like that. And it's a small island. News travels when someone buys a place like the Falls."

Small-town life would be an adjustment. "It's nice to meet you."

"You, too. I promise folks around here are welcoming, and I have a feeling you'll get the place up and running in no time. If you need an extra hand with anything, just stop by Second Chances. That's my shop. I'll be happy to help."

The kindness of her offer was almost painful. A reminder that I wasn't supposed to be on this journey alone. "Thank you," I croaked out. "I hope you're right."

Hunter

I WINCED AS I FLIPPED THE CHICKEN ON THE GRILL BUT KEPT right on moving through the pain. If I didn't start using my arm again, I'd never truly heal. But the months of slow progress were about doing me in.

"Still bugging you, huh?"

My brother handed me a beer, and I took a slow sip, buying myself some time. "My physical therapist says it'll be a few months before I'm back to one hundred percent. But I'll get there." I had to. I had no backup plans or emergency exits. My construction company was my life. And part of that career meant being physical.

Ford nodded slowly. "You're going crazy, aren't you?"

"I'm about ready to crawl out of my skin." I'd gone by the project site to check on my crew no less than half a dozen times in the last few days alone.

"You really think you're ready to start that big resort job?"

I opened my mouth to say something that would probably sound more like I was biting Ford's head off, but then I saw the worry lining my brother's face. I'd put him and my parents through hell after I'd been shot. None of them needed the stress—especially my dad, who'd had a bad stroke a couple of years back. "I'm going to take it slow. I promise."

Ford took a pull from his beer. "I know you, Hunt. You'll go slow for about an hour, and then you'll be bursting at the seams to bring your vision to life."

He wasn't wrong. It was how I always operated. There was no high like seeing the thing in your mind come to life in the buildings around you. And I'd been itching to get my hands on the resort for almost a decade. The more years that passed, and the more significant disrepair it fell into, the more I'd considered buying it. The problem had always been what the hell I would do with it after I restored it. This was the best of both worlds. I'd get my hands on the old girl and not have to deal with the aftermath.

I brushed a touch more marinade on the chicken. "I know I'll only set myself back if I push too hard. That should keep me in check. The last thing I want is to be laid up in your guest room again with Bell clucking over me like a mother hen."

Ford grinned. "At least, you've made it to the Airstream now."

I glanced out at the silver trailer that had been sitting a few hundred yards from Bell and Ford's place since before I was shot. "You know a door means nothing to Bell. She'll just come bursting in, asking if I've had breakfast, did my PT exercises... It's never-ending."

"I heard that," Bell's voice sounded as she appeared in the frame of the back door.

Ford let out a low whistle. "You're in for it now."

"You know it's the truth. Mothering might as well be your second language," I griped.

Bell crossed her arms in front of her chest. "Well, maybe if you weren't so indecisive, you'd have a house of your own by now instead of living in our driveway."

"I'm not indecisive. I just want to find the perfect spot to build."

Ford snorted. "You've bought over a dozen tracts of land over the last couple of years, only to turn around and sell them a few months later."

"Perfection takes time," I argued. And each piece of land I'd purchased was just that: the place where I would finally build my dream home. The house that had been coming together in my mind since I first started working construction in high school. But after purchasing the properties and living on them in my trailer for a couple of months, I inevitably started seeing all the flaws. So I'd sell and start all over again.

I'd tried beachfront, clifftop, forest, mountainside, and rolling farmland. Nothing was exactly right. And I refused to settle.

Bell shook her head and rolled her eyes heavenward. "Land and women. He can never make up his mind where either is concerned."

I pointed the grill tongs at her. "Hey. I resent that—"

"Because it's the truth?" Ford cut in.

I narrowed my eyes at my brother. "If I remember correctly, you lived quite the bachelor lifestyle in LA before settling down with sweet Bell here. I'm not sure you're one to judge."

Bell scoffed. "He really shouldn't. I, on the other hand, can judge you both."

"You're gonna pay for that," Ford murmured in my direction.

I couldn't hold in my laughter. "Thank God, you two got your shit together. We'd all be miserable if you hadn't."

Bell slipped under Ford's arm. "He really is lucky he snagged me."

"I am." Ford brushed his lips across hers.

I rubbed at the phantom pain in my chest and turned my focus back to the chicken, flipping it one more time. I'd always felt at ease with dating when it suited me, being single when that did the same, but as all the people in my life seemed to be settling down and starting families, I couldn't help but feel as if I were missing out.

I'd always wanted that. Nothing about being a perpetual bachelor appealed to me. But I'd always been more than happy to wait until the right woman came along. I'd thought a few might be it, but ultimately, they hadn't been right.

I wanted what my parents had. What my brother and friends had found. A person who seemed to balance them out perfectly. And I didn't have the first idea of what that felt like.

"Earth to Hunter..."

I glanced up at Bell's voice. "Sorry, what?"

"I said I met your new boss."

I took the chicken off the grill and placed it on a platter. "Really? Did she scream '*city*?'" I'd talked to Piper Cosgrove a handful of times on the phone. She seemed nice enough, but I had a feeling that she didn't have the first clue what she was getting herself into.

Bell shook her head. "I didn't get that vibe. She did seem overwhelmed by all the work that needs to be done, though, so go easy on her." Bell glanced at Ford, a mischievous smile stretching across her face. "She's also gorgeous."

Ford sighed. "Do not get some wild matchmaking hair, please."

She shoved at his chest. "I'm a great matchmaker. Look at Kenna and Crosby."

"Kenna almost killed Crosby at least a dozen times before they ended up together," Ford argued.

"But they're happy now, aren't they?"

I shoved the chicken into Bell's hands. "As adorable as this weird fighting foreplay you guys get into is, I'd really love to eat dinner in the next century, and I won't be able to do that if you two have to go lock yourselves in a room."

Bell blushed. "I'll go get the salad."

Ford smacked me upside the head. "I can't wait until you meet someone. I'm gonna cheer when she knocks you on your ass."

"Naw, I'm way too even-keeled for that."

Ford glanced over his shoulder as he headed for the house. "We'll just see about that."

Chapter Three

Piper

THE LITTLE SPEAKER I'D SET ON THE TABLE IN THE MIDDLE of the lodge's main room blared out eighties' pop songs. The synthesized refrains and copious amounts of Diet Coke I'd ingested were the only things keeping me going this morning—that and the slightly feral panic I felt at getting this place ready in time for guests.

Bruno gave me a forlorn look from his bed in the corner. Anytime I got close, he turned his head as if he couldn't bear to look at me. I pretended that was because I was currently wearing both goggles and a face mask in an effort to block out the dust, but it was probably because he was still mad at me for taking him away from his comfy home.

I gave his head a little scratch. "You'll have so much more space to roam here. I promise I'm going to get the lodge up to your standards." He ducked his head out of my reach and stood. "That was not nice." He walked out the back patio's doors.

"Whatever." I returned to my battle with the dust. Climbing onto a chair that looked as if it had seen better days, I used the extension duster to clean the rustic chandelier that provided most of the light for the room. It was gorgeous. The combination of metal and wood appeared to have been in the room for decades.

That was the thing about the Falls. Almost everything I came across had the potential to hold countless stories—over a century's worth. Something about knowing that I would be a part of history lit up every part of me. And only made me more determined to make this place shine again.

The last two decades had been hard on the resort. The owner, Albert Crowley, had fallen on hard times and had slowly let the place go. It had been vacant for years before the bank foreclosed on the property. I hated that Mr. C. had been struggling so much, but I couldn't find it in me to regret that the Falls was now mine.

I stretched up on my tiptoes, trying to reach the very top of the chandelier. I could see a pile of dust just out of my reach, taunting me. I let out a slew of mental curses at being so short.

"What the hell do you think you're doing?"

The barked question startled me so much that I lost the little bit of balance I had. My arms windmilled, the duster went flying, and I was soon falling. I landed with a muffled "oomph" against a hard chest. The man muttered a curse as I struggled to get out of his hold.

Where had I put the pepper spray Nathan had given me? I was pretty sure it was tucked neatly in my purse—that was still in my bedroom. Blast it. "What are you thinking just walking in here and scaring the life out of me?"

The man's jaw flexed, highlighting the sharp planes of his face and the glint in his dark green eyes. "What am *I* thinking? You were practically hanging from the chandelier. You could have gotten yourself killed."

"I was perfectly fine until you scared me. Do you know you're on private property?"

"I was asked to come here. And maybe if you weren't playing that ear-bleeding music so loud, you would've heard me knock."

I straightened. "You're Hunter?" Taking in the man from head to toe, I let out another stream of curses in my mind. He was tall with broad shoulders and a lean, muscled form. But the dark green eyes froze me to the spot. It was as if they could see right past my defenses.

"That would be me," he said with a grimace as he rubbed his shoulder.

"Shit. Did I hurt you?"

"I'm recovering from a shoulder injury."

"Oh, God. I'm so sorry. Are you okay? Do you need an ice pack? A doctor?" Just the first impression I was trying to make, injuring my contractor before he'd even toured the grounds.

Hunter's brows rose at my outburst. "I'm fine." He rolled his shoulder as if testing it. Only a small wince crossed his features. "No harm done." He glanced at the speaker. "Other than to my ears."

I hurried to shut off the music as Cyndi Lauper sang *Time After Time*. "Not a fan of the eighties?"

"Got nothing against the decade. The music leaves something to be desired."

My lips twitched. "I'll keep that in mind." I met Hunter's gaze and swallowed. "I really am sorry about all that."

"Me, too. For scaring you. But you can't be doing stuff like that, especially if you're alone. And you need a sturdier ladder."

I looked at my pathetic cleaning setup. If Nathan had seen me, he would've read me the riot act, too. "I know, but the one in the storage shed looks about ready to give out, and I didn't want to go back into town, just for a stupid ladder."

Hunter scrubbed a hand over the thick stubble on his jaw. "I've got one in my truck you can use for now. And I can pick one up at the hardware store next time I stop by."

"You don't have to—"

He cut me off with a look, and I had the burning desire to stick out my tongue at him. Instead, I simply said, "Thank you."

A low growl sounded as Bruno appeared at my side.

"What in the ever-loving hell is that thing?"

I gave my dog a scratch between the ears. "This is Bruno. Bruno, friend." I touched Hunter's arm. "Friend." Bruno relaxed and sat at my side.

"Is he part bear? Lion?"

I rubbed Bruno's head, and he head-butted my hand. "He's a Tibetan Mastiff."

Hunter's gaze ran up and down my furry friend. "He looks like he weighs more than I do."

"Only one-fifty."

"Only," Hunter scoffed. He took a couple of cautious steps towards me, and held out a hand for Bruno to sniff, and then scratched his head. "He's going to terrify guests."

"He is not. Bruno loves people."

"Yeah, that growl really convinced me. Maybe you can build him a crate."

Bruno ducked out of Hunter's reach as if he understood every word that had come out of the man's mouth.

"Don't say the C-R-A-T-E word. He'll think I'm about to take him to the V-E-T," I whispered.

Hunter's mouth quirked. "Are you seriously spelling so your dog won't understand you?"

"He's very smart."

"I'll take your word for it."

"Whatever," I mumbled. "How about we focus on the resort?"

Hunter moved in closer. "Might help me take you seriously if you lost…this—" He slid my goggles to the top of my head. "—and this." He tugged down my mask.

My face flamed. I'd gotten so used to wearing the damned

things that I'd forgotten I had them on. "I'm not doing well with all the dust."

"Always good to play it safe," Hunter said with a smirk.

I had the sudden urge to chuck my goggles at his too-good-looking face. "I don't really care what you think about my getup."

"Fair enough. How about we walk the grounds and figure out a plan of attack?"

I pulled off my goggles and mask and set them on the table next to my speaker. "Let's go." The sooner we walked the property, the sooner I could get back to work and erase this entire encounter from my memory. But, somehow, I wasn't sure that Hunter would be so easily forgotten.

Chapter four

Hunter

S HE WAS BEAUTIFUL IN A WAY THAT STOLE MY BREATH AND
froze my brain. Especially when she seemed flustered or
riled. And that only made me want to push her buttons.

Dumb. Dumb. Dumb. I didn't have many rules for my life,
but I did have one hard-and-fast one: No mixing business with
pleasure. I cared too much about the company I'd built to screw
it up by sleeping with a client. It didn't matter how gorgeous they
were.

I held open the door for Piper and watched as she walked
through in her cutoff denim shorts and sneakers splattered with
various shades of paint. The multiple colors had me curious.
I hadn't seen any signs of new paint around the resort, which
meant she'd worked on some sort of fixer-upper project before.
Or maybe she was an artist.

I knew nothing about the woman I would be working for,
other than the fact that she'd decided to drop a chunk of change
on a falling-down resort, and she'd come from Seattle. I'd been
expecting *city*. Someone who turned up their nose at hard work

and bugs. But if the layer of dust that clung to Piper was any indication, she had no issues rolling up her sleeves and diving in.

Although, at only a couple of inches over five feet, tackling anything on this property would take her twice as long. I grinned as she adjusted the mass of chestnut hair tied into some sort of bun on the top of her head. This project would be interesting, to say the least.

I fell into step beside Piper. "Where are we starting?"

In a mere handful of seconds, the scattered and flustered woman I'd met a few minutes ago was gone. In her place was someone focused and determined. "Let me walk you through my plan, and then you can tell me where you think it makes the most sense to begin."

"Sounds good to me." I pulled my phone out of my pocket and opened my notes app.

Piper pointed towards the north side of the property. "The ten cabins over there are in decent shape. I'll be spending the next week cleaning them from top to bottom so I can open them for use. I've got three summer-long renters who will be filling some of them. I'm hoping my realtor might find me a few more. That gives me at least a bit of income coming in."

She turned to the south. "Those ten over there are in worse shape. Some of them look like a tornado went through. They need a complete overhaul. I'm thinking you and your team can get those cabins in shape, and then when they're done, move on to the ones on the north side."

I nodded. Her plan was more than sound. "What about the lodge?"

"It's in pretty good condition. I think most of the work there is cosmetic. I can handle that. And some heavier stuff if I need to. I might be able to help your crew if time allows, and you're open to it."

I arched a brow in question. Piper shrugged. "My uncles have a home-restoration business in Seattle. I basically grew up on construction sites."

Each little piece she divulged pulled at me a little more. "If you can prove you know what you're doing, I'm always happy to have an extra set of hands."

Her eyes narrowed in my direction. "I've laid tile, hung my share of drywall, refinished floors, and painted so many walls I've lost count. I can have my uncle send you photos if you need the proof."

"No photos necessary." The fact was, I couldn't wait to see this slip of a woman in action.

"Good. You want to see the damage?"

I started towards the cabins on the south end of the property in answer. "Kids have been coming up here the last few years. Partying, mostly. I'd be shocked if they hadn't caused more than a little damage. Have you had any trouble since you moved in?" As my gaze traveled over the property, I thought about Piper up here all alone with poor cell service and spotty power. She needed satellite internet and generators. An alarm system. But at least she had that beast of a dog. I glanced at Bruno, who'd gone to sniff a bush...or maybe not.

"I've only been here a week, but it's been perfectly quiet." A small smile curved her mouth. "It's been nice. I'm used to city noise. This has been...restful."

"Except when you're blaring Cyndi Lauper."

"Except then." She turned to face me. "I'm guessing word's spread that someone bought the place. Shouldn't that be enough to scare people off?"

"Until you get more folks coming and going, it might not. The partying should stop, but some kids could come up here on a dare. It's supposedly haunted." I didn't want to think about the other reasons someone might come to a mostly abandoned resort. Darker ones.

"I always loved the ghost stories from this place."

I stopped and turned to face Piper. "You came here when Whispering Falls was open?" She didn't look familiar, but it had been years since the place had been up and running.

Her gaze swept the property as if something pulled her into a memory. "My uncles brought me here almost every summer. They got married on the cliff up top."

"Uncles, huh?" The prod was out before I could take it back. I couldn't seem to help the desire to know more about the woman currently weaving through this falling-down property, covered in dust and paint.

She pulled open the door to a cabin. "They raised me. My mom was way too young when she had me, and they stepped in."

She said it so matter-of-factly, my steps faltered. "That was good of them."

"They're the best. I'm sure they'll be out here sooner or later to check up on me. And they'll probably want to survey your work."

"I'll make sure I bring my A-game, then."

"Thank goodness. Now, tell me. Any ghosts in this cabin?"

I grinned at the hopeful look in Piper's eyes. "I think a woman supposedly haunts the lodge. It's rumored she hung herself in the mid-nineteen-hundreds after discovering that her husband had left her."

Any signs of humor fled from Piper's expression. "That's just sad."

"I don't imagine many ghosts are happy."

"I guess you have a point."

"There's supposed to be one that haunts the cliffs, too. A young man, waiting for his lost love to return. A couple more, but I honestly can't remember the stories."

She drummed her fingers on her bare thigh. "I might have

to make up my own. But I'm going to invent one of those happy ghosts. You know, like…what was his name?"

"Casper?"

Piper snapped her fingers and pointed at me. "That's the one. This place needs a happy ghost."

"Might have to start calling you Casper." This woman was a total kook. But it worked for her. Somehow, it was this potent mix of endearing and intriguing, and I didn't doubt she'd keep me on my toes for however long the job lasted. Glancing around the space, I had a feeling it would be a good while. "Someone really did a number on this cabin."

"Pretty much all the ones in this area look like this."

A chill skittered down my spine as memories swept in. A burst of pain and heat in my chest. The cold wood of the floor at my back. Telling Shay to run. Being so damned sure I was about to take my last breath. Everything was hazy after that—brief glimpses of things I couldn't place or make sense of.

"Hunter?"

Piper's soft voice brought me out of my spiral. "Sorry, what'd you say?"

She took a step towards me, looking as if she might reach out a hand, but then stopped herself. "Everything okay?"

"Fine." The words came out harsher than I'd intended, and Piper took an instinctive step back. "Sorry, just thinking about plans for the cabins. Got lost for a second." It was a total and complete lie. The dreams that haunted me had been dialed up a notch over the past few weeks. It was as though my mind needed to exorcise the demons there as my body healed. But that would be a hard task. There were too many people I'd failed. Too many who had stepped in to make up for my shortcomings.

"If you're sure…"

I looked up and met Piper's gaze. There were shadows there I hadn't noticed before. A weight *she* carried. I felt an instant pull to her, a desire to see what took up real estate in that brain of hers. To know if the voices sounded anything like the ones in my head. Yet, even with that tug, I couldn't find it in me to be honest with her. "Why wouldn't I be?"

She blinked up at me. "Sorry, none of my business." Piper started walking again. But as I steered us towards cabin eleven, she stumbled, seeming to miss a step.

I reached out a hand to steady her. "You all right?"

Her head snapped up, and she began walking again. "Totally fine."

Now who was lying?

Chapter
Five

Piper

"START INTERVIEWING FOR SUPPORT STAFF," NATHAN ordered. "You can't do this alone. You look ready to drop."

"I'm not doing it alone. Hunter's here." I angled my body so the camera on my phone pointed towards a corner of the lodge that looked in the best shape. This was, of course, the corner where I'd put Bruno's dog bed, and he grumbled at me taking up space.

"What about the rest of his crew?"

"They're finishing up another job right now. They'll be here in a couple of weeks, but Hunter said he could get started on a few things in the meantime." I hated the idea of him working alone when he was still recovering from a shoulder injury. It hadn't seemed to slow him down, though. I'd stopped by the cabin more than a few times to see if he needed anything, but I could tell that my hovering was driving him crazy. My mouth curved at the image of him scowling at me that filled my mind.

"What's that smile about?" Vic asked, crowding into the frame.

I immediately wiped the expression off my face. "I'm just excited about getting the rehab started."

"Mm-hmm," he answered knowingly.

I pointedly turned my gaze to Nathan. "And you'll be happy to know that I have an interview with a housekeeper this morning. She used to work for Mr. C., so she knows the ins and outs of the property." And she hopefully wouldn't run away screaming when she saw what bad shape the place was in.

"Glad to hear it. Are you sure you don't want us to come out there and help for a few weeks?"

My chest warmed at Nathan's offer, at the knowledge that he and Vic would always be there for me. "If you do that, you'll piss off who knows how many clients. And I know your waiting list is almost a mile long."

"Doesn't matter," he clipped. "We always have time for you."

"I know. And I love you for it. But I'm excited to tackle this on my own." And terrified that I would fall flat on my face.

"All right," Nathan grumbled.

The video was grainy thanks to barely-there cell service, but I could still make out Vic elbowing Nathan. "What is it?" I asked.

Vic grinned. "We got the Henley house."

"No way! That's amazing." My uncles had been dying to get their hands on one of the historic mansions on Queen Anne for as long as I could remember. It needed more than a little tender loving care, but they were up for the job. "Why didn't you tell me it had gone up for auction?"

Vic's expression gentled. "You've had a lot going on lately."

"Never too much to hear about things like this. I'm so happy for you guys."

"Thanks, Munchkin. We'll want your input, as always."

I chuckled. "I live to give my opinion."

"You know," Nathan began, "you could sell the resort after

you rehab it. Come work for Vic and me. No one has a better design eye than you."

I tried to reel in the flicker of annoyance. "This has always been my dream. Owning my own place, getting to make it mine. And there's something really special about it being somewhere that holds so many wonderful memories." My words hung in the air, no one speaking for a moment.

"I know this is what you've always wanted. But we worry about you, Pipe."

The use of Nathan's favorite nickname for me softened his words, but not enough. I pushed to my feet. "It's important to me."

"We know," Vic said, sending Nathan a stern look. "And we'll do anything we can to support you along the way. We just wish we could be there to help you."

The set of my shoulders eased a fraction. "I appreciate that. But I really can handle it. And if I have a crisis, I'll call."

"Good. I don't know how much it will ease this one's worrying, though." Vic ruffled Nathan's hair. "He doesn't like you running that place alone."

I rolled my eyes. "I have Bruno. And pepper spray. No one's going to mess with me."

Bruno lifted his head as if to ask, "*Really*?"

Nathan frowned at the camera. "Maybe I should come out there for a week and get some security installed. Check out this construction crew and make sure they're legit."

I sent Vic a pleading look. "Keep him under control, would you?"

"I'll do what I can, but I make no promises."

I let out a groan. "Just remember, all my money is tied up in this resort. I won't have anything for your bail if you get arrested for punching someone because they showed up at the Falls. You might be stuck there until your trial."

Nathan grinned. "Worth it."

"All right, guys, I need to go. My interview should be here any minute. Love you both."

"Love you, too," they echoed.

"Don't forget to send photos of the Henley house," I called as I hung up. Leaning down, I rubbed Bruno behind the ears. He let out another grumbling rumble. "I know. I miss them, too."

With one final scratch, I pushed to my feet. Surveying the space around me, I gave myself a nice pat on the back. It wasn't looking half-bad. I'd vanquished all the dust bunnies and scrubbed and polished every inch of the place. I hoped that people wouldn't notice some of the rougher edges once I'd filled it with furniture and décor.

I headed outside just as an older Volkswagen Camper van came to a stop with a puff of exhaust smoke. The only thing missing on the sky-blue van was a peace sign painted on the side. Crystals of all shapes, sizes, and colors littered the dashboard. A dreamcatcher hung from the rearview mirror. And the woman behind the wheel looked as if she should be headed to Woodstock instead of a job interview.

I blinked rapidly as she climbed out of the van. Somewhere in her mid-sixties, if I guessed correctly, she wore flowy, wide-legged pants covered in tiny flowers. The number of necklaces looped around her neck would've given me a headache, but she seemed to be full of energy as she crossed the space between us in a few long strides.

"You must be Piper." She extended a hand, taking mine. "I'm Celeste." Her eyes widened. "Ooooooh, good energy." Then she frowned. "But there are some shadows around your aura. Death in the family? No...breakup?"

I couldn't find words for the woman in front of me. I simply kept shaking her hand until I realized that it had been a good fifteen seconds. "It's so nice to meet you. Corrie, my realtor, said you used to work for Mr. Crowley." She didn't look familiar, but I hadn't been overly focused on the staff when I'd come here as a child and teen.

She looked around at the property. "For more years than I can count. I'll admit, it's nice to be back at the old place. I've missed it."

"And you're interested in taking on the housekeeping duties again?" It seemed like a lot of back-breaking work for someone Celeste's age. But I knew I couldn't handle it alone.

She laughed. "I'm stronger than I look. And I've been bored as sin lately. I liked working here—most of the time anyway. Got to meet all sorts of interesting people. And it kept me busy."

"Well, I'd love to have you if you want your old job back. I could use someone who knows their way around."

Celeste beamed. "I know all the nooks, crannies, and hidey holes. And, trust me, in a place like this one, there are a lot."

I laid out the salary terms, and she was more than agreeable. "Welcome aboard."

She reached out a hand to shake, making it official. "Happy to be back. Now, let's talk about regular cleanings."

Celeste and I walked the grounds, surveying the cabins that still needed cleaning in hopes of having a few more summer tenants taking up residence. She was far sprier than I could've ever expected as she started a to-do list on a cell phone that somehow didn't quite fit with the rest of her persona.

She glanced up. "You're starting the restorations on the south-end cabins?"

"That's the plan. Real construction will begin in a couple of weeks, but the contractor, Hunter, is getting a jump start now."

Celeste waggled her eyebrows. "Best-looking construction crew on the island. Good choice."

I chuckled. "Let's hope their work is just as good-looking."

"Oh, it is. And if you need help clearing the cabins of furniture,

I've got two grandsons who work for little pay and need to be kept out of trouble this summer."

"I think I'll take you up on that. Maybe they can come out tomorrow when you start? I was thinking of storing everything in the old barn." The property had housed horses at some point, and I could only dream of doing that again someday. But in the meantime, the barn was in pretty decent shape for storage.

"Perfect plan." Celeste pulled me into a hard hug. "We are going to make magic here." When she released me, she kept a hold of my shoulders and frowned. "You look so familiar."

"I used to come here during the summer with my uncles."

Celeste's hold on me stiffened. "You were friends with the Branton girl."

"I was." A memory sucker punched me out of nowhere. The dark waves as boats searched the water for any sign of Jenn. Hundreds of people gathered to search. But no one had found a single clue. It was as if she had simply vanished into thin air. And those of us who remained were left looking for her for the rest of our days.

That was the thing about being the one left behind. You couldn't help but look for your loved one in the face of every new person you met, scanning everyone you passed on the street, hoping against hope that she'd somehow simply appear again—even if your gut told you she'd never left the island you'd lost her on.

Chapter Six

Hunter

"**Y**OU WERE FRIENDS WITH THE *BRANTON* GIRL." THE
words echoed in my head as I watched Celeste drive
off. Piper stood there, staring off at the water. No
wonder she had shadows in her eyes.

I remembered when it happened—the summer before my
senior year. The whole island had been in an uproar. When a
search hadn't turned up anything, people had decided that the
girl likely had too much to drink and had fallen from the cliffs
into the water below. They were probably right, but as far as I
knew, nobody had found her body.

I'd had friends at the party that night. More than a few. They'd
seen the girl. Not the girl—Jenn. I could still see it written out
on a missing person poster. My friends had said that she'd been
drinking, but no one remembered her wandering off. She was
simply there one moment and gone the next.

I could only imagine what that had done to the people who
loved her. The unknown. They must have guessed that the
outcome wouldn't be good. She was far too young to run off

by herself. But all the questions could make a person go crazy, imagining one fate after the other—each one worse than the previous.

Piper had one arm wrapped around her waist, the other hand clutching at a necklace. She looked so damned alone in that moment. I couldn't resist moving closer. "I'm sorry about your friend."

She didn't jolt or jump. It was as if she had known I was there all along. "I guess there's more than one kind of ghost here."

There was more truth in Piper's words than she knew. There were plenty of events that haunted this land. "Maybe restoring this place to its former glory will exorcise a few of them."

"I'm not sure I want mine to be exorcised."

She kept staring at the sea, not turning to look at me. I came up beside her, the need to see her face clawing at me for some reason. When I took it in, the only word I could come up with to describe it was…*ravaged*. As if grief had carved itself into the bones of her face, refusing to leave.

I had the urge to pull Piper into my arms. To drive out the pain and loss. But I barely knew her. "Is she why you bought the place?"

Her mouth curved. "We used to joke about it. Make all these grand plans for what we'd turn it into. Thought we'd run it together. Build houses and raise our families here. Maybe that's what planted the seed for me. Since college, I've worked towards opening my own place. I wasn't sure if it would be a B&B or a hotel, but when I saw the Falls pop up on a list of foreclosures, it just seemed…"

"Meant to be?"

Piper let out a chuckle. "That. But let's be honest, it's a little bit insane, too."

My lips twitched. "It's ambitious. But I have no doubt you can do it if you set your mind to it."

"From the guy who wasn't sure he wanted me working on his construction crew."

"I've seen the work you did on the lodge this past week. It's sound." It was more than that. It was damned good. I would've hired her in a second if she'd been looking for a job.

Piper turned towards me, the wind picking up some strands of her hair that had fallen free of her ponytail. "Good to know I haven't lost my touch."

"You certainly haven't. And since that's the case, why don't you come take a look at something?"

She laid a hand over her chest with a mock gasp. "Are you asking *me* for my construction opinion?"

"Such a smartass," I said, shaking my head. But that hint of mischief in Piper's eyes chased out the shadows, so I'd take smartass all day long.

She started towards the cabin I'd been working on. "Takes one to know one."

Her steps slowed as we approached number eleven, and I saw the hesitancy with new eyes now. "Did you used to stay in this one?"

Piper pulled open the door. "No. Eleven was where Jenn and her parents stayed."

Hell. Of all the places to start, I'd had to pick this one. "We can start the work somewhere else—"

"No. I think it's fitting that we start here." A small smile curved her mouth. "She always wanted a hot tub on the back deck. I'm going to have to figure out a way to make that happen."

I had no doubt she would. "How would you feel about some more drastic work inside?"

Piper opened her mouth to say something, then seemed to think better of it, shaking her head instead. "What were you thinking?"

I knocked on a wall that separated the living room from the

kitchen and dining spaces. "This isn't load-bearing, but all the cabins have them. Knocking them out wouldn't be a huge change in supply cost, just labor. And it would open up the spaces considerably."

She walked from the living room area to the kitchen space and back again. "It'll give us a lot better light, too." Piper's mind seemed to whirl as she stared at a point on the wall. "Let's do it. I can help with taking down the walls." She paused and glanced in my direction. "Can your shoulder handle that kind of thing?"

The flex of my jaw was involuntary. A necessary measure I'd developed to keep from biting people's heads off when they asked about my injury. "I'll go slow."

I'd need to move at a snail's pace. My shoulder was already acting up with only a few days of work. I'd spent last night icing it and popping a few ibuprofen. I rolled it reflexively. The movement pulled, the minuscule flare of pain triggering a patchwork of memory. The fire in my shoulder. Shay running out the door of a cabin that looked identical to this one.

"And you'll let me help?"

Piper's voice pulled me out of the images overtaking my mind. I gave myself a good mental shake. "Sure. I can always use grunt labor."

She stuck out her tongue at me. "That's boss grunt to you."

I chuckled. "I'll remember that."

Chapter Seven

Piper

I PULLED INTO A PARKING SPOT ON MAIN STREET AND TURNED off my engine. "I'm sorry, buddy, you have to stay in the car. I don't think I can trust you in an antique shop." With my luck, Bruno would knock over something priceless with his tail.

He slumped down in the backseat. He'd seemed to forgive me for our move after his first game of fetch on the beach but being left in the SUV when he wanted to go exploring was never his favorite.

"I promise I won't be long. And I'll get you a treat on the way back." The Mad Baker had these adorable little cupcakes just for dogs that I knew would have Bruno drooling. He barked in response.

I rolled down the windows a crack, then climbed out and shut my door, beeping my locks as I walked away. I passed the bakery and a mail and copy shop before hitting Second Chances. An antique bell tinkled as I pulled open the door.

"I'll be out to help you in just a minute," a voice called from the back.

"Take your time," I returned.

I wound my way down one side of the narrow shop and knew that it wasn't Bruno at risk of drooling. It was me. The furniture pieces had been meticulously restored with a bit of whimsy in many of the color choices—lots of blue-green sea tones with the occasional pink pop. Even the more practical grays and browns had unique accents.

A sideboard made my breath catch, and I bent to peek at the tag. I then proceeded to nearly swallow my tongue. This place was way out of my price range.

"Piper, I'm so glad you stopped by," Bell greeted.

I straightened, releasing the piece of paper that might as well have burned my fingers. "I'm trying not to drool over your gorgeous pieces. Where did you find them all?"

She beamed. "I'm so happy you like them. I hunt just about everywhere. Garage sales, estate auctions. I've picked up more than a few pieces on the side of the road. My fiancé thinks I'm crazy."

"You found some of this stuff on the side of the road?" If that was the case, I clearly needed to start driving the neighborhoods of Anchor.

Bell chuckled. "Well, they didn't look like this before. I've restored just about everything in this shop. Not the little decorative odds and ends, but all of the furniture."

I surveyed the space with new eyes. Bell certainly had the vision and the skill. "That's amazing."

"Thank you. Are you looking for some pieces for your resort?"

"I wish I could buy about half the store, but I'm afraid you're a bit out of my price range. This restoration is going to bleed me dry."

Bell winced. "I know how that is. We just finished a remodel on our house not too long ago. I thought it was going to kill me."

"It always takes longer, and costs more than you think." I'd learned that time and again working with Nathan and Vic. I'd hoped to get lucky with Whispering Falls, but I didn't think that would be the case.

"Isn't that the truth?" She paused for a moment, taking me in. "Come with me." She flipped the sign on the door to *Closed* and threw the lock, motioning for me to follow her. Bell led me through the store and out the back door. Across the alley was a much larger building that looked as if it had been a garage at one point.

She keyed in a code and entered. "This is where the magic happens."

I stepped inside and gasped. There were what seemed like endless rows of furniture. Mostly wooden pieces in various states of distress, but a few were in mid-restoration stages. I found myself pulled to a stripped and re-sanded desk. It only waited for paint. My fingers dusted over its surface. "What color are you going for?"

"She'll be a deep blue-gray when she's done."

"Perfect. You know antiqued brass accents would look great."

Bell arched a brow. "You've got an eye."

"I have an interior design degree, and my uncles have a home-restoration business. They specialize in historic houses and are always trying to blend the old with the new. I love the process."

"Me, too," she said, crouching low to check some invisible detail on the desk. "There's just something about bringing a piece back to life, especially if it was neglected or damaged. It never gets old."

A burn lit along my sternum. "Finding a new purpose for something that was lost or forgotten."

"That's it, exactly."

It was why I'd continued working with my uncles even through college and after I'd gotten a job. It gave me hope. No matter how long something had gone unseen and abandoned, it was always possible to give it life again.

"Piper?"

Bell's voice pulled me from my thoughts. "Sorry, got lost there for a minute. Anything with history will do that to me."

She straightened from her crouch. "I knew I liked you from the minute I met you."

I covered my face with my hands and groaned. "You mean when I unloaded on a perfect stranger in the middle of a hardware store?"

"You were stressed."

"Understatement."

"Well, I appreciated the honest moment."

I chuckled. "I'm glad I didn't scare you off."

She tapped the desk with her knuckles. "You certainly didn't. Tell you what? I hit up the estate and garage sales almost every weekend. Why don't you come with me? We can find you some bargains that you can refurbish yourself. I'm sure if you've worked on old homes, you can handle furniture. And I can give you pointers if you get stuck."

"I'd love that."

"Awesome. Now, tell me, how's Hunter doing on your resort? Not making too much trouble for you, is he?"

"You know Hunter?" Though it was a tiny island, Bell probably knew most people. Still, I had a sudden panicked thought that Hunter might be Bell's fiancé. It was ridiculous for that possibility to send my stomach into freefall, but that knowledge didn't stop the tumbling sensation.

"Pretty much since we were born. He's my soon-to-be brother-in-law."

I didn't want to look too closely at the cool relief sweeping through my veins. The last thing I needed was to get distracted by a man. Especially not when I would be spending every ounce of energy I had getting the Falls back on its feet. "Small world."

"Small *island*," Bell chided.

"True. He's been great. It was really nice of him to start on some projects himself before his crew made it over."

Worry flashed across Bell's expression. "He's not overdoing it, is he?"

"I don't think so. I've been trying to help out as much as I can. He told me about his shoulder injury. He's okay, right?" I wanted to ask more. What had happened? How? It seemed that I had a million and one nosy questions I wanted to ask when it came to Hunter, but I held them back.

"He'll be fine. He's just not great at moderation. Once he has a vision for a place, it's full speed ahead."

I understood that drive. I was chomping at the bit to bring the picture in my mind for the Falls to life. "He's had some great ideas for the cabins already. I think I lucked out finding him and his company."

"Hunter really could be an architect. He just didn't get the degree. He had so many genius ideas for Ford's and my place."

"Let's hope he brings that genius to Whispering Falls."

"I'm sure he will."

∽◎

Bruno barked happily as we rounded the curve in the gravel road, and the resort appeared. "So now you like it here?" He barked again. "I'm glad to hear it."

I pulled to a stop in front of the lodge. Hunter's truck was still gone. I studiously ignored the flare of disappointment. He'd told me that he needed to check on another site this morning but would stop by the hardware store to place another order for my project.

Climbing out of the SUV, I picked up the Mad Baker bag

from the passenger seat. When I let Bruno out, he immediately went for the sack. "Uh, uh, uh. You already had your treat. You can have the second one tomorrow."

He hung his head and whined. I couldn't help but laugh. "Come on, you little sulker. Let's get this stuff inside." I pulled open the door, and Bruno ran past, a growl low in his throat. "Bruno, come."

He immediately returned to my side, but the growling didn't subside. I scanned the room and gasped. Furniture had been toppled over. A few of the dishes that had been in a cabinet were now smashed on the floor.

I started to take a step inside, but Bruno blocked me. Reaching down, I patted his head. "You're right, bad idea." My voice trembled a bit as I spoke. "Cops. We need cops."

I tugged Bruno back to my SUV, putting him in the passenger seat next to me, needing him close. He scanned the property, his eyes alert. Pulling my phone out, I dialed nine-one-one.

"Sheriff's department, what's your emergency?"

I'd forgotten that Anchor didn't have a police force. Instead, they shared a sheriff's department with the rest of the chain of islands. I remembered that it had taken what felt like forever for the sheriff to arrive when Jenn went missing. I shivered.

"Yes, this is Piper Cosgrove. I'm the new owner of Whispering Falls. I've had a break-in."

"Are you currently in a safe place?"

My fingers drifted through Bruno's thick fur. I didn't think I'd ever been so glad to have my defender. "Yes. I'm in my car."

"We have someone fifteen minutes out. Just hold on."

There was nothing else I could do. I remembered another time when the police had been forced to come to the Falls.

Things hadn't turned out so well then.

Chapter Eight

Hunter

THE SCENTS OF SANDWICHES WAFTED THROUGH THE CAB of my truck as pavement turned to gravel. I hadn't asked Piper if she wanted me to pick up lunch, but I figured it couldn't hurt. She was always on the go, and she needed to sit down and have a real meal.

I passed the sign for the resort and noticed that it looked brand new. Piper must've spent some time on it yesterday after I'd left. I hated the idea of her working into the evening out here alone, but I had a feeling any talk of safety precautions wouldn't go over well.

Rounding the bend in the road, my blood turned to ice. Two sheriff's department SUVs were parked next to Piper's vehicle. I pressed the accelerator until I was only a few feet from them. Gravel spit as I slammed on the brakes. I'd barely shut off the engine before I jumped out. "Piper!"

"Over here," she called.

The tightness in my chest loosened a fraction at the sound of her voice. But not enough. I rounded the SUVs and headed for the side of the lodge. "What happened?"

Piper gripped her necklace again, her other arm once more wrapped around her middle. Bruno stood staunchly at her side, on alert. "I'm fine. I think we might have had some mischief-makers. They tore up the lodge."

"Seriously?" Sure, kids had come up here to party, but showing up in the middle of the day just to destroy things didn't fit.

Sheriff Parker Raines greeted me with a nod. "I've got two deputies in there dusting for fingerprints and collecting any other evidence they can find." He turned to Piper. "The powder leaves a hell of a mess, so I apologize in advance."

She gripped her necklace harder. "The place was already a mess. A little dust won't make it any worse."

Piper had spent over a week cleaning the lodge from top to bottom. Touching up paint, re-staining some of the woodwork. And some asshole had come along and ruined all her hard work. I met Parker's gaze. "You got any clue who this might be?"

"No other vandalism was reported in the area." He pulled out his cell phone and opened a notes app. "Have you seen anyone nosing around while you were working? Seen any kids looking for a spot to party?"

"No. The only people who've been around are me, Piper, and Celeste. Celeste's grandsons came up a couple of days ago to help haul furniture and clear out the cabins we're remodeling, but that's it. Not even a nosy neighbor stopped by."

Parker looked up from his phone. "Not exactly any neighbors nearby."

He had a point. No other house or farm was within sight of the resort. I shrugged. "It's Anchor. You know people will use any excuse to find out what's going on around their island."

"True enough." Parker slid his cell phone into his pocket and then turned his attention back to Piper. "You got any sort of security around here?"

She winced and then looked down at her dog. "Bruno and pepper spray are about the extent of it."

Her words had my lungs constricting. It felt as if my rib cage were closing in around them. The idea that I couldn't get air in or out only made my chest feel tighter. I recognized the signs now. I'd had a few panic attacks since getting shot. The first time it'd happened, I'd thought I was having a heart attack. My doctor had informed me that it was post-traumatic stress disorder. PTSD. He'd offered medication, but the last thing I wanted was to put more pills into my body.

I stared at the ground, focusing my attention on a single rock in the grass. I counted as I breathed in for five seconds and then out again. Even when pulling oxygen into my lungs felt like inhaling fire, I pressed on. I tried to push out the images invading my brain. All the things that could happen to Piper if someone broke in and she was here alone. In for five. Out for five.

Soft fingers wrapped around my forearm. "Are you okay?"

My eyes met brown ones so dark I could get lost in them for days. "Fine."

Those dark depths scanned my face, silently telling me she knew I was lying. Her hand squeezed my arm before releasing it. She didn't say a word. And I missed her touch the moment it was gone. Something about it was grounding. And as I turned my gaze back to Parker, I realized that single touch had dialed back the worst of my panic. Distracted me enough that my lungs had forgotten they were struggling to breathe.

I cleared my throat. "We really should get Piper an alarm system. On the lodge, at least."

Piper scowled at me. "Hello, owner of the resort over here. I'm not wasting a bunch of money on an alarm system when people will be coming and going constantly. As soon as I have guests anyway."

Parker covered his laugh with a cough. "I understand. But

it's worth thinking about. Maybe put some cameras in. Security lights. That alone should discourage anyone from making trouble."

"Security lights, I can do. It was already on the list. I don't want anyone tripping if they come back after dark."

I fought the urge to push. "It wouldn't hurt to have a camera or two. This happened in the middle of the day."

Parker nodded. "We have a friend who's great with that kind of thing. He'll help you set it up for free. You'd just need to buy the cameras."

Parker was right. Griffin loved configuring systems to give someone a sense of security. One call and he'd be over here in a flash.

Piper scratched Bruno behind the ears, and he leaned into her leg. "I appreciate the offer, but I'm not ready to spend a bunch of money on cameras. I have other things that need to take priority. When the first round of cabins is done, I'll think about it."

I knew a brush-off when I heard one. She wouldn't take one penny away from restoring this place. "I can run to the hardware store and get what you need for the security lights. When are your first summer tenants arriving? Having vehicles parked on the property should help, too."

Piper looked back at the lodge, a hint of panic sweeping over her features. "They come tomorrow."

I moved in closer, my hand going to her shoulder. Even that part of her was petite. Delicate and fragile—but far stronger than it appeared. Just like the rest of Piper. "We'll get it cleaned up. We've got the rest of the day."

"Thank you. I know it's not your job—"

I gave her shoulder a gentle squeeze. "I'm happy to help. Whatever you need."

Two deputies rounded the corner of the building. The guy was unfamiliar, but I'd seen the female deputy a handful of times.

She nodded at our group. "All done. But I'm not sure we're going to find what we're looking for. There were hardly any prints near the area of the most damage."

"Great," Piper mumbled.

Parker sent her a sympathetic smile. "We'll do what we can to find out who did this. In the meantime, stay safe. You have my card. Call if you think of anything."

"I will." She looked around at the group. "Thank you for coming. I really appreciate your help."

Parker reached out a hand for her to shake. "Anytime. But I hope the next time I see you, it's over a beer at The Catch, not at a crime scene."

The corners of Piper's mouth turned up. "Sounds a hell of a lot better to me."

I glared at Parker. Was he hitting on her? "See you around."

There was an edge to my tone that Parker didn't miss. He slapped my uninjured shoulder and whispered under his breath, "Not how I meant it. Stand down." I grunted in response, and Parker chuckled. "Let's hit the road, guys. Call if you need anything, you two."

We watched as Parker and the deputies drove off. When they disappeared from sight, I turned back to Piper. "I got you a sandwich when I was in town. What are the chances I can get you to eat it before we survey the damage?"

"Slim to none," she muttered. Scrubbing her hands over her face, she sighed. "Sorry. I'm cranky. That was really nice of you."

"It was extra-nice of me. It's a BLT from The Catch."

Her eyes flared. "How'd you know that place was my favorite? The sandwich, too."

I grinned. "I didn't. It's my family's restaurant."

"Really? I always loved going there growing up."

I searched Piper's face, wondering if we'd ever met when we were kids. I'd spent so much time at the restaurant during the summer. Running in to beg my dad to give me French fries to take out to the beach or stuffing my face before heading off with my friends. "You have good taste."

She smiled, but it seemed just a bit sad. "Tell you what? Let's survey the damage, and then we can eat. We'll make a plan of attack over lunch."

"Deal." I started towards the front of the lodge, Piper and Bruno following.

When we reached the front porch, Piper gave Bruno a command to stay, and he whined in protest. She bent, rubbing the sides of his face. "I know. But there's broken glass in there. I don't want you to cut your paws." Bruno licked her cheek, and Piper laughed. "I love you, too."

The laugh was the first truly carefree sound I'd heard come out of Piper's mouth. It made me realize just how much pressure she had put on herself to get this place up and running. It was a heavy weight to carry. She needed to share a bit of that burden or she'd buckle under it all. Anyone would.

I pushed open the door and muttered a curse under my breath. Furniture was overturned, and shards of glass and what looked like dishes were scattered all over the floor. I moved through the space, going from one room to the next, but it looked as if the damage was centered around the main entry room. I turned back to Piper. "Have you checked upstairs?"

"Not yet."

"Let's go." The stairs creaked in the silence as we climbed.

Piper scooted around me when we hit the hall and let out a slew of curses that would've made a sailor blush when she reached what I assumed was her room. Clothes were strewn about, books lay open on the floor, and photographs were everywhere.

"Shit," I muttered.

Piper bent, picking up a photo. "At least they didn't tear them, I guess."

I moved in behind her, looking down at the picture. It was of two girls, their arms slung around each other, beaming up at the camera. Piper's hair was in two braids, and she was missing a front tooth. The blond-haired girl had a high ponytail and was missing the opposite tooth. Posed on the front porch of the lodge, everything about them screamed: happy and carefree.

"That was one of my favorite trips here. They had the stables up and running, and Jenn and I took trail rides every day we were here. We had a picnic at Mount Orcas. Went kayaking. I don't think I've ever had as much fun as I did on that trip."

Hearing her words, I understood a bit more what Piper was fighting for. She was trying to reclaim the innocence and joy that had been stolen from her. And she was trying to gift it to other families. To give them a piece of what she had loved so much about this place.

I moved in just a little closer. "You'll have that kind of fun again."

She kept staring down at the picture, her thumb sweeping across her friend's face. "But it won't be the same."

"No, it won't. And you'll never stop missing her. But you wouldn't want to, would you?"

Piper turned to face me, just a breath away. "No. If I stop missing her, it means I've forgotten."

"So, hold onto her. To all the memories you have. But don't let them weigh you down and keep you from moving forward. That's where you'll find new joy. And she'll be with you every step of the way."

Piper's mouth curved the barest amount. "You're pretty profound, you know that?"

I chuckled. "It's all that time building things. Gives you time to think."

"Maybe you should make a coffee table book. You could call it *Zen Wisdom of a Contractor*."

"Smartass," I mumbled.

"Come on and feed me. It's been way too long since I've tasted one of those BLTs." She stepped around me and started down the hall. "And I hope to God you got me French fries. A BLT is nothing without some of those curly fries."

I shook my head and watched her go. The woman was a force of nature. I was simply along for the ride.

Chapter Nine

Piper

BLINKING AGAINST THE BRIGHT, LATE-SPRING SUN, I silently prayed for the two Diet Cokes I'd downed this morning to take effect. If I'd had the option of a caffeine IV, I would've gone with that. Three hours of sleep wasn't going to cut it.

Hunter and I had spent the remainder of the afternoon yesterday getting the lodge set back to rights. Thankfully, there hadn't been much actual damage, mostly the decorative dishes from the hutch. But the thought that some of them had likely been antiques turned my stomach.

After Hunter had left, I'd spent the rest of the night doing a final once-over of the cabins that would gain inhabitants today. I dusted every surface. Straightened all the linens. Arranged the flowers I'd bought at the market in town.

This morning, I'd gotten up early for a trip to The Mad Baker and The General Store for more treats. I figured going above and beyond for my long-term guests couldn't hurt. The welcome baskets I'd put together had everything they might need while they got settled in their summer homes. Coffee, wine, snacks, and baked goods.

I let out a slow breath as the first vehicle rounded the bend in the gravel road. The minivan pulled to a stop in front of the lodge, and a couple climbed out. I waved with one hand while patting Bruno's head with the other. "Best behavior, remember?" I whispered to him. He just nosed my hand for more pets.

"Welcome to Whispering Falls. We're so happy to have you here." The *we* was a little misleading, but this family didn't need to know that I currently ran the show alone.

"We're happy to be here. And the kiddos are ecstatic. Too many hours in the car," the woman greeted as she pulled open the van door.

A pang hit my chest as a memory rose of Jenn and me, begging to ride in the same car on our trip over. Racing around the ferry to find the best view. I swallowed against the lump in my throat. "That trip from the mainland can be brutal for little ones. But they'll have lots of room to stretch their legs around here."

The man smiled as he appeared from the other side of the van with a sleepy little girl in his arms. "Looks like it. We're the Gragerts. I'm Colin. And this is my wife, Emily."

"Nice to meet you. I'm Piper."

A little boy jumped out of the van and ran towards Bruno and me. "Doggy."

"Ben!" his mom called, panic lacing her tone. "You don't know that dog."

Bruno's tail wagged in excitement at the prospect of a new friend, but he remained seated. I crouched low to meet the boy. "This is Bruno. He loves new friends. Who are you?"

"I'm Ben. I'm six. And I'm gonna be a first-grader this year."

I smiled. "Want to meet Bruno?" The little boy nodded enthusiastically. "Hold out your hand." Ben did as instructed. "Shake, Bruno."

Bruno placed a paw in Ben's outstretched hand, and the boy squealed with delight. "He's shaking my hand, Mommy."

"That he is." Emily placed a hand on her son's shoulder and shook her head. "Sorry about that. He loves animals."

"Not a problem. Bruno loves kids. And he's been lonely without any guests, so I'm guessing Ben will have a new best buddy while you guys are here."

"That will make him a very happy camper."

I gave the Gragerts their key and the welcome basket and directed them towards their cabin. "As Corrie likely told you, we have some construction going on in the cabins on the south side, but the noise shouldn't reach you where you're located. There's a boathouse down by the beach with kayaks, paddleboards, and beach toys for the kids."

I'd done an inventory with Celeste two days ago and had breathed a giant sigh of relief that everything was in such good condition. The one thing I hadn't assessed yet was the sailboat docked in our little cove. It was still floating, but I had no idea if it was truly seaworthy.

"Everything looks amazing," Colin said. "I'm sure we'll be on the beach this afternoon."

I waved them off just as a truck pulled up to the lodge. A grizzled man in what looked to be his seventies climbed out. I waved, but he didn't return my smile. Ambling up the steps, he said, "Checking in. Last name's Simpson."

"Yes, Mr. Simpson. I have your key. And here's a welcome basket with some goodies and an area map. You're in cabin twenty-one. If you have any questions, just come find me."

He scowled at the basket as if baked goods somehow offended him. "You got me in a private cabin?"

"Yes, sir. You're in the cabin farthest removed from the rest."

He didn't say another word, simply snatched up his key and basket and took off back to his truck. Bruno growled at his retreating form. "Oh no, you don't," I warned my dog. "He might be a grump, but we don't growl at guests." Bruno let out a little huff of air.

"Come on. I don't think our next arrival is due for a bit. Let's start on these flower beds." It was a little late to put flowers in the ground, but I was determined to try. I'd loaded up on things from the nursery but hadn't had a chance to plant anything yet since I'd been preparing for today's arrivals.

I picked up gloves and headed for my pile of plants. I'd missed things like this living in my loft. The only gardening I'd been able to do was in a few pots on my balcony. But Vic had taught me all about plants growing up. Our garden at the house on Queen Anne had been a masterpiece, with everything from vegetables to a dazzling array of flowers. I just hoped my green thumb still worked.

I lost myself for a couple of hours, playing with arrangements and then sticking things in the ground. With each plant I rooted, I sent up a little prayer that they flourished. Pops of color would really brighten up the front of the building.

At the sound of tires on gravel, I pushed to my feet. Ridding myself of my gardening gloves, I did my best to wipe off the dirt, but it was a hopeless task. Our next guest would simply have to take me as I was.

A silver sedan came to a stop in front of the lodge, and a man with dark hair climbed out. He was tall and classically handsome. And something about him was almost familiar. An itch at the back of my brain that I couldn't quite scratch. His eyes flashed in the afternoon light. "Piper?"

The voice did it. A flood of memories cascaded over me. A boy just three years older than Jenn and me, leading our trail rides when we were older, and always letting us take the long way back. The son of the couple who'd owned this place. "Nick?"

He grinned. "Are you the new owner?"

"I am. What are you doing here?" Maybe he'd come to visit his old home. I hadn't gotten the details of how the resort had gone under, just that they'd faced some hard times.

A bit of Nick's smile slipped. "I'm renting one of the cabins this summer."

"The paperwork said Richard Crowley."

"Nicholas is my middle name. I've always just gone by Nick."

I motioned for him to follow me up the steps and into the lodge. "So, what brings you back for the summer?"

"Dad's in the assisted living facility in town. Alzheimer's. I live in Portland, but my company is letting me work remotely over the summer. I wanted some time with him before his memories are totally gone."

I couldn't seem to stop from putting my foot in my mouth. "I'm glad you're able to get some time with him. That must be hard."

Grief flashed in his expression. "It's a hell of a disease."

"Please let me know if there's anything I can do to help. Your father was always so kind to us when we visited." Mr. C. had always snuck Jenn and me extra ice cream or a candy bar when we stopped by the lodge in the afternoons.

I'd thought he, his wife, and Nick had built the perfect life here. The kind I wanted someday. But I'd learned one thing all too well—happiness like that wasn't guaranteed. Someone could sneak up and steal it from you, and there was nothing you could do.

"I will. And you let me know if you need help around here. It's been years since I stayed here, but I should remember all the ins and outs."

"Careful what you offer. I might be knocking on your door more than you'd like." I handed Nick his key and the welcome basket. "You're in number nineteen. I put a map in there, but I doubt you'll need it."

"It's been so long; it may come in handy." He paused, shuffling his feet. "They never found her, did they? I tried to keep up with the case but…"

I swallowed against the lump in my throat. "No, there's never been any sign. Her parents still put out an age-progression shot every year. Try to get local news stations to give the case some coverage. But there's been nothing."

He shook his head, staring out at the sea through the back windows of the lodge. "I hate that for them." His gaze found mine. "For you. I don't think any of us were ever the same after that."

Sometimes, I forgot that Jenn's disappearance had marked more than just me and her parents. It had been difficult for Nathan and Vic to let me out of their sight that whole next year. But it had left scars on so many others. I imagined that every single person who'd searched for Jenn remembered her name. Her face. They probably still recalled the fear that had seemed to hang in the air and cling to everything and everyone. The grief of knowing that we might never find her—and we hadn't.

"Sometimes, I think things like that live in your bones. Become a part of who you are somehow."

Nick's gaze traveled to the water again. "I think you're right. And it became a part of what this place was, too. I hope you can bring it out of that shadow. If anyone can, it's you. I remember you and Jenn chattering about how you would own this place one day. My dad loved hearing you two talk about it."

Something about Nick's words stuck. My uncles and I hadn't returned to the Falls after Jenn had vanished, but I wondered if other folks had stayed away, as well. Maybe that was why the resort had fallen on hard times. I wanted to ask, needed to know everything, but it felt too intrusive.

"I'm giving it my all. I can promise you that."

Nick reached out and squeezed my shoulder. "Couldn't ask for anything more."

Hunter

As I ROUNDED THE CORNER OF THE CABIN, I ALMOST collided with an older man carrying a fishing pole. "Excuse me, sir. I didn't see you there."

"No shit, Sherlock. You need to watch where you're going," he grumbled.

I didn't point out that he could've been watching where *he* was going, as well. I didn't think Piper would appreciate that. "My apologies. Did you need help finding anything?"

"The dock. How do I get down to the dock so I can catch some danged fish?"

I pressed my mouth into a thin line to keep from laughing. Apparently, this gentleman's vacation wasn't agreeing with him. "There's a set of stairs just on the other side of the lodge that will take you down to the beach and the dock."

The man grunted in response and took off in that direction. He moved pretty fast for an older guy. Piper would have her hands full with that one. Just the thought of her made me want to go and find her. Make sure she was okay after the ordeal of yesterday. Instead of fighting the pull like a smart man, I headed for the lodge.

As I climbed the steps, I caught sight of a man moving in close to Piper, his hand on her shoulder. The soft smile on her face punched me right in the gut. A sick feeling spread through me. Jealousy, I realized. I hadn't felt envy before over where a woman pointed her smile. Ever. The sensation threw me for a loop. And it wasn't a pleasant ride.

The man released his hold and turned, surprise flickering across his expression. "I'll be damned. Hunter Hardy. It's good to see you."

I reached out a hand for a shake. "Nick. I didn't know you were back in town." We'd run in the same circles in high school but hadn't truly been friends. And when he'd taken off for college on the mainland, we'd lost touch.

"Here to spend some time with my dad."

"I know he'll be happy about that."

Shadows passed behind his eyes. "I hope so."

"I was sorry to hear about his diagnosis."

"Thanks, man. I need to get settled so I can go by the home, but let's grab a beer and catch up."

"You just name the place and time." I was about to offer to get some of the old crew together but stopped myself. We'd all scattered to different places and different lives—some by choice and others because of forces beyond their control.

"Will do." With a wave, he headed to his sedan.

I turned my attention to Piper. "How are you holding up?" The dark circles under her eyes had me worried, but the smudge of dirt on her cheek made the corners of my mouth tip up.

"I need at least thirty more Diet Cokes if I'm going to make it through this day."

"Come on." I inclined my head towards the kitchen and started in that direction. Pulling open the massive fridge in the industrial space, I found a Diet Coke and one of the water bottles I'd stuck in there this morning. I handed the soda to her and kept the water for myself.

"You're a godsend." She leaned against the counter and popped the top on the can. After taking a long drink, she let out an exaggerated sigh. "The best there is."

I chuckled and reached out to brush the dirt off her cheek. "You've got a little—" My breath caught as her gaze locked with mine. Somehow, I'd found myself closer to Piper than was safe, my mouth mere inches from hers. I couldn't look away from those lips. It was as if they had some sort of gravitational pull.

Bruno trotted into the kitchen and let out a friendly bark, breaking the spell. Piper laughed and took a step out of my hold. "Every time I come into the kitchen, he thinks it's treat time. We'll have to give him one, or I'll never hear the end of it."

I reached for the jar on one of the open shelving units, and Bruno immediately plunked his butt on the floor. Piper looked from me to her dog and then back again. "You've been sneaking him treats, haven't you?"

"I don't know what you're talking about. I just saw the jar with the paw and assumed."

"Suuuuure."

I pulled out a treat and bent at the waist. "High five." Bruno met my hand with his paw, and I gave him the biscuit.

Piper's jaw fell open. "When did you teach him that?"

"Bruno and I like to hang out when you go into town."

She shook her head. "I wondered why he wasn't sulking when I didn't take him with me."

"Careful, he might start to like me best."

"Never." Piper crouched to throw her arms around the furry beast. "I'm your favorite, right?" Bruno licked her face in response. "That's right. Hunter can't buy your love, no matter how many treats he gives you." Bruno barked.

"I wouldn't be so sure of that."

She pushed to her feet. "I've had him since he was fifteen weeks old. He'd better not toss me aside for you."

This dog would never love anyone more than Piper. The howl after she'd left was proof of that, so damned forlorn and sad it had me freeing him from the lodge. After some pats and treats, he'd followed me back to the job site and kept me company.

I leaned a hip against the counter. "I've got a proposal for you."

She glared in my direction. "I'm not giving you my dog."

"I wouldn't dream of asking." But another idea had begun swirling in my head as I stared at the ceiling of my trailer last night, worried about Piper all alone up here. "How would you feel about work-for-rent trade?"

"What did you have in mind?"

"I've had my Airstream at my brother's ever since I sold my last piece of property. I'd like to get out of his hair and wouldn't mind being out of the trailer for a bit. Cabin seven isn't in too rough of shape. If you let me stay there, park my Airstream alongside it, I'll give you my work hours for free while I'm here."

Piper's eyes widened. "I know what your hourly rate is, Hunter. That's not a fair trade. And you know I'd let you stay in that cabin for free. It's not like anyone else is using it."

I knew that she'd likely let me stay without any sort of rent, but I wanted to kill two birds with one stone. Piper needed someone up here to have her back, at least until the resort had a fuller roster of guests, and troublemakers knew to stay away. But she also deserved a break. She was giving her all to the Falls, working herself to the bone and sinking every penny she had into the place. My company had more than enough cash flow to cut her a bit of a break.

"A trade works out for both of us. I'm out of my brother's

and Bell's hair, and you get some man-hours for free. What do you say?"

Her lips pressed into a firm line. "Ten hours a week. No more."

"Deal." She didn't have to know the exact number of hours I'd be shaving off her weekly bills.

Piper pointed a finger at me. "And no sneaking my dog treats. I don't want the vet mad at me because he's gained weight."

Bruno gave her a baleful look as if he understood every word.

"You're breaking his heart."

She scratched Bruno behind the ears. "I'm keeping you healthy, so you'll live forever." There was a little catch in Piper's voice as she spoke. I knew immediately that this dog was more child than pet. "So, when do you want to move in?"

"I need to pick up a few things in town. I'll stop and pick up the trailer on my way back. Work for you?" I didn't want her spending another night here mostly alone.

"You might want to pick up a mask and borrow some of my cleaning supplies. That cabin is a mess."

I grinned and took a step closer to Piper, my fingers reaching out and brushing away another streak of soil on her shoulder. "I'm not afraid of a little dirt."

Her breath hitched. "That's good."

But I was damn afraid of just how strong the pull was to touch Piper's skin. The visions that had haunted my dreams of what it might be like to do more than brush my fingers across her cheek or shoulder. Instead of chasing those dreams, I took a step back. The action was almost painful as I lost the feel of that silk beneath my palm. "I'll be back in an hour or so."

"I'll be here."

And that was the most dangerous thing of all. A living, breathing temptation would be just a few doors down.

Chapter Eleven

Piper

ILAUGHED AS BRUNO CHARGED OUT OF THE WATER FOR what felt like the millionth time. He seemed to smile around the stick in his mouth. "Come on, buddy. We have to go back up. I need to check on Hunter and head into town."

Bruno's ears perked up at the sound of Hunter's name. "Sorry, he's on treat restriction. But I'm sure you'll have him wrapped around your paw again soon."

I climbed the beach stairs, Bruno dutifully on my heels. When we reached the top, he made a beeline for a sun-soaked spot on the back deck. Before I'd even made it to the side of the lodge, he was snoring. He'd be down for the count for a couple of hours, at least. The surprisingly intense afternoon sun would ensure that he was dry by the time he woke.

I rounded the building and caught sight of the Airstream shining in the afternoon light. Making my way to the cabin, I took a moment to soak in the unique blend of scents in the air and take in the feel of the sun on my back. Sure, I was exhausted, but I was also grateful. The magic of this place had found its way back into my bones.

When I reached the cabin, I almost swallowed my tongue. Hunter appeared in the doorway, shirtless. His golden skin seemed to gleam in the afternoon light, his muscled chest on display. As my gaze traveled over the expanse of skin, I froze. An angry red scar shone on the right side of his chest, between his pec and his shoulder.

My gaze snapped up to Hunter's face. "Your shoulder injury?"

Hunter's jaw worked back and forth before he answered. "I was shot."

"What?" The single word came out more like a whisper. I'd assumed he'd been injured on the job, maybe had lifted something he shouldn't have. "How? Why?" I gave my head a good shake. "I'm sorry. None of that is my business."

"It's more your business than you might think."

I opened my mouth to ask yet another question and then snapped it closed, letting the silence ask it for me.

Hunter sighed and then looked away, towards a cabin in the distance. "One of my friends, Shay, has a mentally unstable brother. He was fixated on hurting her, however he could. He and a friend of his took her. I didn't know it at the time. I was out of good cell range and had come up here because I wondered if I'd have to buy this place to get my hands on fixing it up. I was just about to start looking around when a text from my brother popped up on my phone."

Pain flickered in Hunter's dark green eyes. "I almost left to go help in the search when I saw the car. Parked right by that cabin over there." The air seized in my lungs. "My gut told me that something was off. I had to see. Just to make sure."

He still didn't look my way, but I couldn't take my eyes off him and that soul-deep pain that seemed to call to mine. His Adam's apple bobbed as he swallowed. "Michael killed his friend, and he would've killed Shay, too. He had a gun, and all she had was a lousy fork. And yet, she didn't give up. I knew we didn't have time to wait for the cops. He could've done anything to her in the time it would have taken them to get here."

"What happened?" The question slipped out of my mouth before I could stop it.

"I charged in there, thinking I could be the hero. That things would be different this time."

His words might as well have been lead weights falling into my stomach. "Is she? Your friend…?"

"She threw herself off the cliff up top and prayed she cleared the rocks."

I held my breath, waiting for whatever came next.

"She made it. Because her man got to her in time."

There was such bitterness in Hunter's words. I knew it wasn't directed at the man who had saved Shay, it was directed inward. I understood that kind of self-hatred. The anger that ate you up inside. Because if you had done one thing differently, maybe the person you cared for wouldn't have been hurt. "You can't blame yourself."

Hunter's gaze snapped to mine. "Can't I?"

I didn't look away. So many people faced with that kind of pain pouring out of a person turned away. I wouldn't do that to Hunter. The least I could do was look him in the face, confront his pain. "Well, you can. But it's not going to do you much good. She's still here. And so are you. You're going to have to find a way to make peace with it."

"Have you made peace with it?"

It was a fair question, but it wasn't an easy one to answer. "I thought I had. But coming back here… I realized I'm still working through some things." I'd hoped to find my answers as I brought the Falls back to life, working through broken boards and pieces of memories.

Hunter let out a long breath. "Maybe that's why I'm here,

too. To work through it and make my peace with this place. With what happened. At least, it's a start."

I sensed that there was more to the weight that Hunter carried. Guilt had carved its way into his marrow, and it would take a hell of a lot to work it out. I had the sudden urge to wrap my arms around Hunter and tell him that everything would be okay. But nothing about the set of his body said that he'd welcome touch right now.

"Are you sure you're ready for that? I don't want to force you into something that will cause you pain." That would make me the lowest of the low. I wasn't sure I could handle working at the place where I'd almost died just months ago.

"I can handle it." Hunter's words came out as more of a growl.

"Okay, then. Maybe we'll both exorcise some demons as we work on this place." I wouldn't mind having company while I did it. Someone who understood in a way no one else could.

Hunter's expression softened a bit. "Maybe we will."

I just hoped like hell the process didn't kill us.

Chapter Twelve

Hunter

WE WORKED IN SILENCE, PIPER HELPING ME UNLOAD my belongings and bring them into the cabin. She did it without a word, simply began picking up boxes that I'd set aside and carrying things from the trailer's small kitchen as if she knew that I needed someone. No platitudes and encouragements, merely the presence of someone else. The knowledge that I wasn't alone in this.

I set my duffle of clothing in the bedroom and came out to find Piper arranging my kitchen. She frowned at the sparse array of pots and dishes.

"What's with the scowl?"

She turned to face me, leaning a hip on the counter. "If you're going to be here for a while, you need more than a frying pan and one set of cutlery."

"I have a pot, too," I pointed out. Piper would be amazed at what I could whip up with one pot and a single frying pan. An image of cooking for her flashed in my mind. Eating across from her at the small, rickety table in the corner. The picture quickly morphed into what else we might do on that table.

"You need a better setup. I'm about to go to Goodwill. Want me to get you some things?"

Her words brought me out of the fantasy playing out in my brain. "What?"

Piper let out an exasperated sigh. "I'm making a run to Goodwill. Do you want me to pick you up some more dishes and things?"

I didn't want to lose this touchpoint. Not yet. Something about having Piper close warmed the cold spot that had taken up root in my chest since the shooting. I also had a feeling that if I let her run wild, she would return with more items than would ever fit in my trailer again. "Why don't I come with you?"

Her dark eyes widened a fraction. "Sure. You want to go now?"

"Yeah." I grabbed my t-shirt from where I'd tossed it on the worn couch and pulled it over my head. Just as I regained my vision, I caught sight of Piper tracking my movements. Hell. The last thing I needed was the knowledge that this attraction was two-sided. But it was more than attraction. It was lust mixed with a healthy dose of understanding. And it packed a potent punch.

She cleared her throat, making a beeline for the door. "Let's go." She let out an ear-piercing whistle, and Bruno came running from the other side of the lodge.

"We can take my truck."

"You okay with dog slobber in said truck?"

I gave Bruno a good rub. "A little drool never hurt anybody."

"You say that now. Just wait until you're mopping it up."

I pulled open the door to the backseat, and Bruno jumped right in. "I'm not afraid." We climbed into the cab, and I started the engine. "What do you need at Goodwill?"

"Books, books, and more books."

I glanced briefly in her direction as I started down the gravel road. "Random, but okay."

Piper let out a mock gasp. "Books are *never* random. And there's a big ol' empty library in the lodge that I just finished cleaning out. It's time to fill those sad shelves. I want guests to have a place they can pick up a book for the week they're here. Somewhere to curl up and get lost in a good story on a stormy day."

I could picture the image she painted. "I like it. You should get some board games, too. You could loan those out."

"That's a great idea. Guests could take them into the dining room and play at one of the tables in there. Jenn and I used to get into vicious gin rummy battles with my uncles when we came up here."

It was the first time I'd heard Piper talk about her friend without sadness in her voice. "My brother and I used to play with our parents a lot. Bell still goes over and plays with my dad now and then."

"I like her."

"Bell?"

Piper nodded. "I stopped by her shop the other day, and she was incredibly kind. Went out of her way to make me feel welcome."

"She's the best. And she's got a good crew of friends. You'll like them all."

Piper toyed with a string on the frayed hem of her jean shorts. "It'll be nice to meet more people."

I couldn't help but wonder if Piper felt she was trying to replace Jenn every time she made a new friend. It had to be a battle, holding that memory but also trying to move forward. "I'm sure Bell will bring you into the fold. Kenna and Shay are great. So's Caelyn, but she and her husband, Griffin, are leaving for Europe in a couple of months for a summer trip."

Piper let out a low whistle. "That sounds dreamy."

"Delayed honeymoon. And they're taking Caelyn's siblings that they have custody of."

Piper's entire demeanor changed, softened somehow. "That's wonderful that they're doing that."

Every word and reaction just drew me in more. Closer. I wanted to know everything about the woman sitting next to me. "Have you been with your uncles since you were a baby?" It was nosy and none of my business, but I asked anyway.

"Yup. Since the moment I was born. My mom lived with Nathan and Vic while she was pregnant so they could go to every doctor's appointment and be there at the birth."

"She was lucky to have them."

"She is. And she knows it."

I made the turn towards town and Goodwill. "Do you have a good relationship with her?"

Piper arched a brow in my direction. "You're just full of questions today, aren't you?"

I shrugged but grinned. "I'm curious."

"You know what curiosity did to the cat."

"Good thing I'm not a cat."

Piper laughed, and the sound seemed to coat the air. "Our relationship is good for the most part. She lives in California now. She's a lawyer. Married. No kids. I think going through that so young made her a little gun-shy. But her husband worships the ground she walks on and is happy with or without children."

"Do you see her much?" I had a million questions I wanted to ask, but I tried for one at a time.

"They usually come up to Seattle over Thanksgiving. It's more normal than you'd think. Nathan and Vic were always open about how I came to be. And they always made me feel loved and wanted."

"I didn't mean that I thought it was weird—"

"I know," Piper cut me off. "But it's different from how most people were raised. But sometimes, different is good. And for me, it was the best."

"I'm glad."

"What about your parents? Do you see them much?"

I pulled into the parking lot of Goodwill and found an empty spot. "At least once a week for family dinner. Sometimes more. My dad had a stroke a few years ago, but he's finally made a real recovery. He's back to being in my and Ford's business every chance he gets. I'm sure he'll be up to check out the resort before long."

Piper smiled as she climbed out of the truck. "He's welcome anytime. I'd love to meet him. Your mom, too."

"Careful what you offer. And if my mom asks you if you want to see baby pictures, the answer is no."

Piper laughed as she headed inside. "The answer is going to be yes."

I groaned. "Shouldn't have said a damned thing."

"But you did." She wound her way through the aisles, picking up a cart as she went.

"A basket won't do? You need a cart?"

"Didn't you hear me say I needed to fill the shelves in the library? I might need two carts."

I couldn't hold in my chuckle. "Maybe I should go get us some snacks. We're going to need sustenance for this journey."

"That's not a bad idea." Piper made a beeline for the young adult and children's section, picking up one book after the other. "I'm going to need all of these." She began shoving books into my hands.

"Whoa," I said, examining the pile. "These all look like they're the same book."

She froze in her pillaging and looked up at me. "How dare you say that about the genius that is Ann M. Martin? This is The Baby-Sitters Club series. Each book is a different and equally amazing adventure."

I pressed my mouth into a hard line to keep from laughing. "A fan, I take it?"

She held a book to her chest. "They were amazing.

Especially the extra-long mystery ones. Those were the best. You really missed out by not reading these."

"I read the Hardy Boys," I said, feeling suddenly defensive.

"Oooooh, we should find some of those, too. Can you look? Pick out some of your favorites." She paused. "Wait, your last name is Hardy. That's why you liked them, isn't it?"

My lips twitched. "I was convinced I was the long-lost brother."

And that was how we lost ourselves for the next hour. Picking out favorite stories from our childhoods and then moving on to the adult fiction sections. We chose books that looked interesting or had ridiculous covers. We made a game of who could find the funniest titles and embarrassing inscriptions.

By the time we'd finished, Piper's cart was piled high. She sighed. "I'm really glad most of these are twenty-five cents."

"They certainly know a bargain around here."

"We have to get your kitchen supplies, too."

I eyed the stacks of books. "I'm not sure anything else will fit."

Piper squeezed my biceps. "You've got muscles. You can carry them."

I snorted. "Thanks?"

"Come on, it's a compliment."

She steered me over to the kitchen wares section. I didn't say a word as she piled things into my waiting arms. Piper mumbled the reasoning behind each selection, and when she was done, she clapped. "I think that's everything."

"We've barely left anything for any other shoppers, so I *hope* that's everything."

She stuck her tongue out at me. "You're going to be happy you have that citrus juicer, just you wait."

I didn't argue that I could just cut a lemon or lime in half and squeeze it with my hands, but I didn't want to ruin Piper's happy buzz. The cashier's eyes widened as she took in our haul. "You certainly found what you were looking for."

"That we did," Piper answered.

The cashier began scanning the books. "Oh, I loved these growing up. Especially the mystery ones."

Piper looked over her shoulder at me. "Told you."

"I wasn't arguing. Get all the babysitting books you want."

She beamed. "Thank you. I will."

As we made our way to my truck, a voice called out my name. We paused, and I caught sight of a woman headed our way. I could barely hide the wince. "Hey, Court."

"What are you doing in town in the middle of the day?" She asked the question as if she knew my schedule when that couldn't be further from the truth.

"Just running some errands. Courtney, this is Piper. She just bought Whispering Falls. Piper, this is Courtney. She manages the craft shop around the corner."

"Nice to meet you," Piper greeted.

Courtney's smile faltered a bit. "You, too. Welcome to Anchor." Her gaze cut back to me. "You're doing the remodel?"

I hated to admit I was. Courtney would take that as a sign that the only thing between Piper and me was work. She would likely take it as assurance that I was single and that there was still hope for us. "I am."

"That's nice that you're helping with errands. Hunter's the best, isn't he?" Courtney asked Piper.

"He is, and his knowledge of the Hardy Boys comes in really handy."

"The Hardy Boys? The books? I didn't know you liked those." Courtney sounded legitimately frustrated that she hadn't known something about me.

"Well, we'd better be going," I said, placing a hand on Piper's lower back to get her moving. "It was nice to see you, Court."

Courtney's eyes zeroed in on my hand. "Nice to see you, too. Come by the store sometime. We can grab lunch."

I made a noncommittal noise and waved. There was zero chance I was stopping by that store.

"Ex-girlfriend?" Piper asked when we were out of earshot.

I blew out a breath. "We didn't date long and broke up months ago."

"She wants to get back together?"

"She has hinted in that direction."

Piper shook her head as she loaded books into the back of my truck and tossed a treat from her pocket to Bruno. "You need to just straight-out tell her that you're not interested." She paused. "Unless you *are* interested."

"I'm not." The words were out of my mouth so fast, my head should've spun.

Piper leaned against the back of my truck, no idea the kind of picture she painted. Her dark brown hair flowed around her, just a bit wavy from the braid it had been in all day. Her golden skin seemed to glow, kissed by the sun from all the gardening she'd been doing. Carefree and heart-stopping.

"Then be honest with her. Don't be one of those guys who moans and complains about a girl who won't leave him alone when he hasn't told her he's done."

I stiffened. "I ended things. Isn't that clear enough?"

"What did you say when you ended things?"

I set my bag of dishes and kitchen gadgets in the truck bed. "I don't know. Something along the lines of it not being what I was looking for."

Piper snickered. "You might as well have told her you'd be looking for it one day if she just waits around long enough."

"I was trying to be nice."

"*Nice* is cutting her loose so she can find a person who can make her happy. What you're doing is stringing her along."

Hell. That hadn't been what I'd intended at all. But I couldn't argue that Courtney clearly hadn't gotten the message that we were done. "I'll talk to her."

Piper clasped her hands under her chin. "He's growing up right before our very eyes."

"Smartass."

"Takes one to know one." She looked down the street. "How would you feel about another stop?"

"Sure. What were you thinking?"

"I wanted to stop by the care home that Mr. Crowley's in. Maybe bring him some treats from The Mad Baker."

God, Piper's heart was good. Things that people would rarely think to do in her position, she gladly added to her list, even with a million other tasks and thoughts weighing on her. "I think he'd love that."

"Do you know where it is?"

I nodded. We unloaded the rest of the books and then picked up some cookies to take with us to the assisted living facility. It was located in a larger historic home on the island. It gave a warm and welcoming feel instead of the more sterile one you might find at a larger facility.

We walked up the front steps, and I held the door open for Piper. She introduced herself to the man behind the reception desk. "I'm Piper Cosgrove. I'm the new owner of Whispering Falls. I used to know Mr. Crowley. Is he up for visitors? I'd love to drop off some cookies."

The man smiled. "He's in the conservatory. Come on in." He led us through a living area and tv room out to a space encased in glass, with a bunch of plants. "Albert, you have some visitors. This is Piper and—"

"Hunter," I offered.

"Hi, Mr. C.," Piper greeted, moving in closer to the man in the wheelchair. "I just bought the resort, and I wanted you to know that I'm going to take really good care of it. You don't have to worry."

"You bought the Falls?" he asked, looking up at her.

"I did. We're bringing it back to its glory. Hunter's helping."

He looked from Piper to me and back again. "That's good. Real good."

She pulled the bakery box out of the paper bag. "We brought you some cookies. I wasn't sure which kind you liked, so I got you a bit of everything."

Albert's hands trembled as he opened the box. "Double chocolate."

"I'm partial to those myself."

He looked up at Piper. "I used to sneak you candy. You and your friend."

A flicker of grief passed over Piper's features. "You did. Ice cream, too."

Albert's hand shot out, gripping her arm. "You have to be careful. It's not safe. Bad things happen at the Falls. Bad things. Don't go back there."

A nurse ran over. "It's okay, Albert. Everything's all right."

"No! It's not. Not safe. Not safe." He kept muttering the words over and over to himself as the nurse rolled him out of the room.

Piper's hand covered her mouth. "Oh God, I didn't mean to upset him. I didn't think he'd remember me at all. If I'd known—"

I didn't think, just pulled her into a hug. "It's not your fault. It's that damned disease."

"Sometimes, I forget how many people Jenn's vanishing haunts, other than me."

I rubbed a hand up and down her back. "There's no way it couldn't. She was so young. Innocent. That rocks a community."

Piper took a step out of my hold, brushing at her eyes. "I wanted to honor her, but maybe I'm just making this worse for everyone involved."

I gripped her elbow, ushering her outside. "Don't say that. You're giving this island a gift by bringing back the Falls. And you're giving a gift to yourself and Jenn. When anything is worth having, you have to walk through a few storms to get there. And I didn't take you as someone who gave up easily."

Piper's eyes blazed with a dark heat. "I'm not."

"Then don't let something like this make you doubt yourself."

She looked at me as if she saw through every shield I'd thrown up. "You gonna walk through your storms, too?"

"I already am." And, somehow, having Piper there made it just a little bit easier. The journey not quite so lonely.

Chapter Thirteen

Piper

THE RAIN POUNDING ON THE ROOF FIT MY MOOD. AND IF Hunter wanted me to walk through the storms, it seemed fitting that I did so when the weather played along. A sneeze rocked my body. I should've worn my mask to brave the attic, but now I was too tired to go back down and get it.

It had been a long time since my nightmares had chased me, but last night had been a doozy. One after the other. Each one worse than the previous. I'd finally given up on sleep altogether around four in the morning. I'd decided it was the perfect time to tackle the attic.

Bruno had taken one look at the piles of junk and had abandoned me in favor of his dog bed downstairs. I didn't blame him one bit. There were some hidden treasures up here, though. Four rocking chairs that would be perfect for the front porch after some touchups. Some old artwork that I could definitely find a home for in the cabins. And now, I was tackling the array of trunks.

I took a rag and carefully cleaned off the top of one. If the combination of dark brown wood and aged leather was anything to go by, the contents should have one hell of a story. Unlatching the lock, I lifted the lid. Scents of dust, aged paper, and cloth filled my senses.

Cream lace had been folded meticulously over the top of the contents. Carefully, I took it out and placed it on the rocker behind me. The trunk held an array of items. A stack of journals. Some loose papers. What looked like baby clothes. And a small wooden box.

I pulled the box out first, the wood creaking as I opened it. There was a pile of jewelry inside. Nothing fancy, but pieces that I imagined held sentimental value to whoever had owned the resort before the Crowleys. I couldn't resist pulling out the antique cameo.

A woman's profile stared back at me, her hair piled high, the shadow set against an apricot background. My fingers traced the grooves. It was beautiful. And something about the sad, sorrowful eyes called to me. I slipped the chain over my head.

There was something special about wearing a piece of history from this place. I could imagine another woman running the resort as more of a boarding house. Families coming to stay for the summer or even a year. I loved picturing myself becoming part of that history.

I set the jewelry box aside, closing the lid. The worn leather journals called to me next. I grinned as I picked up the first one, hoping for tales of past ownership or perhaps family histories that reached far beyond this tiny island. Flipping open the cover, I saw that it was even better. An old ledger from when the resort had first been open in the early nineteen-hundreds.

My fingers ghosted over the names scrawled across the page in varying degrees of legibility. It appeared as if there had only been the lodge and three cabins to begin with. As I flipped through the pages, that number jumped to five and then eight.

There was an entire stack of ledgers in the trunk. I'd likely be able to track the resort's growth up to the point the property changed hands or things went digital. I hauled the pile into my lap and then carefully placed them into a tote I'd brought up with me for discoveries just like this one.

They would be the perfect addition to a table in the lodge's main room. Guests could flip through and get an idea of the history of where they were staying. I hoped that there might be old photos in the trunks, as well. Having images from the past to display would complete the effect.

I pushed to my feet, slinging the bag over my shoulder. As I did, the door to the attic slammed closed. The ferocity of the noise made me jump and startled a little shriek out of me. My hand flew to my chest as I caught my breath. I let out a laugh. "Just a draft."

Crossing to the door, I pulled, but the piece of wood wouldn't budge. I tugged harder. Nothing. A chill skittered up my spine. "Stay calm," I whispered to myself. The doorknob itself still worked, but the door wouldn't budge.

The knob seemed sturdy, so I put my entire body weight into my next pull. The wood groaned but didn't move. My breaths started coming quicker. Not a single soul knew where I was right now. I didn't have my phone—not that it would have worked up here anyway.

I moved to the small window in the corner and looked out. It faced the wrong direction, and with the rain, everyone was inside. Even Hunter and his crew that had arrived earlier today. The attic walls suddenly felt as if they were closing in. As if there were a little less space in the room.

I angled my body under the window to try to shove it open. It didn't move even a millimeter. I pushed harder, the wood splintering and biting into my palm. "Shit." I winced and shook out my hands.

Closing my eyes, I took a deep breath. Everything would be okay. A scratching at the window had a scream tearing loose from my chest. My eyes flew open to see nothing more than a branch scraping against the glass.

The room that had, just a moment ago, felt filled with history and treasures, now seemed ominous and foreboding. I hurried back to the door, giving my all to try and open it. Nothing seemed to work. Out of breath and fingers blistering, tears pricked the corners of my eyes. "One more try. Come on, Piper."

This time, I looped both hands around the door handle and placed a foot against the doorframe. I sucked in a deep breath. Shoving as hard as I could with my foot, I held firmly to the knob with my hands.

It came open with a crack, and I went flying to the floor. My head hit the wooden planks with such force I saw stars. I blinked away the tears in my eyes as I sat up. Gingerly, I touched the back of my head and winced. I would have one hell of a goose egg.

But I didn't waste a second. I scrambled to my feet, ignoring the dizziness, and thundered down the stairs. When I reached the bottom, I almost collided with a broad chest. Two hands reached out to steady me. "Whoa. You okay?"

Heat rose to my cheeks as I took in Nick's worried expression. "S-s-sorry. I was going through some stuff in the attic and got trapped. I think I freaked myself out."

Understanding filled his eyes. "The door get stuck?" I nodded. "There are more than a few doors in this place that will do that. You have to be careful." He released me, but concern still creased his features. "Are you sure this is a good idea? You tackling all of this alone?"

I straightened, brushing the dust off my flannel shirt. "I can handle it. Just a little scare. I'll get Hunter to take a look at the door."

He glanced up the steps. "Did you see anything that Dad might've left behind? I've been hoping to find his journals. I feel horrible that I couldn't make it out before the sale to clean out any old belongings."

I winced at the reminder of my visit to Mr. Crowley yesterday. "I didn't see anything that jumped out as his, only some ledgers from the early nineteen-hundreds. Everything up there looked pretty old. But you're welcome to head up and look. Just prop the door open."

Nick chuckled and started towards the stairs. "I will."

"Nick?"

"Yeah?"

I tugged at the corner of my shirt before speaking as if that might give me the right words. "I went to see your dad yesterday. I just wanted to drop off some cookies and tell him I was looking after the Falls. But he got upset when I was there. I'm so sorry. It wasn't at all what I intended."

Nick stiffened. "It's not your fault. It was really kind of you to stop by." He sighed, scrubbing a hand over his jaw. "Dad is easily confused and upset. And there's not much we can do to help. He took a swing at me the other day when I went to visit."

"I'm so sorry." The words were painfully inadequate, but I didn't know what else to say. Nick had to watch his father disappear right before his very eyes. I wasn't sure which was worse: having someone vanish without a word or seeing them go.

Nick gave me a sad smile. "Just know it's not only you that he acts out with. I'm trying to find the right balance between being there to support him and not upsetting him unnecessarily."

I couldn't imagine having to walk that invisible and ever-changing line. "I won't go back. I don't want to add any stress. But let me know if I can drop things off for you. Or if there's anything else I can do to help."

"Thank you. It means a lot. And for what it's worth, I'm glad you're the one who took over the Falls. It seems right somehow."

It felt right to me, too. Even amidst the break-in, the nightmares, and getting stuck in the attic, it felt right. I just had to walk through the storms first.

Chapter Fourteen

Hunter

"HOPE YOU FIND THOSE FISH YOU'RE LOOKING FOR, Mr. Simpson," I called. The older man just grumbled something as he took off in the direction of the pond.

My foreman chuckled. "What's his deal?"

"Just grumpy. But it's amusing to see what kind of responses I can get from him if I deign to say hello."

Cal grinned. "I think this job is going to be full of interesting characters."

I didn't doubt that he was right. And the most fascinating one of all was headed in our direction. "Hey, Casper."

"Hey," she called, dodging a puddle that the rain had left behind.

"This is my foreman, Cal. Cal, this is the new owner, Piper."

Cal inclined his head in her direction but not before widening his eyes at me a fraction. "Pleased to meet you. I hope this one hasn't been causing you too much trouble without the rest of the crew to keep him in line."

"He's been a constant headache. I'm glad I'll finally have some help dealing with him."

"Hey," I said with mock affront. "I am an angel."

Cal snorted. "Only your mama calls you that."

"I'm regretting handing you the reins for the past couple of months. The power has gone to your head," I chided.

Cal rubbed his hands together with glee. "And now you're never getting it back."

Piper brushed some dust off her sleeve. "I like him."

"Don't fall for his charming smiles. It's all an act." I reached out and brushed off her shoulder. "Where have you been? You're covered head to toe in dust."

She grimaced. "The attic. Where I got stuck. I think I need you to look at the door when you get a chance."

"You got stuck? As in you couldn't get out?"

Piper nodded, blushing. "I might've had a tiny freak-out."

Understandably. The quick look I'd taken of the place had told me it was full of cobwebs and who knew what else. "Are you okay?"

"Fine." But her eyes drifted to her hands.

I reached out to lift one, examining her palm. "Shit, Piper. You need to get these cleaned out." The skin on her palms and fingers was torn and still bleeding in a few places.

"I didn't think it was that bad. I'll clean it in a minute."

I glanced at Cal. "I'll be back in a few. Get the guys started taking out the wall in number six and the floor in number eleven."

"You got it, boss."

I placed a hand on Piper's lower back, ushering her towards the lodge. "Do you have a first-aid kit?"

"In the kitchen."

When we made it inside, Bruno got up from his bed and stretched, then followed us towards the kitchen. I was sure he thought he'd get treats. With a quick look at Piper, I headed for the pantry. "You stay."

"Are you talking to my dog or me?"

"Both of you." I found the first-aid kit without too much trouble and went back to the kitchen.

Piper's glare was pointed directly at me. "I don't take kindly to orders."

"Noted." I set the kit on the island and then lifted Piper onto the counter.

She squealed. "That wasn't an invitation to manhandle me."

I pinned her with a stare. "You need to take better care of yourself."

"I was going to deal with this before you went all crazy worrywart on me. It's not like gangrene is going to set in within minutes."

I examined one of the worst tears in the skin. "You never know. And I'd hate for you to lose one of these pretty fingers."

She huffed out a breath, holding up both her hands. "Fine. Do your worst."

I made quick work of washing my hands and taking some supplies out of the kit. I scooted Piper closer to the sink. "Hold your hands over here so I can rinse any dirt out." She silently obeyed. I tested the temperature and then turned the gentle spray on her. She winced slightly. "I'll take a look at that door when we're done here."

"Thank you."

"We'll probably have to replace it. Sometimes, that old wood is tricky."

She sighed. "Just one more thing to add to the expenses list."

It wasn't just Piper's hands that had me worried. It was the dark circles under her eyes. "Didn't sleep well last night?"

She squirmed in place. "Bad dreams."

"They're not fun."

Her gaze met mine. "You have them?"

"More than my share." They seemed to be easing off a fraction lately, though, ever since I'd told Piper what had happened that day at the cabin.

"I'm sorry."

"Sucks for both of us." I pulled off the cap of the anti-bacterial spray. "This might sting." I sent a blast of it over her hands.

"Holy hell, that doesn't sting. It burns with the power of a thousand blazing suns."

I took her hands in mine and bent to blow on the abused skin. When I straightened, we were close. Too close. Our mouths just a breath away. "Feel better?"

She nodded. "Thank you."

I couldn't seem to move. Some invisible force held me in place. Just as I was about to do something monumentally stupid, Bruno nosed between us. Piper smiled down at her dog. "He's feeling neglected."

And saving me from myself, apparently. "I'll give him a little TLC after I bandage your hands."

I swiped ointment over each tear in Piper's skin, fighting the urge to let out a slew of curses. She'd done a number on herself. "You're going to have to take it easy over the next couple of days. I'll rewrap these cuts if you have trouble."

She scowled down at her hands. "I have some painting I need to do. That shouldn't hurt them too bad."

I wanted to tell her to let the crew handle it, but Piper would go crazy if she weren't productive. "Just make sure you keep the cuts covered."

"Yes, Dr. Hardy. Where did you get your medical degree, by the way?"

"The school of hard knocks."

"Hard knocks on the head, maybe."

I chuckled. "You're all done. The worst patient I've ever had. Even Cal didn't complain this much when a new guy on the crew sent a nail through his foot."

Piper's eyes widened. "Seriously?"

"It wasn't a pretty sight."

"I'll bet."

I helped her down from the counter. "Will you do me a favor before you head back to work?"

She eyed me carefully. "What would that be?"

"Have a snack. Maybe drink some juice. You had a scare. You need to get your blood sugar back up."

Piper's expression gentled, and she stretched up on her tiptoes, pressing a kiss to my cheek. "I never say no to a snack."

The brush of that mouth against my skin seemed to burn. And I was sure I'd feel the imprint of her for the rest of my day. I cleared my throat. "I'll grab Cal and deal with the door."

"Thanks again. For everything."

I nodded but didn't meet her eyes as I headed out. I was too scared that if I looked into those dark depths, I'd stay in the kitchen and do something that couldn't be undone. Instead, I strode out of the lodge and towards Cal.

He let out a low whistle as I approached. "Now I know why you were more than happy to work this job alone for the past few weeks."

"Shut up. You know I don't go there."

He arched a brow. "I have a feeling you might be breaking that rule of yours this time around."

But I couldn't. It was too risky, on too many fronts.

Cal kept right on going. "I'm going to have to tell Ashley to stop setting you up with her friends."

"That alone will be worth listening to you give me shit. Your wife's friends are going to be the death of me." I couldn't begin to total up the number of ambush setups Ashley had leveled on me. Every time she invited me over for dinner, I knew there was a risk.

"You were singing a different tune when she introduced you to Carly."

I leveled Cal with a stare. "Carly seemed all nice and sweet, and then it turned out she had a freaky foot fetish."

He barked out a laugh. "Everyone's got their kink."

"Well, that is not my kink." I gave an exaggerated shiver.

"I really thought things were gonna work out with you and Courtney. That seemed like a good fit. And that was thanks to Ash. She's pretty set on you two being perfect for each other."

Things with Court had been good for a while. I couldn't put my finger on exactly what hadn't worked for me. Things had almost been *too* easy. It hadn't felt like I knew the real Courtney, and she hadn't known me. Within the first handful of conversations, I had felt like I knew Piper on a level that most people didn't get to. And there was something about that. An addictive feeling. And I couldn't wait for another hit.

"You're thinking about the boss lady again, aren't you?" Cal smirked.

"Shut up and come help me fix a door."

With Cal on my heels, I wouldn't get away with anything. But maybe that was exactly what I needed—someone to keep me from diving into the deep end without a life preserver.

Chapter Fifteen

Piper

I TOOK A SIP OF THE HOT CHOCOLATE AND SURVEYED THE bookshelves. They were coming along nicely. I was slowly but surely creating a welcoming space for all the guests that would pass through this room. I blinked my eyes, attempting to clear away the burn. Sleep had not been a frequent visitor over the past few days.

That wasn't quite right. Sleep had come, but on its heels came the nightmares. I was in a gray sea in the worst ones, submerged in the salt water and searching for Jenn. But I couldn't find her anywhere. Just as the fire engulfed my lungs from lack of air, I'd wake up gasping for breath.

I wasn't eager to experience that one again. My hope was that if I were tired enough, no dreams would come. So, here I stood, organizing my library. Bruno snored from his new spot in the corner where I'd moved his bed. No nightmares seemed to plague him.

I picked up a few thrillers and put them in place on the shelf. The organizational system was unique. Memoirs and biographies.

The shelf I dubbed *murdery books*. Young adult. Books that felt like a warm hug. History of the area. It would be fun to add to the sections over time. To see what genres were most popular.

A flash of muted light in the window caught my attention. I moved towards the glass, peering out. Nothing. I scanned the grassy area behind the lodge; my eyes straining to make out anything in the dark. The moon was only a sliver and barely gave even a hint of illumination.

A translucent form sprang up on the other side of the window, startling a scream out of me. An image of a woman in a white dress fluttered and then went out. As soon as she disappeared, flames burst to life less than a dozen feet from the back deck of the lodge. A white gown billowed against the fire.

I didn't think, couldn't rationalize the images flashing before my eyes. I simply moved, running out the glass double doors onto the deck, Bruno hot on my heels, now barking. The flames flew higher, engulfing what I could now see was a mannequin. Out of the corner of my eye, I caught a figure running away.

Shouts sounded, and Nick ran up the deck steps. "I'll get the fire extinguisher. Stay back."

My gaze jumped to the lawn. The heat from the past few days had completely dried the grass. Images of those flames engulfing the main building danced in my mind. I ran around the side of the lodge to get the long hose. Cranking the water as high as it would go, I jogged towards the flames.

"Stay, Bruno," I commanded.

I reached the blaze at the same time as Nick, and we unleashed streams of liquid simultaneously. I focused first on the grass in front of the blaze, hoping I could prevent it from catching. As soon as I'd doused that patch of land, I turned the water on the fire itself. Nick's extinguisher soon emptied itself, but I kept working on the dying flames.

"What the hell?" he asked, out of breath.

"I don't know." Anger laced my words, but my heart galloped in my chest, seeming to bounce around my rib cage. "Thank you for coming out to help." I didn't want to think about what would've happened if he hadn't shown up.

"Of course." He studied what remained of the fire. "This could've been really bad. Is that a doll?"

"I think it's a mannequin."

"Piper," Hunter's voice called from the darkness.

The vise that had gripped my chest relaxed a fraction at the deep timbre of that single word. "We're okay."

Nick jogged up onto the deck again and flicked on a floodlight.

"I think we've got your vandals." Hunter held two teen boys by the backs of their shirts. One looked ready to pass out or vomit, but the other had a pompous look on his face.

Mr. Pompous leered in my direction. "We weren't doing anything. You can't hold us. It's kidnapping."

Bruno let out a low growl and planted himself in front of me.

Hunter kept pushing the boys along. "The smell of gas on your hands says otherwise. Nick, can you call the sheriff?"

"You got it."

Hunter shoved them towards the deck's steps. "Sit. If you move, I'll cuff you with cable ties."

My eyes widened at the ferocity in Hunter's tone, but I didn't take my attention off the dying fire. It was mostly out, but I wanted every last ember gone. Hunter rounded the pyre and gave my neck a squeeze. "You okay?"

I nodded. "Just gave me a good scare."

Hunter's gaze traveled from me to the fire and then to the lodge. "If you hadn't been awake, this could've taken the whole resort."

I swallowed against the lump rising in my throat. He was

right. A little wind, a few sparks, and the entire resort could've gone up in flames. I turned to the boys. "Why? Why would you do something like this?"

"I-I-I'm sorry, ma'am. We just wanted to play a little joke. You know the ghost stories and everything," the scared one said.

"Shut up, Aaron. Don't say a fucking word," the other one hissed.

Hunter stalked towards them, and I caught the glint of silver in the waistband of his jeans. A gun. The idea that Hunter thought he needed that to protect himself, to protect me, sent a shiver down my spine. He leaned towards the boys. "Oh, you're gonna talk. And you're also going to pay for what you've done. You could've killed someone."

"Jasper," Aaron whispered.

Jasper scoffed. "Yeah right. It was just a prank. My parents will pay for the damages. It's not like it's a big deal."

"It's too late for that," Nick said, coming out of the lodge. "The sheriff and a deputy are on their way."

"Shit, man," Aaron moaned. "I told you this was a bad idea."

I dropped the hose and jogged back to the side of the building to turn off the water, Bruno sticking with me every step of the way. I gave him a scratch behind the ears. "Love you, too, buddy."

When I returned, Mr. Simpson had arrived and was leveling a scowl at everyone. "What in God's name is going on out here? Do you know what time it is?"

"I'm so sorry, Mr. Simpson. It would appear we have some troublemakers at work." Understatement of the century. "The sheriff is on his way. I apologize if we disturbed your sleep." Thankfully, I didn't see any lights on at the Gragerts' cabin in the distance. Hopefully, they'd slept through everything.

Mr. Simpson glared at the teenagers. "I hope you throw the book at them." And with that, he turned and stalked off.

I rubbed at my temples where a headache was beginning to pulse. "Maybe this place is cursed."

Nick winced. "I was hoping you'd have better luck than my family did."

Hunter strode towards me, wrapping me in a hug. "The Falls isn't cursed. And I'm guessing these two are the same ones who broke in. We've caught your culprits, and we can fix the rest."

I sank into his hold, soaking up every ounce of warmth that poured out of him. I was exhausted, and I simply needed someone to prop me up for a while so I could rest. So, I let myself be held. Shielded from the realities of the world by his embrace for just a minute.

"Thank you," I mumbled against his chest.

"For what?"

"Everything?" I said it as a question because I wasn't quite sure how to put all the things Hunter had done for me into words. It was more than a working relationship. It was the kind of friendship I hadn't had in forever.

He brushed the hair back from my face. "You've helped me, too. More than you realize."

I could just make out the dark green of Hunter's eyes in the glow of the lodge's light. Something in them seemed to spark and burn. I wanted to lean a little closer, lose myself there. "I guess we make a pretty good team."

Hunter flashed a grin. "We can even catch bad guys and save the day."

I groaned but did it while chuckling. "I wish there was a secret bad guy pit we could toss them into. I think dealing with the legalities of this is going to be a nightmare."

Lights from an emergency vehicle flashed through the darkness, and Hunter pulled me closer against him. "But you won't have to deal with it alone."

It terrified me just how relieved that promise made me.

Chapter Sixteen

Hunter

PARKER SCOWLED IN THE DIRECTION OF THE TWO TEENS sitting on the deck steps. "The parents are on their way. I can't question them until they get here. And given the damage and potential charges, they may ask for a lawyer."

Piper pressed harder against my side. "What are they going to be charged with? Don't get me wrong, there needs to be some consequences for their actions, but I don't want to take things too far."

"It's up to the prosecutor. But they'll likely be charged with arson. It's up for debate whether it's a misdemeanor or a felony. They set the fire close to an inhabited building, and that's a heavy strike against them," Parker explained.

Piper nibbled on the edge of her thumbnail, and I knew she felt bad for the boys. But one look at that kid, Jasper, and I knew any empathy was a mistake. The teen had a malicious glint in his eyes and didn't seem to contain even an ounce of remorse for an action that could've killed someone. I squeezed Piper's shoulder, bringing her gaze to mine. "You need to see this through. Trust me."

She nodded slowly. "Okay. They do need to at least cover the damages. I'll have to reseed a big chunk of the lawn."

"And those two need to take responsibility for their actions." It might be too late for Jasper to learn, but his friend—the one who'd let himself be talked into this mess—still had a prayer of turning into a halfway decent human being.

Headlights swept across the lodge as a luxury sedan pulled into the parking area beside the building. A couple hurried out of the vehicle. The woman crossed the area more quickly than the man. "Are the boys okay? They weren't hurt, were they?"

"Ma'am, I'm Sheriff Raines. The boys are fine, but they were apprehended in the process of committing a crime, as I explained."

The woman straightened. "There has to be some kind of mistake. They wouldn't."

Her husband came up alongside her and wrapped an arm around her shoulders. "Just what do you think they did?" He glanced at the teens sulking on the steps and then moved his gaze to the fire damage on the lawn.

"Mr. Leclair," Parker greeted. "Jasper and Aaron built a bonfire to burn a mannequin outside the Whispering Falls lodge. They projected a hologram over the windows in an attempt to frighten the woman inside."

Mr. Leclair chuckled. "A prank? You called us out of bed for a prank?"

Piper stiffened in my arms, and I had to bite the inside of my cheek to keep from decking the man. Parker straightened. "The fire was set extremely close to a building with someone inside. That, sir, is a felony."

All humor fled Mr. Leclair's expression. "That's ridiculous. I'll pay for the damages. It doesn't look like there was much. But I'm taking the boys home tonight."

"I'm afraid that's not possible. While they're minors, they

committed a crime. Jasper and Aaron will be taken to Shelter Island and booked. You may accompany us and be present for questioning. Or you may choose to have a lawyer present if you prefer."

"This is bullshit. If you think you can use this to extort money out of us for this piece-of-shit lodge—"

"Be very careful how you finish that sentence," I growled, letting my arm slip from around Piper's shoulders. "Your son and his friend could've killed someone tonight. Jasper has shown zero remorse. And I can see why. But that's going to change because this isn't in your hands."

"Hunter," Parker warned.

My gaze shot to him. "Am I wrong?"

"You're not, but we don't need anything stoking the animosity right now. All right?"

I gave a jerky nod.

Mr. Leclair glared at me. "You're the owner?"

Before I could answer, Piper stepped forward. "No, I am. And I was in the lodge alone when the incident occurred. If one of our guests hadn't been nearby, the fire might have taken off, and there wouldn't have been anything I or anyone could do. Hunter's right. People could've died tonight."

A muscle in Mr. Leclair's cheek ticked. "I'm sorry you were frightened. I'll have a word with Jasper about his manners."

I snorted. This went way past manners. That kid had a desire to hurt people. Got a thrill from terrifying them and didn't care how the story ended.

Parker stepped forward. "I'm afraid it's gone past that. Leveling charges isn't up to Ms. Cosgrove. It's up to the prosecutor. The only decision Piper has to make is whether or not to press civil charges."

"Civil charges?" Mrs. Leclair asked. "This is insanity. They're just boys. Up to a little mischief."

Parker leveled her with a stare. "That is far from the truth, ma'am. And the court will feel the same way."

"Warren, do something," the woman screeched at her husband.

"I'm going to call our lawyer." He turned to the teenagers. "Don't say a word, you two."

Jasper's eyes cut to Piper and me. "Told you."

Piper's fingers grabbed hold of my t-shirt. "There is something seriously wrong with that kid."

"I know." I pulled her against my side again as if that alone could keep her safe. God, what if she'd been sleeping? The entire lodge was made of wood. It would've gone up in flames in a matter of minutes. I did my best not to hold her too tightly, but I wasn't sure I'd be able to let her go. Not tonight. Not knowing what a close call this had been.

"Deputy Hughes, let's get these two in the SUV so we can head back to the station," Parker said.

The female officer nodded and headed towards the teenagers. Mrs. Leclair gaped at Parker. "You're putting them in a cop car?"

"It's procedure, ma'am. But you can follow us to the docks and ride with us in the boat."

"I—I never. Warren, this is outrageous."

Mr. Leclair's glare was glacial. "The department will be made aware of their missteps in this case."

Parker shrugged. "You do what you have to do, but I've got a job to do, and you're not going to stop me from doing it." He turned to Piper. "I'll be back to talk to you tomorrow. You have my number if you need anything."

We watched in silence as the entire group left. Bruno let out a bark and growl from the lodge when the boys walked past. I rubbed a hand up and down Piper's arm. "At least we know Bruno has your back."

Piper's mouth curved. "My knight in shining armor."

"Hey, what am I? Chopped liver?"

She patted my chest. "You were very heroic. I don't think I'll ever forget the image of you dragging those kids across the yard. The younger one looked like he might pee his pants."

"There's hope for that one. *If* he stays away from Jasper."

"If his parents have any brains, they'll *keep* him away."

"Hopefully, Parker gets in touch with them soon."

Piper looked up at me. "I didn't even ask. Are they locals?"

I ushered her towards the lodge. "I don't think so. I've never seen any of them before."

"That makes me feel better somehow."

I pulled open the back door. "Why?"

Piper made her way towards the kitchen. "I don't like the idea of people who live here being so callous."

"There are bad eggs everywhere. Even on Anchor." I knew that better than most. And how those people could hide under your nose without you even realizing it.

Piper stopped, tugging at my t-shirt. "What is it?"

"Nothing."

She tugged harder. "Don't lie. You can tell me it's none of my business, but don't lie."

As I stared down at her, I felt that now-familiar pull. I wanted to spill it all, every last secret. Wanted to lay everything at Piper's feet. "I've been blind about things like this twice. The guy that helped Michael kidnap Shay was on my crew. I didn't sense that anything was off about him until it was almost too late."

"And the other time?" she whispered.

My jaw worked back and forth as I tried to get the words out. "A little over a year ago, someone stalked my brother and Bell." I swallowed against the burn in my throat. "He tried to kill Ford. Kidnapped Bell. Turned out, it was my best friend. I never saw it. Not a damned thing. People can hide their darkness." I shrugged. "Or maybe I'm just shit at reading people and seeing the truth."

Piper gripped my t-shirt harder, her gaze never leaving mine. "You loved someone who did something horrible. That doesn't make you bad. It doesn't make you blind. It makes you loyal. It makes you someone who wants to see the best in people."

Each word hit like a physical blow. The way this woman saw my failures. "You don't know how bad it was," I croaked. All I could see was the terror in Bell's eyes after she'd been rescued. The pain in Ford's face as he recovered from his injuries.

"I don't have to." Piper placed her hand on my chest, right over my heart. "I know what's in here. I've seen it. You're a good man, Hunter. One day, you'll forgive yourself for the things that weren't your fault and see the truth."

Chapter Seventeen

Piper

I WOKE WITH A GROAN, MY FACE PRESSED AGAINST A HARD surface. No, *smushed* into it. A chest? Oh, God. Was there drool coming out of my mouth? My eyes flew open. Yep, there was a small spot of drool on the t-shirt-covered chest beneath me. Hunter's chest.

Everything came back in flashes. The fire. The sheriff's department. Those awful parents. Hunter's heartbreaking confession. After he'd given me that peek into his world and the shadows haunting him, I'd done the only thing I could think of. I'd made hot chocolate.

We'd sat on the overstuffed couch in the library and talked about everything and nothing. Our childhoods and favorite spots on the island. Favorite movies and foods we couldn't stand. I'd learned that Hunter had a soft spot for old-school romcoms and hated eggplant. He usually took at least one long hike on the weekends, and he'd never live down the time he dressed up in a full cheerleader outfit for his school's powder puff football game.

Somewhere along that train of discovery, we'd fallen asleep. And we'd done it curled around each other as if our bodies had instinctively known just how to fit together. I did my best to keep my breathing slow and steady. But my heart hammered against my ribs as I tried to get up without waking Hunter.

He mumbled something in his sleep and pulled me tighter against him. I didn't want to admit just how good it felt, his warmth and strength forming a cocoon I never wanted to leave. As Hunter turned into me, I froze, another body part altogether making itself known. The action must've roused him because his eyes popped open.

"Morning," I whispered, not knowing what else to say.

"Well, hell," he muttered.

The look of pure panic on his face had me dissolving into laughter. "Oh, God. Hunter. I drooled on your shirt."

His chest started to shake. "Better than waking up with a hard-on."

The laughter came harder until tears streamed down my face. "At least, we're in it together."

"You have to stop laughing," he groaned. "It's not helping."

"Sorry." I awkwardly pushed myself up, trying not to touch any body parts that should be off-limits for my hands.

Hunter scowled at me. "It also doesn't help how damn attractive you look all rumpled and mussed."

Heat licked through me at his words, and I wanted nothing more than to lay right back down. Instead, I forced myself to stand. "I'll let all the women who come around know that bedhead is what does it for you."

"No women come around."

"It was a joke."

"Yeah, yeah," he muttered but didn't look very happy.

"Sorry about your shirt."

He looked down and grinned. "I can handle a little drool."

He might be able to handle it, but I didn't think I'd ever forget how good it'd felt to have him pressed up against me. His long, muscled body surrounding mine. I gave myself a good mental shake. "Glad to hear it."

Bruno got up from his bed in the corner and padded over. I gave him a little rub. "I'd better let him out. And I need to get ready for some cleanup."

"I can help with that," Hunter offered, sitting up.

"That's okay. Celeste should be here in an hour. I'll have extra hands."

"You sure?"

"Yeah. You've got your crew." And something in me needed a little distance. It had been too easy to lean on him. But I needed to figure things out myself. Fix them with my hands. And that meant cleaning up the mess from last night.

"Okay. Just come find me if you need me."

"I will." I watched as Hunter headed out the front door. And everything felt just a little colder once he was gone.

⌒◎

I dumped another shovelful of charred ground into the wheelbarrow. Each trip to the dumpster stoked my anger a little more. The lack of care these kids had shown. The cruelty. Not having a single care that their actions might destroy someone's dream. One of the few pieces of Jenn that I still had.

My hand went instinctively to my necklace. Even that was fading. The words engraved on my half of our heart wore away more and more with time—just like everything else.

Even though I had photos and a few videos, her face was a little less defined in my mind. I used to be able to see her so clearly. The way she moved through the world as though it were at her mercy. For a long time, I swore I could even smell the green tea lotion she'd worn since the fifth grade. But that had faded, too. For the last several years, it all felt like a movie I had watched years ago instead of something from real life.

But being back at the Falls had changed things. I'd gotten glimpses of the past. I'd round a corner and a memory would hit me. Just the other day, I could've sworn I heard Jenn's laugh. Bright and booming, completely uninhibited—just like she had been.

And these two teenagers had almost cost me that. They didn't care. They'd only been looking to get a charge out of scaring someone half to death. I hadn't heard from Parker yet today, but I hoped the kids were getting a scare of their own. And a healthy wake-up call.

A low whistle cut through the air. "It's even worse close-up," Celeste said as she approached.

I stared down at the burnt ground, wondering how much I needed to clear away so that the new grass would take. "It could've been worse."

"What were those boys thinking?" she asked, shaking her head.

"Not much, as my uncle, Nathan, would say."

Celeste chuckled. "Glad to see you haven't lost your sense of humor. This place can take it out of you."

I paused in my shoveling and took in the lines of her face. "What do you mean?"

She shrugged and picked up the second shovel, spearing the ground with it. "There's been a lot of pain here. It's a reason so many people tell those ghost stories. Some folks wouldn't stick around to make things right."

I lifted another piece of singed sod into the wheelbarrow. "I'm not going to let that kind of thing stop me."

"Even the ghosts that haunt you?"

My grip on the shovel tightened. "I'm not haunted." The words sounded like a lie even to my ears. The truth was that I'd gotten the first good sleep I'd had in weeks last night. On a couch, pressed up against Hunter.

"You don't need to lie to me, honey. Just tell my old nosy self to mind my own."

I forced myself to send a smile in Celeste's direction. "This place doesn't just hold pain, you know. It holds a heck of a lot of good, too. At least, it does for me. I hope it does for you, too."

She dumped dirt and grass into the wheelbarrow. "It's got a healthy mixture for me, too. The Crowleys became good friends while I worked here. Got lots of beautiful memories with that sweet family. But it hurt like hell when we lost Mrs. C. Even more to see this place go down in her absence. And now, we're losing Albert, too."

"I'm sorry. I didn't know you guys were so close." That was the thing about places like this. With so much history and so many people crossing through its orbit, memories touched us all every day.

"It gives me hope that you'll bring it back. A little piece of both of them carrying on."

"I hope it gives me the same. A way to keep Jenn alive. A place where I can remember her."

Sympathy filled Celeste's expression. "You're sure she's passed?"

The question took me by surprise, a hard blow to the gut that stole my breath. It was why I didn't talk about her often. Especially not with anyone but Nathan and Vic. People asked questions. They were curious. And if you weren't careful, they could ask something that would slice you right open.

"No," I croaked. "I'm not sure. I just mean keeping her memory alive." Everything in me tightened as I spoke the words. A mixture of anxiety, fear, and guilt swirling through me, constricting my muscles.

"Excuse me," I choked out. "I need to get some water."

"Piper—" Celeste began. But I was already charging away. I didn't head for the lodge. Instead, I walked alongside it, making a beeline for the forest. I needed air. To move. If I didn't, I'd crawl out of my skin.

As I rounded the building, I almost ran straight into Hunter. "Sorry," I mumbled and kept right on going.

He caught my elbow. "Hey, what's wrong?"

"Nothing." I tugged my elbow from his grasp and strode towards the trees.

By the time I hit the tree line, Hunter was by my side. "If you think I'm just going to let you take off alone, looking white as a sheet and with so much pain in your eyes, you've got another thing coming."

"It's not your job to take care of me. You know that, right?"

"You being prickly right now isn't going to keep me from giving a damn. You know *that*, right?"

I whirled on him. "Back off. I need to be alone."

"Can't do it. Not gonna let whatever's eating at you get you alone."

I let out a growl and shoved at his chest. "You don't get to see. Not this. It's mine."

His eyes bored into me as if searching for a million things I wouldn't voice. "You got to see my mess. All of it. Every last thing. There's bravery in letting someone in."

"I'm not brave. And if I hadn't been so scared all the damned time, Jenn would still be here. I would've gone with her. And then I wouldn't have to lie to everyone when I say I think she's still alive. I wouldn't lie when I feel every single second that she's gone."

The words flew from me, and with them, the tears. Ugly, wracking sobs. I broke. And there was nothing I could do to stop it.

Hunter

I CAUGHT PIPER JUST AS SHE STARTED TO CRUMPLE, HER knees giving out. Too much was coming at her from all sides. Things that weren't hers to carry. I lifted her into my arms and strode towards the barn where Celeste's grandsons and I had stored all the cabins' furniture. Piper wouldn't want to chance any of the Falls' guests seeing her this way.

I slid open the barn door with my foot and made my way inside. The air was cool and smelled stale, but it would have to do. I eased down onto one of the sheet-covered couches and placed Piper in my lap.

Sobs continued wracking her body, and I didn't have the first clue how to fix it, to make it better. The small movements I made were simple instinct, rocking her back and forth as I ran a hand over her hair. "That's it. Let it out. Been holding it inside for too long."

So much blame. God, that stuff was toxic. I'd only been living with it for the past two years, and it was already eating me alive. It had been working on Piper for a decade. And it had grabbed hold of her at such a vulnerable time. Fourteen years old. Barely a teenager. An age when you were still trying to figure out who you were.

She pressed her face harder against my chest as if trying to escape the world, to crawl inside me. I wrapped both arms around her and held her as close as possible. "It's not your fault. It never was."

"It is." Her voice shook, the words barely audible between her cries.

I kept rocking with her, waiting out the sobs, knowing they couldn't last forever. But she wouldn't be able to truly hear me until she worked the hysteria out of her system. She'd bottled it up for too long.

So, we sat there. I rocked, and she cried. I didn't stop the small motions until her heaving eased, and the tears slowed. "You coming back to me, Casper?"

"I'm sorry," she whispered.

I squeezed her shoulder. "Don't you dare apologize. You don't owe a soul an apology."

"Even putting glue in Bobby Smith's hair in kindergarten?"

I chuckled, something in my chest releasing at Piper cracking a joke. "Okay, you can feel guilty for that. Unless he deserved it."

"He put a frog in Jenn's lunchbox. He definitely deserved it."

Her voice hitched on Jenn's name, and I brushed the hair away from her face. "You ready to talk about it?"

I wanted nothing more in that moment than for Piper to let me in. To let me share her burden and ease a little of her pain. Because I was falling for this pint-sized spitfire with more heart and work ethic than I'd ever seen before. And I couldn't find it in me to tell myself that it was a bad idea. The only thing I cared about right now was Piper.

Her breath shuddered through her. "I miss her. And I can't help but wonder how different things would've been if I had just gone to that damn party. Maybe she'd be here with me, sharing the workload to restore this place. Or perhaps we would've had an epic falling-out in high school that we never recovered from. But at least she'd be alive. Because as much as I wish it weren't true, I know she's not."

I couldn't imagine having to come to terms with that without seeing any evidence. The only proof had been in the empty space Jenn had left behind. "I'm not going to tell you not to question yourself. There's no way not to. But you can't blame yourself for her disappearance."

Piper looked up at me with bloodshot eyes. "Then whose fault is it? They still don't know what happened. Maybe someone took her. But maybe she had too much to drink and fell off one of the cliffs into the sea. Whose fault is it then? The water's? I need someone to dump all of this anger onto."

"And it's just as easy to turn it inward."

She lifted a shoulder and then let it drop. "That punching bag's always present."

I cupped her cheek with one of my hands, swiping my thumb across the tracks that her tears had left behind. "I'm not a fan of anyone taking potshots at you. Even you."

"You really do have a strong protective streak, don't you?"

"When it comes to people I care about, yeah."

Shadows flitted across her eyes. "Jenn and I were the same way. Always the most protective of each other. The second Ethan invited her to that party, I should've told her she couldn't go. I knew there'd be drinking, maybe even drugs. It was so stupid."

Everything in me locked. Even my heart seemed to stopped pumping. "Did you say Ethan?"

She blinked up at me. "Yeah. He was one of the boys who invited us to the party. Jenn had a crush on him."

This wasn't happening. Couldn't be. What were the chances? I'd known my friends had been at the bonfire that night. I'd known they'd seen the girl who'd gone missing. But what were the chances that the one person who had invited Jenn to the party was the same one whose sickness I hadn't seen? The best friend I'd had all my life, who'd returned the gift of friendship by almost killing my brother and terrorizing my soon-to-be sister-in-law.

"Oh, God, I'm sorry. Do you know him? I didn't mean to insinuate anything. He was perfectly nice. Just older, and we weren't ready for that crowd."

"We went to high school together." It wasn't a lie, but it was so far from the truth. I couldn't seem to find the words to tell her everything. Not now. Not yet. I needed to know more. And it wasn't like Ethan was some crazed killer. He'd become fixated on Ford and Bell in a sick way, but he hadn't done that to anyone else.

I kept telling myself the same thing over and over, but even that felt like a lie.

Hunter

T HE BUZZER OF THE REINFORCED STEEL DOOR BROKE
through the muted whispers of the people in line. A guard
with a clipboard stepped forward. "Hunter Hardy?"

I didn't answer for a moment. Couldn't seem to find my voice.
Instead, I simply nodded and stepped forward.

"Identification?"

I'd already shown it when I arrived at the prison. I'd been
searched and had had to sign what felt like endless paperwork.
But here I was, showing my driver's license again.

The guard read the name and then glanced at the photo to
compare it to the man standing in front of him. "You're in stall
three. Your prisoner is waiting."

"Thank you." The words came out on a croak, but it was the
best I could do. It was a miracle I'd even been able to get in to see
Ethan today. It was only because he had already put me on his
visitors' list. His parents had begged me to go and see him, but I
hadn't been able to do it. To face the friend who had almost cost
my family everything. To finally be forced to examine whether

or not there had been darkness in him that I'd seen all along and chose to ignore.

But I couldn't wait any longer. I needed answers. Explanations to give Piper. She'd looked slightly confused when I told her that I was headed to Seattle for a meeting today. Just one more lie to add to the pile. But I needed more information before I could tell her everything. I needed to know if there was any chance that Ethan had stolen her best friend from her.

If there was, I didn't see how she'd be able to get past it. Every time she looked at me, she would see the best friend of a killer— the person who had changed her life forever.

My steps towards the small prison phonebooth-type setup were slow and measured. As if I were counting down to something that might destroy me. I came to a stop at the stall labeled number three. My gaze met familiar brown eyes, yet something about them seemed different. They appeared slightly unfocused but at the same time took in every movement around him.

I wondered if it was a side effect of the medication Ethan was on. That had been one of his parents' pleas. They'd told me he was different now that he was on medication. Better. The prison had a psychiatric ward and doctors who could treat and monitor him. But I wasn't sure they could cure the part of him that wanted to harm the people I loved.

I slowly eased onto the metal stool, pausing before I picked up the phone. When I did, Ethan mirrored my movements. He cleared his throat. "Hey, man."

The greeting was so normal. So familiar. The same acknowledgment I'd received a million times. Hearing it now, through glass and a phone line, was almost an out-of-body experience.

"Hey."

"I'm glad you came."

I stared at the person who'd shared so much with me while growing up. It was almost ironic. Both Piper and I had lost our best friends though in completely different ways. "I need to ask you about something."

Ethan's jaw worked back and forth, and he tapped out a silent rhythm on the desk. "Can't talk about them. It's not good for me."

I saw it then. The anger still bubbling beneath the surface. The medication might be keeping him in check, but it hadn't destroyed the root of it all. The insidious anger and fixation on Ford and Bell. "I'm not here to talk about that."

Ethan's fingers stilled for a moment before picking up the tapping again. "What is it?"

I gripped the phone tighter. "Do you remember Jenn Branton? The girl who went missing?"

His staccato beat picked up speed. "Sure."

"You saw her the night she vanished, right?"

He gave me a jerky nod. "Me, Tim, and Nick. We all saw her. Everyone else, too. Half our class was there. Cal and Ashley. Marco. Jill and Lex. I hung out with her for a while but then we went our separate ways. You know how those parties were."

I could almost see the night playing out. Like the million parties before it. A bonfire and plenty of beer. Someone would always bring music, but we never let it get too loud. Didn't want to risk the party getting broken up. Some sort of high school drama always came to light. Someone always got too drunk and did something stupid. Only this time, the consequences had been far greater.

"Tell me what happened."

"What's this about?"

"Just tell me, Ethan. I need to know." I wouldn't give him the why. Not yet. It would give him something to hold over my head. Possibly get me to keep coming back if he was feeling particularly manipulative.

"It was the usual. Drinking. Flirting. I remember Cal and Ashley having one of their fights."

A smile almost pulled at my mouth. Cal and his now-wife, Ashley, had endured a drama-filled early relationship. But after a breakup, they'd realize just how much they loved each other and get it together. "What else?"

"It was a million years ago, Hunt. I don't really remember. I know the girl showed up. Tried to play at being older than she was. Had too much to drink. We told her she should head back to her cabin."

"Who was *we*?"

Ethan's tapping stopped, his fingers curling into his palm. "I don't know. Everyone."

"And you just let her go off alone? No one walked her home?" I knew we were all idiots back in high school, but letting a drunk girl wander off near some cliffs? That was insane.

"I don't remember. I told you, it was a long time ago. Why do you keep asking all these questions?" His words came faster and faster, frustration lacing his tone.

I knew my time was limited, and I only had one real shot at this. A surprise attack was my best option. I kept my gaze trained on Ethan's face, looking for any tells. "Did you hurt her?"

He froze. "I didn't hurt her. I don't hurt anyone. No one who doesn't deserve it. No one!"

Ethan's voice rose with every word until a guard moved in behind him, placing a hand on his shoulder. "Calm down."

"Fuck you!" Ethan threw the guard's arm off. "I don't hurt people! They deserve it!"

Two more guards appeared in a flash and pushed Ethan to the floor, pulling his arms behind his back. Soon, someone in a different uniform appeared, holding a syringe. What seemed like seconds after they injected Ethan with the substance, his body went lax. Someone rolled in a stretcher, and they lifted Ethan onto it.

I couldn't tear my eyes away from the scene. Didn't understand how I hadn't seen all of this long before it was too late. And I still didn't have any answers. Not ones I could be certain of, anyway. But time had run out. I couldn't keep this from Piper. Not if I ever wanted her to trust me.

I rose without waiting for a guard to tell me to leave. Everything was a blur as I exited. The sun flared in my eyes as I walked outside, but I relished the burn. That and the clean air. I'd never go back there. Not for all the money in the world.

As I walked to my truck, I pulled out my cell phone and hit a contact. It rang three times before someone picked up. "Raines."

"Parker, it's Hunter. I need to ask you something."

"Everything okay?"

I beeped my locks and climbed into my vehicle. "Not really. You remember the Jenn Branton case?"

"There's not a law enforcement official on these islands who doesn't. But I was the low man on the totem pole back then. It was my first month on the job. Mostly handled grunt work."

"Do you know that Piper was Jenn's best friend?"

A door closing sounded over the line. "Hell. I didn't remember the name."

Piper would be glad that not everyone could place her right away. That her pain could remain private in most cases. I shifted in my seat. "Did you know Ethan was there that night? He invited Jenn to that party."

Parker was silent for a moment before speaking. "Jenn Branton's case is still open. When we arrested Ethan, the fact that he was a person of interest in that case popped. We questioned him about it during his interrogations. We also reached out to other witnesses who were present the night the Branton girl vanished. We have no reason to believe that Ethan had anything to do with her disappearance. More than one person saw him get in his truck and leave the party."

My shoulders sagged in relief, but the feeling didn't sink all the way in. It probably never would. I'd forever wonder if Ethan had hurt other people. Worry that I could've stopped him from inflicting pain.

"What's all this about?" Parker asked.

"I'm at the prison. I had to know if he had something to do with it. Before I talk to Piper."

"You're falling for her."

I gripped my keys a little harder, the teeth of them digging into my palm. "I care about her."

"Then level with her. She doesn't seem like the type to hold something like that against you."

I hoped not. But grief did funny things to people. Things you didn't expect. "I will. Thank you for being honest with me."

I was about to hang up when Parker spoke. "Ethan's actions aren't on you. Just like Shay's brother's or Sam's weren't. I know it can be hard to let that shit go. Constantly asking yourself if you could've done something differently. But when the time came, you acted. You tried to help when others would've turned away. That's more than anyone could ask for. If I wasn't so sure you loved your job, I'd ask you to think about joining the department."

"I think I'll leave the catching bad guys up to you. But thanks." It was all I could force myself to say. Because, deep down, I knew those what-ifs would always haunt me.

Chapter
Twenty

Piper

A BREEZE PICKED UP, TAKING AWAY A BIT OF THE SUN'S bite as I headed down the steps of the lodge. Waving to the Gragerts as they headed to their van, I made my way towards one of the cabins Hunter's crew was working on. Cal looked up from fixing the railing on the front porch steps. "Hey, Piper. You need something?"

"Hi, Cal. This is looking really nice." The entire front porch had been redone. They'd replaced the rotted boards and sanded and stained everything. And the color they'd chosen was perfect.

He stood from his crouch. "Everything's starting to come together. A few more weeks and we'll have another few cabins you can rent out."

My stomach gave a healthy flip. I wasn't ready for a major guest influx. I still needed to hire a cook. I hadn't started on activities other than reading and board games. Maybe I could see if Hunter knew of anyone who could check out the small sailboat docked down below.

"I see the panic taking root in your eyes. Don't worry. It's all going to work out."

"I'm glad you believe that." I could use a dose of Cal's optimism right about now.

"You're pouring everything you can into this place. And you're doing it with heart. No way you can go wrong if that's the case."

"Thanks, Cal."

He gave my shoulder a squeeze. "Anytime. Now, what can I help you with?"

"I was looking for Hunter. I wanted to run something by him but wasn't sure if he was back."

Cal scrubbed a hand over his jaw, his gold wedding band gleaming against the deep brown of his skin. "He's not back yet, but I can have him come and find you when he is."

Something about the movement and the shifting of Cal's gaze told me that something was up. Something more than just a meeting on the mainland. But I had no right to pry. And that burned. I wanted the right to know everything. Instead, I swallowed back the questions I wanted to ask. "Sounds good. I'm going to take Bruno down to the beach for a little fetch, and then I'll be up working on the attic."

"No getting locked inside this time."

Heat rose to my cheeks. "I think the new door will save me from that fate." I didn't share that even though Hunter and Cal had replaced it, I still propped it open with a trunk when I was working in there.

Cal grinned. "Glad to hear it. I'll send Hunt your way when he's back."

"Thanks." I waved and headed back towards the lodge. Bruno's head rose as soon as I walked inside. "You want to go to the beach?"

He leapt from his dog bed and began dancing around me. I

laughed as I bent to retrieve the ball launcher from the corner. "I thought you might. Let's go get a workout in."

Heading out the back doors, Bruno raced ahead of me and then ran back as if telling me to hurry up. I caught sight of Mr. Simpson walking along the cliffs and towards the highest peaks. "Enjoy your walk, Mr. Simpson," I called.

He startled and whirled around, glaring at me. "I don't have a young heart, missy. Don't go sneaking up on me."

"Sorry. Just wanted to tell you to enjoy your afternoon."

"I will if I don't have a heart attack," he griped.

I couldn't help the little chuckle that escaped. He might be a grump, but every time I brought muffins to the guests from The Mad Baker, his eyes lit up like Christmas. I simply gave him a wave and headed down the stairs to our beach.

Little coves like this one were scattered all along the cliffs' edges. But the one at the Falls was the best. Long and wide, with plenty of space for our small boathouse and for guests to roam. As soon as I reached the sand, I chucked the ball towards the water.

Bruno let out a happy bark and took off into the surf. There weren't waves exactly, more like a strong tide, the sea ebbing and flowing. It was perfect for kids and dogs alike. Bruno shook out his fur as soon as he bounded out of the sea.

I lost myself in the rhythm of it all. Simply soaking in the sun and sea air, and the pure joy of playing fetch with a dog that loved the water. I completely lost track of time. Suddenly, a voice broke my trance. "He seems happy."

I turned to see Hunter, hands shoved into his jeans' pockets and dark circles rimming his eyes. "What's wrong?"

He watched as Bruno darted out of the surf and charged towards us. "I'm honestly not sure how to answer that question."

A distance that had never been there before loomed between us. I had no idea what had put it there, and I wanted it gone. "If you start talking, I bet you'll find your way."

He picked up the tennis ball and threw it as hard as he could. Bruno took off again. "I wasn't in the city for a business meeting."

"Okay…" My heart picked up its pace, anxiety fueling the erratic rhythm.

"I went to see my old friend, the one I told you about a couple of weeks ago."

Oh, God. He'd gone to the prison. And he'd faced it alone. I reached out for his hand. "Hunter—"

He stepped out of my grasp. "Don't. Not yet."

The movement stabbed an invisible blade, and it went deep. I hadn't realized until that moment how far gone I was for this man. Not until he moved away from my touch.

"I never told you my friend's name." He paused as if waiting for me to say something, but I kept silent. "It's Ethan Green."

It took a few seconds for the name to click. "The same Ethan that Jenn had a crush on?"

He nodded, pain lancing his expression. "I had to go. Needed to see if there was any chance he could've hurt her. He has it in him. I never would've thought it. But last year showed me how wrong I was."

My blood ran cold, and my hands trembled. "Did he?"

"I don't know for sure. But I don't think so. Parker doesn't think so. But he could've, Piper. He could've done something to her, and we might never know. And all that time, I was by his side. He could've been hurting God knows who, right under my nose."

I moved before Hunter had a chance to evade my touch again and threw my arms around him, pulling him close. I couldn't engulf him the way he did me, but I wanted to give him the same comfort. "Whatever Ethan did or didn't do is not on you. I need you to hear that."

This beautiful man had broken under the weight of his guilt. A burden that wasn't his to carry. I held him close. Felt his heartbeat against my cheek. I understood for the first time that I couldn't shoulder the blame for Jenn, either. It was pointless and killing us both. Eating away at the good in our lives because we couldn't let it go.

"What if he did?" Hunter's voice cracked on the question. "How would you ever be able to look at me again?"

I looked up at him, placing a hand on his thickly stubbled cheek. "Because I know your heart. And I know that heart is good. I believe that the truth will eventually surface. We'll find Jenn one way or the other. But no matter what happens, no matter who's responsible, I don't want to lose you because of it."

Hunter's gaze locked with mine, his expression searching, hopeful. His lips hovered just a breath away. "I don't want to lose you, either. It's been eating me up inside since I heard you say his name."

"I hate that you didn't tell me what was going on inside that head of yours." Instead, he'd been drowning in it all alone. I understood the impulse. You didn't want anyone to see when the things swimming around inside you were dark and ugly.

Hunter winced. "I'm sorry I wasn't honest from the beginning. Panic set in, and all I could think about was finding the truth."

My fingers twisted in the hem of his shirt. "Don't do it again. I don't want you dealing with this alone."

"Yes, ma'am."

"How was seeing him?"

Hunter's Adam's apple bobbed as he swallowed. "Surreal. And hard." His dark green eyes flashed with pain. "He's sick. And I'm not sure how I didn't see it for so long. It's like I look at the past with a different lens now. I wonder if so many things were his sickness or just life."

"You'll drive yourself crazy if you overanalyze every detail of the past."

The corners of his mouth turned up the barest amount. "And you don't do the same?"

I released my hold on his t-shirt and placed a palm over his heart. "I'm beginning to see how that might not be the healthiest."

He nodded and pulled me closer to him. "How about we find some healthier ways to deal?"

"What did you have in mind?"

"Let's go knock down a few walls."

Bruno barked as if in agreement, his ball falling from his mouth.

"I could knock down a few walls." But what I really wanted to do was stay here in Hunter's arms, listening to the water roll in and losing myself in his warmth.

Chapter Twenty-One

Piper

BELL AND I WOVE THROUGH THE ROWS OF FURNITURE and décor. The vastness of it all was a little overwhelming. She paused in front of a dresser. "The key is to focus your eyes on one thing at a time. If you try to take it all in, you're going to freeze."

"I'm going to dub it estate sale overwhelm."

She chuckled and opened the top drawer. "That's a good name for it. Ford's mom, Kara, is the one who taught me how to find the treasures amidst the trash."

I ran my hand over the top of the dresser, examining the corners. "It sounds like you're close with them."

"We pretty much grew up together. Ford actually dated my sister before she passed away in a car accident."

My fingers stilled. "I'm so sorry, Bell."

She looked up at me, a ghost of a shadow passing over her eyes. "Thank you. I miss her every day. Don't think that will ever stop. I wouldn't want it to. But I've made peace with it the best I can."

I understood that. Feeling someone's absence every single day. At times, I still picked up the phone to call Jenn. Especially when something funny happened, and I was dying to tell her. "The holes they leave behind is kind of like a memorial. It reminds you that they were there."

Bell pushed to her feet. "You lost someone?"

I focused my gaze on the dresser's trim, trying to estimate how difficult it would be to repair. "My best friend has been missing for ten years. Disappeared from the Falls, actually."

Bell's eyes widened. "Jenn Branton?"

I nodded, not sure what else to say. The words didn't come as easily as they did with Hunter. Every piece of the ordeal felt too private, too raw.

"I helped search for her. All my friends did. I'm so sorry, Piper. I can't imagine how hard that was. How hard it still *is*."

"Thank you. Being back here has helped in a lot of ways. Hurts, too. But mostly it's helped. The memories of her are stronger here, somehow. Because every summer we had those few perfect weeks. Now, I have a chance to give that to others."

Bell reached out and squeezed my arm. "That's a beautiful way to look at it. And I think this dresser would be perfect for one of the cabins."

When Bell had come to pick me up this morning, I'd given her a tour of the grounds, showing her what I needed most and taking her through all the furniture I'd stored in the barn. She'd pointed out more than a few pieces that weren't worth saving, so I needed replacements.

"I don't have the first idea of how to fix this." I toyed with the little piece of trim that had come loose.

She waved me off. "That's easy. I'll show you. And it will help us drive the price down. I know the guy who runs these sales, and he always prices things too high."

"I'm glad to have an expert with me."

Bell chuckled. "I don't know about that, but I'm learning. Hunter's pretty knowledgeable about this stuff, too, if you run into trouble. His dad is the one who taught me how to bring broken pieces back to life."

Just the mention of his name had heat rising to my cheeks. There was no reason for it, other than the fact that I knew I was falling. Somehow, I worried that Bell would be able to see it written across my face. "Good to know, but he's pretty busy with the cabins right now."

"He seems to be holding up okay."

I could see just how much Bell cared for Hunter by the worry etched deep in the lines of her face. A small flare of jealousy lit inside me. Not that I thought there was anything romantic going on between the two. It was clear she saw him as a brother. But in this closely woven circle she'd built for herself, there was a mixture of family and friends.

I'd had that once. But after Jenn had disappeared, my relationship with the Brantons had become strained. It had been too hard for them to spend time with me. I understood, but it didn't change that it was another loss. And my uncles and I had never found another relationship like we'd had with them. One where you shared holidays and vacations, knew the other would always be there if you needed help.

I shook my head, pulling myself from the memories. "He's doing really well. Cal stops him from overdoing it with his shoulder." My mouth curved at the memory of Cal scolding Hunter the same way a worried mother would.

"I'm glad. He can push himself too far. And his headspace seems good, too."

I halted my examination of the dresser and met Bell's gaze. I didn't want to betray a confidence, but this was Hunter's family, not some curious stranger. "He's taking too much on himself. Blaming himself for not being able to help Shay… For what happened to you."

Her mouth went slack for a moment. "For what happened to me?"

"He told me about Ethan. It weighs on him."

"Oh, God." She sat on a chair next to the dresser. "I thought he'd gotten past it. Let it go."

I moved closer to Bell. "He's working on it. And I think he's making progress. Everything that happened with Shay, getting shot, I think it just brought it all to the surface again. But he's dealing with it. Talking it out and starting to release."

She looked up at me, a hint of tears in her eyes. "You're good for him."

"I think we're good for each other. It's easier to talk about it with someone who's been there. Who understands."

Hunter was the most unexpected gift of this entire process. There were many of them: Finding out how strong I was both physically and emotionally, remembering so many things about Jenn, bringing something broken back to life. But Hunter was the greatest gift of all. A friendship where I felt seen and understood after missing that for so long.

Since coming to Anchor, I'd realized a lot about how I was living my life. There wasn't a single friend I missed from Seattle. Sure, I traded texts with a couple of people, but no one who truly knew me. I'd been keeping people at arm's length without even realizing it for a long time. Choosing friendships and relationships that I knew wouldn't lead anywhere.

Bell reached out and squeezed my hand. "I'm glad you two found each other."

"Me, too."

⌒◯

"You're too big for this bed," I groused.

Bruno answered by laying his head on the pillow next to mine.

"Seriously?" The dog slept like a freaking human. He let out a deep sigh. "I'm glad someone's comfortable." I, meanwhile, had been relegated to a third of the queen-sized bed.

Turning off the lamp on the bedside table, I burrowed under the covers. Even though the nights were cold on the island, I couldn't resist sleeping with the window open, enjoying the smell of the salt air, and the sounds of the sea.

Getting comfortable, I stared up at the ceiling. I should be exhausted. I'd spent all morning with Bell, spending too much money on furniture and restoration supplies. And then whiled away the afternoon, creating a workspace in the barn so I could start making some of those pieces presentable. The first two cabins Hunter and his crew had been working on were done. It was time for the finishing touches, of which I had almost none.

"Tomorrow," I mumbled to my snoring dog. "Tomorrow, I'll get to work."

Just as I was drifting off, the sound of floorboards creaking had my eyes flying open. Bruno let out a low growl next to me. I froze, straining to hear. There it was again, as though someone very slowly walked across the attic. Then moved quicker.

Bruno's lip curled, exposed his teeth, but I gave him a hand command for quiet, and he obeyed. My pulse sped up as I clutched the sheets. Pepper spray. Where was the pepper spray Nathan had given me? My purse. As quietly as possible, I sat up, feeling around the floor for my slippers. Easing my feet inside, I stood. I didn't want to turn on a light and clue in whoever was upstairs to the fact that I was awake.

I tiptoed across my room, thankful for the strong moonlight guiding my path. Pulling open my purse, I dug for the small canister. I squinted in the dark, trying to remind myself how to use the thing. Once I had it firmly in hand, ready to dispense the debilitating spray, I headed back over to the bed. Having a massive dog at my side didn't hurt either.

"Bruno, come. Heel."

With that command, he was by my side in a second. The floor above us creaked again, and Bruno let out another growl. "Quiet," I whispered. Bruno obeyed, but the hair along his spine rose.

I sent out a silent prayer that I could make it downstairs before whoever was in the attic realized that someone was up and about. Holding onto Bruno's collar with one hand and my pepper spray in the other, I hurried downstairs as quickly as possible. More than one stair groaned, but it couldn't be helped.

I pushed open the front door and left it that way. My body had automatically started moving towards Hunter's cabin without me even making a conscious decision. Somewhere along the line, he'd come to mean safety to me.

I released Bruno's collar and knocked on Hunter's door. No sounds came from inside. I peeked quickly around the side of the cabin and breathed a sigh of relief when I saw that his truck was there. I wasn't sure what I would've done if I realized that he had left for the night.

Just as I was about to knock again, the door opened. Hunter stood there, wearing only worn flannel pajama pants. I swallowed hard. Seeing Bruno and me, he came instantly awake. "What's wrong?"

"I, uh, I think I heard someone in the attic." As soon as the words were out of my mouth, I felt like an idiot. "Sorry. I should've called the sheriff's department, not woken you up."

"Of course, you should've woken me up. You and Bruno stay here. I'll go check it out." He moved to a small lockbox resting on a bookcase in the living area. Punching in a code, he pulled out a gun.

"No. No way. You're not going in there alone with a gun." My rib cage constricted at the thought. Hunter, alone, with God knew who else.

He slipped his hand under the fall of my hair, squeezing the space where my neck met my shoulder. "It's probably just those kids again. Let me check it out, and then we can call Parker if we need to. I'll be safe. I promise."

I nodded slowly. "Be careful."

"I will."

I didn't wait inside. Instead, I grabbed Hunter's cell phone from where I saw it charging in the kitchen and paced the gravel drive in front of his cabin, not taking my eyes off the lodge. A minute later, the light in the attic flicked on. I held my breath, waiting for gunshots or screams, but there was nothing.

The light went off. Had I imagined it? Was nothing up there? A minute later, Hunter appeared, and I rushed over to him. He looked as if he were trying to hold back laughter.

"What is it? Am I losing my mind?"

Hunter shook his head and tugged at my arm. "Come with me." He looked at Bruno as soon as we got inside. "Go to your bed." Bruno whined but did as ordered.

Hunter led me up the stairs, and my nails dug into his arm. "Just tell me already."

"Where's your patience, Casper?"

"I don't have any," I muttered.

Hunter moved into the attic, a full stream of moonlight lighting its space. Slowly and quietly, he pulled me towards the back corner. "Look."

I gasped. "What in the world?" In the pile of sheets that had covered the trunks and furniture up here was now a nest. A mother raccoon and three babies lay curled together.

"There's your intruder."

I covered my mouth to hold in my chuckle. "I really thought it was a person."

"Just these little guys. I think we should leave them be for now. I've got a friend who works for Fish and Wildlife. I'll ask him what we should do with them."

"I bet they'll move out once the babies are ready. It's fine if they stay up here for now."

Hunter tipped his head down so he could meet my gaze. "You've got the biggest heart. Soft, but so damn strong, too."

"They're just babies."

"Piper?"

"Yes?" I couldn't breathe. He was so close that I could feel the heat of his body. Smell the scents of sawdust and pine that clung to him.

"Are those sloths on your pajamas?"

My gaze shot to what I was wearing—my favorite sloth pajamas that were about the nerdiest things you could imagine. The tank had a scrawled message, *Slothy Sleeper*, and little sloths clung to branches on both the top and the shorts. My face flamed. "I like sloths."

Hunter chuckled, deep and rich. "I can tell." He bent and pressed his lips to the top of my head. "So fucking adorable."

Somehow, I cringed and warmed at the same time. The feeling of his lips against my hair warmed my insides, but the knowledge that I was only adorable in his eyes cooled me right off. Maybe it was for the best. I needed to stay focused. And Hunter was the type of distraction that could ruin a person.

Hunter

"Boss, I think we've got a problem," Manny called from outside a cabin we were supposed to get started on today.

I took another pull from my travel coffee mug before starting towards him. The last thing I needed today was an unexpected issue. Jobs like these were riddled with them, but I was exhausted. After closing off the door to the attic last night and watching Piper retreat to her bedroom, I had been wide-awake.

Even after a walk in the cold night air back to my cabin, I still felt the heat of Piper's body so close to mine. And images of those long, tanned legs had danced in my mind all night. How someone could be as petite as Piper but still seem to have legs for days was beyond me. But it was all I could see last night. That and those wide, dark eyes. Ones that seemed to beg me to kiss her.

"Hell," Cal muttered as he came out of the cabin. "This shit isn't good."

The look on his face had me picking up my pace. "What's going on?"

"Have a look for yourself."

I headed inside and froze. Spray paint covered the walls. *Bitch* and other choice words that had anger heating my blood. But it was the message scrawled across the living area that stopped me cold. *You'll pay* had been written in angry, red letters.

Manny stepped in behind me. "There are two more with the same kind of thing."

My chest heaved, but I did my best to keep my voice even. "Call the sheriff and tell the guys not to touch anything."

A hand clamped down on my shoulder. "You okay?"

Cal was trying to be a good friend, but it wasn't what I needed. I needed to break something. "No, I'm not fucking okay. How does something like this happen when I'm one hundred yards away?"

Cal winced and ushered me outside. "These cabins haven't been remodeled yet. We haven't installed any lights over here, and it's not like spray painting something makes a lot of noise."

He was right, but it didn't change the fact that I wanted to kick my own ass. "I don't even know when this happened. When's the last time someone even went inside these cabins?"

"I don't know, man. We'll talk to the crew and get a timeline worked up for Parker."

"You talk to the guys. I need to go find Piper." Something clawed at my insides. I hated to have to ruin her day. The hits just kept coming for her, and I couldn't seem to stop them.

I made my way towards the barn that Piper had turned into a workshop. As I got closer, the notes of some god-awful eighties pop song drifted out. Moving through the open door, I wove through empty stalls to a space that looked as if it might've been a tack room at one point. Piper shook her hips, slightly off rhythm as she sang along to the lyrics.

She was in her groove, enjoying the process of bringing the

Falls back to life. Her shoulders weren't strung tight with stress. She wasn't worried or scared. But now I had to destroy all of that.

I cleared my throat, and Piper whirled around, her hand going to her chest. She pointed a sanding block at me. "That was not nice."

Normally, I would've smiled. Made some crack about her music. But I couldn't find it in me to do that.

Her expression fell. "What's wrong?"

"Someone's been in a few of the cabins slated for reno."

"Someone's been in all of those cabins. It was party central, clearly."

"It's more recent than that."

Piper set the block down on the dresser she had been working on. "What is it?"

My jaw worked back and forth. "Spray paint and ugly words. Some threats." I wasn't sure I'd be able to handle seeing what else had been written on the walls of the other cabins.

"Threats?" Her voice had gone quiet. "Against who?"

The ugly words scrawled across the walls had a female connotation. It could only be one person. "You." I moved in closer, wanting to wrap her in my arms but not sure if she needed that.

"Why?"

Piper made the smallest move. As if reaching out for me but then stopping herself. It was all I needed. I strode forward and pulled her into my arms. "I don't know, but we'll figure it out." I had a sneaking suspicion the two teenagers from the fire were to blame. But we'd likely have a hard time proving it.

She rested her cheek against my pec. "Every time I start to feel as if I've got a handle on things, something knocks me off course."

I tightened my hold on Piper. She'd been working so damn hard. From sunrise to sunset, trying to make this dream a reality.

Only it seemed the world was determined to stack things against her. "But you keep pushing on. You'll do that again."

"I know. But for just a minute, I want to feel sorry for myself. When I walk out those doors, I'll be strong. But right now, I just want to wallow. Can you let me do that?"

"I can let you do that." I simply held her, rubbing a hand up and down her back, keeping her close so she didn't feel alone in this.

After a couple of minutes, she sighed and stepped back. "Thank you. I needed that."

My mouth curved. "I don't mind holding you, Piper. I'll do it anytime you want."

A hint of pink hit her cheeks, and she turned away towards the door. "I'll keep that in mind."

By the time we made it back to the cabins, two sheriff's department vehicles were parked in the driveway, and Parker was talking to Manny and Cal. I had the sudden urge to slip Piper's hand into mine. To pour reassurance and strength through my palm. But I held back. I knew the walls of my resolve were crumbling but now wasn't the time to think about or act on it.

Parker gave a chin lift in greeting. "Sorry you're having more trouble."

"Me, too," Piper said. "I haven't seen it yet. How bad?"

Parker mostly hid his wince, but a flash came through. "Someone isn't happy, that much is clear."

"Are those tourist kids still around?" My money was on them.

"The parents rented a house for the summer, so I'm guessing yes."

"And I'm also guessing they aren't sitting in a jail cell." There was no way those enabling parents had let their precious baby and his friend stay in jail.

"They made bail the next morning."

"Why am I not surprised?"

Parker slid his phone out of his pocket. "Because you're not a stupid man."

Piper moved in closer, seeming to subconsciously seek out my heat. "You really think they'd come back here after getting arrested? That seems a little extreme."

I couldn't resist. I wrapped an arm around her shoulders. "Kids like that don't take kindly to the word *no* or consequences of any nature."

"Hunter," Parker began, "we don't know it was them. I'm going to stop by and question them when I leave here, but we don't even know when this happened."

"Sometime over the past three nights," Cal offered. "I talked to the guys. Rick went in to measure for materials four days ago. There was no paint then."

Parker nodded and typed that into his phone. "Could be worse, but it's still a hell of a window. I'm not optimistic about finding a damn thing. I'll try to get a search warrant for their vehicles and rental property. Maybe we'll get lucky and find paint. But I wouldn't hold my breath."

Those two teenagers were stupid, sure, but they weren't morons. They would've gotten rid of the evidence. "Your guys looking for prints?"

"They're dusting now, but you know what those cabins were used for. There will be hundreds of prints. We'll try to find the boys' now that we have their prints on file but…"

Parker's words trailed off, but he didn't have to finish. The chance of finding any evidence was slim to none. I angled my body so I could meet Piper's gaze yet not loosen my hold on her. "Let me call my friend, Griffin. You need cameras. He'll have workarounds that won't be expensive or intrusive." And I'd mitigate the cost of a system if I had to.

"Hunter—" She started to argue.

Parker cut her off. "It's a good idea. Best kind of protection and deterrent. And if you have more trouble, we'll have a hell of a better chance of bringing them to justice."

"Fine," she grumbled. "But only a couple. I don't want to turn this place into a prison. That's not what it's supposed to be. And I'm not putting alarm systems on the cabins. It's too expensive, and it'll only be a headache trying to give guests the codes."

She had a point there. But I'd still try to convince her to put one in at the lodge. "Thank you." I pressed a kiss to the top of her head and pulled out my phone. "I'll be back in a few." I wasn't going to lose my opening to get some security in here. I'd bribe Griffin with whatever he wanted to get his ass over here now. Anything and everything to make sure Piper was safe.

Chapter Twenty-Three

Piper

"**W**HY DIDN'T YOU TELL US ABOUT THIS WHEN IT first happened?" Nathan barked into the camera.

Vic rested a hand on his arm. "Don't yell. That's the last thing Piper needs." He turned his gaze to me. "But he does have a point. We've talked almost every day, and you failed to mention a bunch of hooligans trying to burn down the Falls."

I let my fingers sift through Bruno's fur as if he might be able to help me. Bruno only turned his head away. "I didn't want to worry you. I want to tackle this on my own. I was worried if I told you, you'd be on the first ferry out here."

"We would've been," Nathan muttered.

Vic's expression softened. "I know it's important for you to stand on your own two feet while you see this project through. But no one does something like this alone."

"I'm not alone. I have more than a few people helping. I just need you to trust that I can do this."

Hurt flashed in Vic's eyes. "I know you can do this."

Hell. I hadn't meant to do that. The last thing I ever wanted to do was cause Vic or Nathan pain. "I'm okay. I promise. And it means the world to me how much you both care. This is just a journey where I need to lean on myself."

Nathan's hand squeezed Vic's shoulder. "She's charting her own course. And we need to let her. Piper knows we'll be here if she needs us." His eyes met mine. "It's not weak to ask for help when you need it. That just makes you wise. No one walks this kind of road alone. We'll promise to let you drive this path on your own if you promise to let us in on what you're going through."

"I think that sounds like a fair deal to me."

"Good," Nathan returned.

I smiled. "Tell me about the Henley house."

Hurt feelings and fears mended, we dove into a conversation about my uncles' latest restoration project. The discoveries they'd made, the hurdles they'd encountered, and how they planned to overcome them. I told them about the estate sale and all the furniture I was restoring. And by the time we hung up, I felt better than I had since before Hunter told me that someone had vandalized the cabins.

I set my phone down on the sheet-covered couch next to Bruno and surveyed the damage. The crew had been focused on one of the three cabins that had been spray painted. The walls didn't matter so much because we planned to paint over them anyway, but the floors were another story altogether. They would require sanding to remove the paint.

It was time-intensive, back-breaking work, but it was something I could do so the crew didn't have to waste their time on it. I tapped the screen of my phone and turned on some music. Strapping on my knee pads, I got to work.

It wasn't long before my back was screaming. As I stood to stretch, a familiar face poked around the door. "Hey, Nick."

"Hey, I just wanted to—" His eyes widened as he took in the walls around me. "What happened? Is this why the sheriff was here again?"

"Not the prettiest décor, right?"

He stepped inside. "When did this happen?"

"Sometime over the past few days. You haven't seen anyone lurking around, have you?" I'd begged Parker not to question the few guests I had. The last thing I needed was to send them fleeing. But Nick was different. I knew he'd hang strong.

"No, and I've been up pretty late working. I would've said something if I saw anyone lurking around."

I figured as much. "I appreciate that. Did you and your parents have issues with people causing trouble when you owned the place?"

He sighed and eased down onto the couch, giving Bruno a pat. "Our experience might not be yours. A lot has changed over the years."

"I know that. But I'd still like to know what I might need to expect." Even if it was brutal.

"Owning this place was a rollercoaster. The highest highs, and the lowest lows. But even in our best years, it was a struggle to stay in the black. Something was always breaking, or a guest was creating problems. My parents worked themselves to the bone to keep this place afloat. Sometimes, I think it's why my mom got sick."

I sank to the floor. "I'm sorry things were so tough. I never would've guessed."

Nick gave me a sad smile. "Don't get me wrong. There were a lot of happy memories, too. Things I'll carry with me always. It was just…hard. That's why I didn't take over for my dad."

"He wanted you to?"

Nick nodded. "I feel guilty as hell that because I didn't, this place got foreclosed on. But this isn't the life I want. I don't want to struggle every day. I worked hard in college so I could get a good, secure job when I got out. I've built a career in video game design that I'm proud of. I've just been a shit son in the process."

"You haven't," I argued. "You can't live your life for someone else's dreams."

I couldn't imagine giving up the Falls for anything. Yes, it was a crazy childhood dream, but I'd fallen in love with everything about creating a respite for people who needed it. Even creating a warm place for people like Nick, who were dealing with the harsh realities of life.

He sighed. "I just wish there was more of a middle ground."

"You've found it. You're here, seeing your father every day, supporting him however you can. And I promise, the Falls is in good hands."

Nick met my gaze. "Just take care of yourself. A resort isn't worth your health or safety."

But it wasn't just a resort to me. It was more. A dream. A way to honor a friend. The place I was finding more of who I wanted to be. And I'd give my all to make it into everything I knew it could be.

Hunter

STEPPING OUT ONTO THE SMALL FRONT PORCH OF THE cabin I currently called home, I handed Cal a beer. He took it without looking away from the water. "Thanks, man. This isn't too shabby of a spot."

"It doesn't suck." I eased down into one of the two Adirondack chairs I'd borrowed from Piper's stash of furniture. They looked a little rough but were sturdy enough.

"You gonna tell me about your visit to Seattle, or am I just going to have to guess?"

I'd told Cal about my plan to see Ethan, but we hadn't talked about it since. A combination of too much going on and me not wanting to think about it. Piper wasn't holding it against me, and that was what had mattered. I didn't want to relive the scene of the guards taking Ethan to the floor. Of seeing the sickness in his eyes.

"It's still hard to believe that I didn't see it."

Cal took a pull from his beer. "I didn't either. And I worked with the man for years."

But Cal and Ethan had never been close. Friendly, but not tight the way Ethan and I had been.

"Do you think he had something to do with the Branton girl's disappearance?" he asked.

"I don't think we'll ever know for sure. Parker said he had an alibi that night. Said he checked with the people who were there."

"He called me after they arrested Ethan, but I'd left the party before Ethan." Cal picked at a piece of peeling paint on the arm of his chair. "Ash and I got into a hell of a fight that night. I took off, pissed as all hell, and went for a drive to cool off."

"So you didn't see him with Jenn?"

Cal rubbed a hand over his closely cropped hair. "They were cozy at one point. I remember that much. But she talked to a lot of people. Had too much to drink. Hell, the whole thing makes me sick to my stomach. I should've made sure she got back to her cabin, but I was too focused on Ash."

"You were a teenager. No one thinks straight at that age." I thought about the two teens who had been causing trouble around here and knew that was true. Parker had been denied the search warrant he'd requested because of lack of evidence. There came a point when you had to face some real consequences in life. Otherwise, you never grew up.

"It changed me. That night. Realizing what had happened right under my nose. Scared some sense into me."

I glanced over at my friend. "That's when you started working on Billy's crew, isn't it?"

Cal nodded. "Started learning a trade. Put my head down and got serious about studying. Stopped feeding into the drama with Ash."

I tried to think back to that time and realized that Cal had somewhat disappeared after that. He didn't party anymore and rarely hung out with our crew. "It's crazy how one night can change so many people's lives."

"That's the truth. Changed things for Ash, too." A small smile curved Cal's mouth. "She realized life was short, and she didn't want to live without me."

"Thank God for that. You'd be a miserable S.O.B. without her."

Cal turned to look at me. "She's pregnant."

"What?"

"Just two months along, so we're not telling many people yet."

I set my beer down on the chair and grasped Cal's shoulder. "I'm happy for you, man. You're gonna be a hell of a dad."

He shook his head as if he still couldn't believe it. "I hope so. All I can think about is all the bad in this world and how I'm going to protect my kid from it."

"You can't. All you can do is help them deal with it."

Cal arched a brow. "You hiding a kid somewhere that I don't know about?"

I chuckled but what flashed in my mind was a little girl who looked just like Piper but with my green eyes. Hell, I needed to get a grip. "No kids. I just know how hard my parents tried to protect Ford and me, but it's impossible. Kids are gonna fall down. You have to teach them to get back up."

"I'm gonna do my best."

"Do you and Ashley need anything? You know you can always take time off for doctors' appointments and the like. How's she feeling?"

"Appreciate that. She's got some morning sickness, but it hasn't been too bad so far, as long as she eats the minute she wakes up." He glanced at his watch. "I gotta get home, or I'm gonna be late for dinner."

"Don't piss off the baby mama."

Cal barked out a laugh. "Ain't that the truth?"

I waved him off and checked the time on my phone. It was almost seven, but I didn't see any signs of movement at the lodge.

No lights on, either. I pushed out of my chair and headed in that direction. Maybe I could convince Piper to let me cook her dinner.

Opening the front door, I called out. "Casper, where are you?"

There was no answer.

I whistled. "Bruno?"

There was no jingling of dog tags. Piper might not hear me if she had earbuds in listening to that awful eighties music, but Bruno would've come running. I left the lodge and made my way towards the barn and Piper's makeshift workshop.

Pulling open the door, I listened for sounds of life. Nothing. I still strode by the stalls, calling Piper's name. My chest grew tighter with each step. Her SUV sat in front of the lodge, so she hadn't gone into town. I peeked into the tack room. It was dark.

Flicking on the light, I surveyed the space. There was no sign of her or Bruno. Turning off the light, I headed out, my strides eating up the ground. I saw Mr. Simpson coming out of the forest, and he immediately scowled at me. I didn't give a damn. "Have you seen Piper?"

"No," he grumbled.

"Are you sure?"

"I'm old, but I'm not blind. I haven't seen her."

I didn't give him another thought, I just started for the cabins. Pulling out my phone, I tried her cell. The service was horrible here, but the call connected. Instead of ringing, it went straight to voicemail. In all the time I'd worked with Piper, her phone had never been off. Too many people might need to get in touch with her for resort business.

I started jogging in the direction of the first cabin we'd finished. She might be decorating and getting it ready for guests. Pulling the door open, I called her name. Nothing. I moved through the cabin just in case, checking each room. Endless possibilities flew through my head. She'd fallen off a ladder and was unconscious. She'd fainted because she'd forgotten to eat. And then the possibilities that were much worse. That someone had hurt her.

Flashes of that day months ago filled my memory. Shay terrified with a gun pointed at her head. Trying to wrestle the weapon away from her brother. The pop and the burning pain. Watching as Shay tore out of the cabin, her brother on her heels. Knowing that she likely wouldn't survive.

I did everything I could to push the memories away. They didn't have a place here. Not now. I needed to focus. I combed through each of the newly renovated cabins, but there was no sign of Piper anywhere.

I headed for the lodgings currently being worked on. The first one was empty. By the time I reached the second, I thought I might throw up. Pulling open the door, I was about to call Piper's name when Bruno's head rose from the sheet-covered couch. It was the one piece of furniture we'd left in place because it was too difficult to get out the door.

Bruno let out a little whine but stayed curled around Piper's sleeping form. A war of emotions flared to life within me. Relief that she was okay. Frustration that she'd clearly worked herself so hard that she'd passed out on a dirty couch. And irrational anger. One that burned hot and fierce. That she'd scared me. That I cared so much.

I took a slow, steadying breath, trying to bring the rage under control. Piper needed a bed and a good night's sleep. I slowly walked over to the couch and motioned for Bruno to get down. He hesitated for a moment but then obeyed.

Carefully, I slid my arms under Piper's body, cradling it against mine. As I lifted her, my shoulder twinged, but I ignored it. I maneuvered her out the door and towards the lodge. Just as I managed to get the door open, she stirred.

"Hmmm. What?"

"Go back to sleep." I headed up the stairs towards her bedroom.

Piper's eyes blinked open. "No. I was just resting my eyes for a minute. What are you doing?"

"Carrying you to bed," I growled. "Because, apparently, you can't get yourself there."

She stiffened in my arms and then wiggled to get down. "I was taking a break. Resting. I didn't need you to come in there and kidnap me."

"Kidnap you?" I set Piper down in her bedroom, her boots landing with a thunk on the floor. "You were passed the hell out. You wouldn't have known if a murderer had come in and was about to slice your throat. I was simply taking you to bed. Where you clearly should've been anyway."

"A murderer might be preferable to you," she grumbled and started for the door.

"Oh, no, you don't."

I caught her by the elbow, but she tore away from my grip. "You don't have a say in what I do or when I do it. I was taking a nap in one of *my* cabins. It's not against the law, as far as I know. And, if it is, you can call Parker to arrest me."

"Don't be an idiot. You've run yourself ragged. You're going to pass out where you stand if you don't start taking better care of yourself."

Piper's dark eyes blazed. "I'm perfectly capable of taking care of myself."

"Doesn't look that way to me."

"Argh! Overbearing, infuriating *men*!"

She gave my chest a little shove, but I caught her hands by the wrists and tugged her flush against me. We both froze for a moment as though time and the world around us stopped. Nothing existed but her and me and the breath of distance between us.

Piper crossed that invisible line we'd been playing chicken around for weeks. She moved with a speed I barely followed. And then her lips were on mine.

She tasted like strawberries and a hint of something I couldn't place, but I didn't have time to search my brain for the answer. Because her tongue slid into my mouth, teasing me. My hands moved to her ass, lifting her, and her legs wrapped around my waist.

God, her body felt like it had been made for mine. Even with the layers of clothing between us, I knew that this woman could ruin me with one kiss.

I pulled back, breathless. "Piper. Wait."

Her fingers threaded through my hair, tugging at it. "I don't want to wait."

I searched her face. "You're not going to regret this in the morning?"

Her mouth quirked. "I've been thinking about this since the first day you walked through the door." A flicker of doubt passed over her features. "Are you going to regret this in the morning?"

"There's nothing about you I'd ever regret." Screw my rules. The fact that we worked together. Practically lived together. The world around us could burn, and I wouldn't give a damn. Just as long as Piper was in my arms.

Chapter Twenty-five

Piper

MY HEART HAMMERED A STACCATO BEAT AGAINST MY ribs. Hunter had said he couldn't regret me, but he also hadn't moved. He simply stared as if he were peering into my soul. Looking for everything I'd ever held back. And what I'd kept out of view from Hunter's probing gaze most was that I was falling for him. I knew this one act could tip the scales. But I didn't care. I wanted to fall.

He must've seen that in me because he finally moved. A man given the green light to go after what he'd wanted for weeks but had held himself back from. He took two long strides towards the bed and lowered me slowly to the floor. Every inch of that movement created a delicious friction between our bodies.

My hands went to his t-shirt the second my feet hit the hardwood. I tugged at the cotton as I struggled to toe off my boots. Hunter's fingers were on the button of my jeans. Our movements were desperate, fumbling. All I wanted was to feel his skin against mine. His body over mine, surrounding me.

I pulled off my shirt, letting it fall to the floor. Hunter froze, his gaze going to my chest, his hands following. "So damn pretty." He swept his thumbs across my nipples, the thin lace of my bra leaving nothing to the imagination. The buds tightened and peaked under his ministrations.

My fingers fisted in the waistband of Hunter's jeans as I sucked in a breath. Each swipe of his roughened thumb twisted the invisible cord in me tighter. He rolled a peak between his thumb and forefinger, and I let out a sound I didn't recognize.

"Like that?"

His voice was deeper than I'd ever heard it before. Darker. Wanting.

"I'll give you forever to stop."

He chuckled and pinched the bud. I gasped. "You're not playing fair."

The dark green in Hunter's eyes sparked. "Where would the fun be in that?"

The man had a point. I made quick work of unbuttoning his jeans. And just as I was about to tug them and his boxer briefs down, he slipped his wallet out of his pocket, tossing a condom onto the bed. "Always be prepared."

"Somehow, I'm not sure this is what the Boy Scouts had in mind when they came up with that slogan."

"They should've."

I shook my head and tugged at his pants again. As they fell, and he stepped out of them and his boots, I couldn't help but stare. Hunter's body could've been carved from stone—each ridge and valley of muscle covered by golden skin.

My fingers explored. Sweeping over the ripples of his abs, ghosting over his pecs and nipples. My hands stilled as I reached the scar. It looked too close to his heart. I swallowed against the burn in my throat. Leaning forward the barest amount, I pressed my lips to the puckered flesh.

Hunter sucked in a sharp breath. "Piper." It was both a plea and a warning. As if the gesture was too tender for him to handle.

In a flash, I was sailing through the air, landing with a whoosh on the mattress. Hunter hovered above me, his hand slipping between my thighs. "You keep touching me like that, and this is going to go way too quick. Hell, I feel like I'm in high school again."

Something about the knowledge that I affected him like that, that I had the power to bring this strong man to his knees, stirred something in me. Made me brave. I lifted my hips to meet his fingers. "More."

It was only one word, but it was all Hunter needed. He grabbed the condom from the bed and tore at the packet. I watched in fascination as he rolled it on, the smooth, strong motion causing everything inside me to tighten.

As he bent over me, I grabbed his neck, pulling him closer. I wanted to feel everything. To know every part of his body. To imprint it in my brain so that I'd never forget.

His tip bumped my entrance. "Yes?"

"Yes." The word was both a whisper and a plea. The answer to everything when it came to this man. I wanted all of him in every way possible. It didn't matter if this was reckless or irresponsible. It felt as if I wouldn't be able to breathe if I didn't feel him inside me.

He entered me on a slow glide. My hands went to his broad shoulders, holding on, trying to steady myself as I adjusted to the stretch. It was just shy of too much—the delicate balance between pleasure and pain. And I only wanted more. "Move, please move."

Hunter's hips shifted as he started to move. The angle, the friction, it sent sparks dancing through every muscle. My body instinctively mirrored his as though we already knew each other in every way we needed to. We found a rhythm that was only ours.

My hips rose to meet his, and Hunter drove deeper, hitting a spot inside that had pinpricks of light dancing across my vision. I couldn't help but reach for more. More of every ounce of sensation. More of him.

He picked up speed, seeming to have the same need, and somehow buried himself impossibly deeper. I welcomed the bite of pain. Anything that would mark me, so I never forgot. My heels dug into the divots of muscle above his ass, silently asking for even more.

Hunter gave it all to me. His hand dipped between our bodies, circling that bundle of nerves. Teasing and toying, finding just the right spot. He pressed down, and I came apart, the invisible cord inside me unraveling in a cascade of nothing but sensation.

I let go. For the first time in years, I let go of everything and drowned in feeling. I didn't try to push it away. To manage or control it. I let it overtake me. And as I fell, I knew I'd never be the same.

⌒◎

I woke to a muttered curse.

"Seriously?" Hunter grumbled.

I tried to turn over, to see what he was upset about, but couldn't. Because, somehow during the night, Bruno had wedged himself between our bodies. He let out a happy sigh, and I couldn't hold in my laughter.

"This bed is not big enough for both of us and a giant dog."

Hunter had a point. But I'd slept like a rock. "He just wants to be close to you. He's showing you his love."

Hunter groaned as he tried to move Bruno's massive form. Bruno took that as an invitation to lick Hunter's face. "Stop it. Bruno, no. That's not allowed."

Bruno barked and launched himself off the bed, thinking

it was certainly breakfast time. Hunter rolled towards me, his arms coming around me and pulling me close.

I buried my head against his chest. "I haven't brushed my teeth."

"Don't care." He gave my hair a gentle tug, tipping my face up to his. "Want those lips."

His mouth brushed against mine in a slow caress. My body started to hum at the memory of last night, but Bruno barked again, breaking the spell and disrupting the moment. Hunter threw him a glare. "How does he not suffocate you when you sleep?"

"He is a bit of a bed hog."

"We need to get him a bed for up here, so he doesn't want to sleep with us."

I stilled, taking in Hunter's sleep-rumpled face. "So…this isn't a one-time thing?"

"Fuck, no." His hand went to the back of my neck, squeezing. "Is that what you thought?"

I shrugged. "I don't think I had time to think about what this might be. But I didn't want to assume, either."

His hand slid down the side of my neck, his fingers dancing lightly across my collarbone. "There's something here. Last night, hell, I've never had something so explosive with someone before. And I care about you, Piper. I want to see where this goes."

Fear swept through my system, chilling my blood and locking my muscles. But there was no reason. Nothing I could find as I searched my mind. I wanted this man. And while working together made things complicated, this job wouldn't last forever. "I want to see where it goes, too."

Hunter grinned, the green in his eyes sparking. Leaning forward, he took my mouth in a long, slow kiss. "Glad to hear it."

Just as his hand slipped under my t-shirt, Bruno barked again.

"I really should get up. I need to let him out and get him his breakfast."

Hunter rolled to his back and stared at my dog. "You really are a cock-block. You know that, right? Us guys are supposed to look out for each other. Have each other's backs."

I patted Hunter's bare chest. "Maybe you need to get him a girlfriend."

He paused, seeming to consider it.

"Don't even think about it. The last thing we need is another dog running around here."

Hunter rolled on top of me, his body pinning me to the mattress. "I'll do whatever I have to for more of this."

Chapter Twenty-Six

Hunter

I ROLLED MY SHOULDER AS I HEADED UP THE STAIRS TO THE lodge. I might have overdone it today. My physical therapist wouldn't be pleased. But I was anxious to make up for lost time. Dealing with the spray paint on the floors of the cabins we had been renovating had cost us a couple of days.

As I reached the entryway, I heard the sound of a hairdryer coming from Piper's room. I jogged up the stairs and pulled open the door to her space just as she switched off the machine.

She met my gaze in the mirror through the open bathroom door. "You know the polite thing is to knock."

"You wouldn't have heard me anyway." My gaze traveled down her body clad only in a towel. "I came over to ask you to dinner, but I'm reconsidering that. Maybe we should stay in."

Piper shook her head. "I'm starving. Feed me. Then you can have your wicked way with me."

I moved in closer, my fingers ghosting over the edge of the towel, slipping underneath to feel her silky skin. "Wicked, huh?"

Her breaths came just a touch faster. "Definitely wicked."

A low moan came from under the bed, and I froze. Piper burst out laughing. "It's just Bruno. He's terrified of the hairdryer."

I stepped back and bent so I could peek under the bed. Bruno looked miserable. "This is just sad. Where's the fierce guard dog?"

"All a burglar would have to do is bring a hairdryer, and Bruno would go running for the hills."

I straightened and pulled Piper into my arms. "Can I take you out to dinner?"

She traced a finger along my stubbled jaw. "Is this a date, Hardy?"

"It's a date, Cosgrove."

"I think that would be acceptable. What do I need to wear?"

I gave the corner of her towel a little tug. "I think this is just about perfect."

"You would. The rest of the world might find it slightly inappropriate."

"They're idiots, then."

"Idiots who could get me arrested for indecent exposure."

I released my hold on her towel. "We can't have that. Even though you know I'd bail you out of jail."

"Good to know." She pressed a kiss to the underside of my jaw.

"I was thinking Rocco's. Best Italian around, and it's pretty casual. Jeans are more than fine."

"Sounds perfect. I could use some pasta."

I stepped back and sat on Piper's bed, toeing off my boots. "I'll just wait here."

She smirked at me. "Looking for a free show?"

"Always."

"Who am I to deny a desperate man?"

And she didn't. I lay on the bed as Piper dressed and put on makeup. The fact that I was fascinated watching as she dusted something shimmery across her eyelids and something slick across her lips, told me I was sunk.

Yet, at the same time, it seemed as if we'd been in this rhythm forever. In Piper's presence, I was totally at ease. There was no pretense. And as we drove towards town, it was a mixture of silence and conversation but never anything that felt forced. All of the other relationships I'd been in had been lacking that. As if I'd never fully settled into them. Everything was different with Piper.

I pulled into a parking spot just a few doors down from Rocco's and squeezed Piper's hand. "Wait here."

Climbing out of my truck, I rounded the vehicle and opened her door. She smiled, her eyes twinkling with mischief. "What a gentleman."

"Hey, my mom taught me how to treat a lady."

"That's a good mom you've got there."

"The best." I took Piper's hand in mine how I'd wanted to so many times before. A silent message that she was mine, and I was hers.

Just as we were about to reach Rocco's, I came up short. The couple walking towards us did the same. The woman in her late fifties gave me a shaky smile. "Hunter, it's good to see you."

Neither of us should've been surprised. Our island was a mere thirty square miles. And there was only one downtown area. But I'd only seen them a handful of times since Ethan's sentencing. "It's good to see you, too."

It was a lie. The words burned my throat when set free. I'd never understand why they had chosen to remain on Anchor when it had so many bad memories for them. It lit an irrational anger in me because I was forced to remember every time I ran into them. Made to deal with a resurgence of memories filled with all the betrayals and failures. I didn't want to remember. Especially on a night like tonight.

James Green stayed silent, his eyes hard, but his wife tried for conversation. "I heard you're working on the Falls."

"I am. This is the new owner. Piper, this is Cathy and James Green."

She didn't know that these were Ethan's parents, but she likely knew enough to get the underlying tension. She moved closer to me. "It's nice to meet you both."

Mr. Green squared his shoulders, ignoring Piper's greeting. "Have you been to see Ethan?"

"Honey—" Cathy began.

He cut her off with a single, sharp look. "They were best friends for their entire lives. It's not an unreasonable thing to ask."

"I saw him." I'd known Mr. Green all my life, and I knew that he wouldn't let it go until I gave him the truth of it.

"Maybe you'll keep it up the way a true friend should," he muttered.

Piper's hand spasmed in mine. I gave hers a reassuring squeeze. "I won't be going back. I'm sorry if that hurts you, but it isn't healthy for me."

Mr. Green's face reddened. "You're out, breathing free air, going on *dates*, and he'll be locked up for the rest of his life."

He said it as if I had been his son's partner in crime. Maybe because we had been involved in so many things throughout the course of our lives. But we weren't in this together. "I didn't try to kill two people, James. My brother and the woman who will soon be my sister. You can't ask me to forget that."

James muttered a slew of curses and then stormed off. Cathy wrung her hands, her gaze darting from her husband's disappearing form to me and back again. "I'm so sorry. He's just—he's upset."

"I understand. But you know why I can't be Ethan's support system, right? I upset him when I was there. It wasn't good for either of us."

Tears glistened in Cathy's eyes. "I understand. He's sick. He didn't mean to..."

Her words trailed off, and my chest squeezed painfully. "I know." That wasn't entirely true. Ethan hadn't meant to hurt Bell and Ford, but his mind had twisted itself to make him want to. It killed me that he had experienced that and that his parents were left to deal with the aftermath. All of it. But it didn't change a damn thing about today or my ability to be in Ethan's life in any capacity. I simply couldn't.

She sniffed. "I'll let you two go. Enjoy your dinner."

My appetite had fled the moment I saw their faces. Piper tugged on my arm, turning me to face her. She framed my face with her hands. "You okay?"

"Not really."

"Understandable. Want to get some takeout somewhere and go back to the lodge?"

I loved her for that, so willing to do whatever I needed, regardless of our plans. "No. I don't want this night to be ruined. I want to sit across from you at a restaurant and ask you all sorts of get-to-know-you questions. I want to stuff ourselves silly. And I might even try and get a peek down your shirt to see that pretty cleavage."

Piper snorted. "I hate to spoil this scenario, but you've already seen my boobs. You've had your mouth on them."

A lick of lust flared to life in my gut. "I'm gonna repeat that tonight."

"If you're lucky... Come on, Casanova. Feed me before you try to get lucky."

❦

"I'm pretty sure I consumed a week's worth of food in one meal," Piper groaned as we headed out into the cool night air.

"Pietro doesn't like any of his customers going hungry."

"I think he's especially partial to you."

The owner of Rocco's and I had become friends over the years. Mostly because I came to his restaurant at least twice a week. "He likes anyone who enjoys his food."

Piper held up a massive bag of leftovers. "I'm officially a fan. And we'll be eating these for days."

"I don't mind that in the slightest."

"Me, either."

I beeped the locks on my truck and opened Piper's door for her. "What would you say to a walk on the beach when we get back?"

"Ooooooh, very romantic. I'd say yes. Can we bring Bruno?"

"I don't think we could keep him away." The damn dog had wormed his way into my heart, slobber and all.

As we headed out of town, we rolled down the windows and let the sea air flow through the cab of my truck. Piper beamed into the wind. "I don't think I'll ever get tired of that smell."

"Lived here all my life and I'm not sick of it." I couldn't imagine anywhere in the world I'd rather be. This island had given me so much and had almost anything I'd ever need.

"Sometimes, it's the simplest things that make all the difference."

"You're not wrong about that."

I pulled into a spot in front of the lodge, and Piper jumped out of my truck before I could open her door. When she opened the door to the lodge, Bruno tore out, hackles raised and barking. "Bruno, what is it?"

Everything in me tensed as I watched the massive dog tear off to the cabins just across the gravel drive. "Stay here."

"I don't think so."

Piper took after her dog, me hot on her heels. Bruno ran up the steps to one of the cabins we'd just finished renovating and kept barking. I went to open the door and then realized it was already open a crack. I pushed it open more and flipped on the light.

Piper gasped. "No..."

The space was demolished. Damage that could've only been done with a sledgehammer. Sink smashed to bits, and countertops ruined. Holes in walls. And grooves in the floor.

"Why?" she whispered.

I turned and saw tears streaming down her face. "Come on, Casper. We need to get out of here and call Parker." I didn't want her to see the destruction. All the hard work we'd put into this space now gone in the blink of an eye. This wasn't just maliciousness. It was rage. And it was focused on Piper.

Chapter Twenty-Seven

Piper

THIS WASN'T HAPPENING. ALL I COULD DO WAS SIT ON the steps of the lodge and stare as the sheriff's department deputies moved in and out of the three destroyed cabins. I had insurance. I could fix it. But I wasn't sure that mattered.

The one thing I wouldn't be able to get back was time. Weeks of it. And when every second counted, this latest destruction might be a death blow to my business. Bruno pressed into my side, seeming to understand that I needed his comfort. I buried my face in the fur of his neck. "Maybe this was a mistake."

"It wasn't."

My head snapped up at the sound of Hunter's voice.

He eased down onto the stairs beside me. "We'll fix this. Get it back."

"There might not be enough time. I have to be realistic."

Hunter wrapped a hand around my jeans-clad thigh, the warmth of his palm soothing something in me. "My guys will be pissed on your behalf and more than willing to work overtime. We'll get it back."

I let myself lean against Hunter. "I'm exhausted. Just so damn tired." Tears burned my eyes. "Why does someone hate me so much? This seems beyond two teenagers."

"I agree," Parker said as he strode up. "I sent a deputy to the Leclairs' rental house, and they swear the boys were home playing video games all evening. And this just seems like more to me. I'm going on a gut feeling, but I've learned not to ignore those kinds of things."

Hunter's hand tightened on my thigh. "We had a run-in with the Greens tonight. James isn't very happy with me. I'd like to think there's no way he'd do something like this, but he knows this is the job I've been working on."

Parker tapped a few things into his phone. "I'll talk to him myself, but I'll go gentle."

"Appreciate that."

I wrapped my hands around Hunter's arm and squeezed. The weight of his friendship with Ethan, the ties to his parents, it was all weighing him down. "Did the cameras catch anything?"

Hunter and his friend, Griffin, had been working on getting them set up, but the only ones that were operational were the ones on the lodge. We didn't have a strong enough internet connection for the others, so we'd been left waiting for the internet company to come out and beef up our setup.

Parker gave a small shake of his head. "Nothing that will help us."

"I'm starting to feel like we need armed guards around here," Hunter mumbled.

My gaze swept over the Falls—this place that I wanted so badly to rebuild. To give people a piece of the idyllic respite I'd had here growing up. Instead, all I managed to bring this place was anger and strife.

Parker looked up from his phone. "We're dusting for prints—"

"You won't find any," I interrupted. Whoever was doing this

knew enough to avoid detection. And I was losing hope that we'd ever figure out who it was.

"We'll find them," Parker promised. "I'm not giving up. We'll keep at it until we get some answers."

"Thank you." My voice caught on the words.

An SUV rounded the bend in the gravel road and stopped in front of the lodge. Before the engine had even turned off, a figure jumped out of the passenger side. Bell rounded the SUV and made a beeline straight for me. Pulling me to my feet, she wrapped me in a hug. "I'm so sorry. I can't believe this happened."

My throat burned at her kindness and care. "Thank you. How did you—?"

"Hunter texted Ford to bring over some plywood to board up the damaged windows."

I glanced over Bell's shoulder to a man currently pulling some boards out of the SUV. He was tall and leanly muscled. The build was so similar to Hunter's, I knew it had to be Ford. His hair was lighter, though. I stepped out of Bell's embrace. "It was really nice of you to come."

She scowled at me. "It has nothing to do with nice. We have our friends' backs around here. And I'm about to kick the ass of whoever did this."

"Whoa there, Trouble. I really don't want to have to bail you out of jail." Ford wrapped an arm around his fiancée's shoulders.

"It would be worth it."

He shook his head and grinned at me. "She'd do it, too." He stretched out a hand for a shake. "I'm Ford. Sorry we're meeting under such shitty circumstances."

"I'd much prefer we did it over barbeque, quite frankly."

Hunter came up beside me and wrapped an arm around my shoulders. "Me, too."

Bruno came up beside me, and Ford's eyes widened. "Holy shit. Is that a bear?"

The chuckle escaped without any effort. It was the first smile or laugh I'd experienced since we found the destruction. "This is Bruno." I turned to my dog. "Sit." Bruno's butt hit the ground. "Shake." Bruno held out a paw, and Ford took it.

"Well, I'll be damned."

"He's a hell of a dog," Hunter remarked.

Bell looked up at Ford. "We need a dog."

Ford tipped his face to the heavens. "Can we get through the wedding first? The last thing we need is a puppy peeing on everything."

"Puppies are pretty much a full-time job," I warned.

"But they're so cute." Bell crouched and took Bruno's face in her hands, scratching his neck. "And so sweet. Right, Bruno?"

"So sweet he could eat you in a few bites," Ford mumbled. "I think we should go for something smaller."

"Chicken," Hunter chided.

I looked up at him. "You know, you were pretty scared of Bruno the first time you saw him."

Ford barked out a laugh. "I like you, Piper. Call him on his BS."

Bell straightened from her crouch. "Is there anything we can do to help?" She glanced over at Parker, who was talking with a deputy.

"I wish there was—"

"We could always use a few more hands on the crew," Hunter interrupted me.

"You've got it," Ford answered immediately.

Bell nodded. "Me, too. I'm great with a paintbrush."

"You guys don't have to do that. Really. We'll figure it out." I didn't want Hunter's family suckered into cleaning up my mess.

Ford opened his mouth to argue, but Hunter shook his head and pulled me tighter against him. "Really appreciate you dropping those by. Both of you. I'll call you tomorrow and let you know if Parker finds anything."

Bell tugged me from Hunter's hold and wrapped me in another hug. "You call if you need anything."

"I will. Thank you." But I knew I wouldn't. The more I leaned on those around me, the heavier the weight that settled on my chest. A little voice inside taunted me that they too could disappear.

Hunter and I were both silent as we watched Bell and Ford climb into their SUV and drive away. I let myself sink deeper into his hold, trying to soak up some of that steady strength so I could face everything anew tomorrow. "I like your brother."

"He's the worst." The corners of his mouth tipped up. "But also the best."

"I think that's the way it's supposed to work with siblings." It was how things had been with Jenn and me. I'd fought the hardest and laughed the loudest with her. Something about being completely at ease with another person, taking down all those walls of politeness. I'd never had another friend like her. I doubted I ever would.

Parker turned away from the deputy that he was talking to and came back to us. "We should be out of the cabins by to-morrow afternoon. I'm going to send everyone home in a bit to get some sleep, but we'll be back at eight a.m. tomorrow. If that works for you."

I nodded, my throat thick. They needed hours more to pro-cess everything that had been done. How angry would a person have to be to create that much destruction? "That works for me."

He met my gaze and locked there. "You need to be careful. This feels more and more personal with each incident. Don't go off on your own, okay? And keep an eye out."

"That's impossible. I have a million and one things to do, and I can't take a buddy with me everywhere I go. I'll take pepper spray and Bruno. That will have to be enough."

"Piper…" Hunter warned.

"No. I'm not stopping my life because someone's an asshole. If I have a prayer of still making this work, I need to keep pressing on. Otherwise, everything will fall apart." My words fell faster and faster, a touch of hysteria edging into my tone.

Hunter framed my face in his rough hands. "It's not going to fall apart. We're going to make it work. You have Celeste, who's here during the day. Just take her with you for whatever you're doing. And I'll be here the rest of the time."

I could feel the spark between Hunter and me slipping away. I was turning into a weight around his ankle. "We'll talk about it tomorrow. I honestly can't deal with this right now." It was the best I could give him.

There was an edge to Hunter's gaze that I'd never seen before. "Don't think I won't stalk your ass if I have to."

I glanced at Parker out of the corner of my eye. "Can you arrest him for that?"

Parker grinned and held up both hands, walking slowly away. "I'm staying out of this one."

"Some help the local sheriff is," I mumbled.

Hunter brushed his lips against mine. "People care about you, Piper. You're just going to have to get that through your head."

Chapter Twenty-Eight

Hunter

"NICK," I CALLED AS I JOGGED TOWARDS HIM.

He paused on his way to his car and turned around. "Hey, man. I'm so sorry about what happened."

Parker had needed to question everyone at the resort. Thankfully, none of the three guests had canceled their stays. Mr. Simpson had groaned and complained, but the Gragerts and Nick had been incredibly sympathetic. I think that was the only thing that allowed Piper to hold onto her sanity at the moment.

"Appreciate that. I actually have a favor to ask you."

"Name it."

That was the thing about living on Anchor—when the chips were down, everyone came together to help however they could. Nick might've been off the island for years, but he still knew where his roots were.

I inclined my head towards the barn. "Piper's in her workshop and I don't want her alone. I need to run into town to rally some troops and place an order for supplies. Do you think you could find a reason to keep her company for a couple of hours?"

"Is Parker worried someone has it out for Piper personally?"

"It's looking that way. He tried to tell her to keep someone with her so she wasn't alone, but she's stubborn and not exactly listening to reason." I'd had to stop myself from finding hand-cuffs and locking herself to my side this morning. I admired how determined Piper was to make this place sing again and to honor her friend. But not at the expense of her safety. Her ac-tions were bordering on reckless.

"Not a problem. I can tell her Dad wanted me to talk to her about the history of the place."

"That's perfect. She'd never turn that down. She loves your dad."

Grief flashed across Nick's face, and I immediately felt like an ass. "He doing okay?" I asked.

"As well as can be expected. It's a rough journey."

I could only imagine. I knew how helpless I'd felt when my father lay in a hospital bed after having a stroke, barely able to move and communicate. It had to be a million times worse hav-ing your loved one's mind slowly disappear. "I'm sorry you're going through this."

"Appreciate that. But it's good that I can be here this sum-mer. Spend some time with him. Watch the Falls get back to its former glory."

"I'm glad."

He clasped my shoulder. "Don't worry about Piper. I've got her back."

"Thank you. I appreciate it more than I can say." With a lift of my chin, I jogged towards my truck.

The crew was already here, and I'd been right. My team was pissed as hell that someone had destroyed their hard work. And they were worried about Piper. She'd become the guys' favorite after she impressed the hell out of them by taking down walls and refinishing floors right alongside them. So, they were ready to do anything they could to help her out.

I headed towards town, stopping at the hardware store to make some replacement orders. I begged Jill, who managed the place, to put a rush on anything she didn't already have in stock. She'd taken pity on me and agreed. Then I pointed my truck toward The General Store. Sliding into a parking spot, I hopped out and jogged up the stairs.

I waved at Molly behind the front register and then headed to the small kitchen in the back. "Caelyn, you back here?"

"I am," she called.

Weaving my way through the aisles, I found Caelyn sliding some sort of egg concoction onto an English muffin and then handing it to her husband, who sat at one of the stools. She smiled at me. "You want one?"

My stomach rumbled at the sight. "That would be a yes." The only thing I'd managed to consume this morning was coffee.

She pointed her spatula at the stool next to Griffin's. "Have a seat. Coffee? Orange juice?"

"I'd love some juice." I gave Griffin a nod of greeting. "Hey, man."

"Morning. Any word on when the internet company's coming out to the Falls so we can get the rest of those cameras up and operational?"

"I'm going to call them as soon as they open this morning. We had another incident last night."

Griffin straightened on his stool. "What the hell is wrong with these kids?"

"I'm not so sure it's them. This time, someone destroyed three of the cabins we renovated. It's going to take us weeks to get that work back."

Caelyn paused her chopping and looked up. "I can't believe

someone would do that. Poor Piper. Is there anything we can do to help?"

She hadn't even met Piper, and yet I felt the sympathy coming off Caelyn in waves. "I was hoping you might say that."

"Just name it," Griffin said. "Whatever you need."

"I know it's last minute, but I was thinking of trying to get as many people together this afternoon and tomorrow as I could to set things back to rights. A lot of our friends and family know their way around a hammer or paintbrush."

Griffin nodded. "I can come over after I pick up Mia from gymnastics. Do you mind if I bring the kids? Will more than knows his way around a reno."

Caelyn and Griffin had custody of her three younger siblings, and they were the lights of their lives. "Of course. There's plenty of room for them to run and play, too."

Caelyn slid my breakfast sandwich makings onto a bagel. "I'll be done here in a few hours. I'm happy to help however you need, but I'm not the best with repairs."

"I actually wondered if you'd be willing to make sandwiches for everyone who's going to help out today and tomorrow. I'll reimburse you for ingredients and all that."

She brightened. "That, I can definitely do. Don't worry about paying me back. I'm happy there's a way I can help. And I can call Kenna and Crosby. I'm sure they'll want to help, too."

"I wonder if lawyer boy can swing a hammer," Griffin grunted.

Caelyn rolled her eyes. "I'm sure you can teach him. Or he can help me with the kiddos." She looked at me. "Tell everyone you ask that there'll be childcare if they need it. We can organize a soccer game or something like that."

My throat tightened a fraction. I knew it wasn't this way for everyone. That with only a couple of sentences, an entire community would rally around you. It made me realize just how fortunate I was. "Thank you. I know it's going to mean the world to Piper, and it does to me, too."

Caelyn handed me my sandwich. "You were there for us when the chips were down. You know we'll always have your back."

Griffin grunted in agreement.

I inhaled my sandwich with a speed I was sure would've made Piper laugh and then headed out of the store. I had one more stop to make before I could return to my crew. If one person could get the call out for help, it was my mother. She could befriend just about anyone, and they couldn't resist wanting to help her in any way they could.

I wove through the older historic neighborhood until I reached the house I'd grown up in. It had barely changed in all the years since I'd left, but something about that was comforting. I jogged up the path and knocked on the door.

A few seconds later, my mom pulled it open and smiled at me. "Well, look what the cat dragged in. It's about time you came by. Come in, come in." She waved me forward. "You know you don't have to knock."

I wrapped her in a hug. "Knocking's polite."

"Knocking isn't for family."

I kissed her cheek and released her. "Whatever you say."

"That's right. Now, come on into the kitchen. We're just finishing up breakfast. You want something?"

My mom couldn't resist trying to feed anyone and everyone who came through her front door. I patted my stomach. "Just came from The General Store. I'm stuffed."

"That Caelyn has a gift."

"That she does." I patted my dad's shoulder as I sat down at the table. "Morning."

"Thought that was your voice. Shouldn't you be working?"

He looked the best he had since his stroke, and every time I saw him strong and without any slur to his speech, I breathed a sigh of relief. "I'm making the rounds to rustle up some help."

My mom eased into her seat. "What do you need help with? You haven't had any more trouble, have you?"

"I wish I could tell you we hadn't." I walked them through everything that had happened last night and what I was trying to pull together today and tomorrow.

"That poor girl," Mom whispered.

"She's definitely been through the wringer. But she's strong. She'll get through this."

My dad studied me closely. "You care about her."

Shit. If my mom latched on to this, I'd never hear the end of it. But there was no way around it, and I wouldn't hide Piper. I'd planned on them both meeting her soon enough anyway. "I do. She's the surprise of a lifetime."

The corner of Dad's mouth quirked up. "Your mother was, too."

My mom pressed her lips into a firm line, but she practically bounced in her chair. "We'll be there this afternoon. I'll call Caelyn and see what I can bring food-wise. I'll bake some things this morning and pick up some snacks at the grocery."

"We should get some things to grill for when the workday's done," my dad offered.

Mom nodded. "That's a great idea. I can pick up sides, too. Maybe Pietro could make us some salads."

Pietro had become a huge fan of Piper's in just the two hours we'd spent in his restaurant, so I knew he would. I leaned over and pressed a kiss to my mom's cheek. "I knew I could count on you to rally the troops."

"I really should've been a drill sergeant."

"Not arguing with that," Dad muttered.

She waved him off. "Oh, hush, you."

I pushed back from the table and stood. "Thank you both.

I really appreciate it. I need to head back to the crew, so they don't give me a bunch of shit for bailing on them."

My mom had already pulled out a notepad and was making what I was sure was a grocery list. "You go on. We've got this handled. We'll see you this afternoon."

"See you soon." I headed out the front door and back down the path. For the first time in twelve hours, I felt hopeful. Piper would learn what it was to have a community at her back.

Chapter Twenty-Nine

Piper

VOICES DRIFTED THROUGH THE BARN'S HALLWAYS, BUT they weren't close—they seemed far away. I looked up at Nick from where I stood, sanding a sideboard. "Do you hear that?"

He'd stopped by a few hours ago and hadn't left since. He'd been telling me story after story of the Falls' history and then more about his family's time here. It was kind of him, but I wanted to be alone for a while. To lose myself in my music and have a good wallow while still being productive.

"Sounds like the crew."

"Maybe. But I don't usually hear them all the way up here."

Nick followed me as I stood. "Do you think they'll be able to fix everything that was broken? I'd be happy to help if they can show me what to do. It's been a minute since I've done that kind of work." He glanced around the barn. "But I've honestly missed it more than I thought I would."

I couldn't imagine leaving all of this behind for another life. "They'll be able to fix it. The question is whether they can do it fast enough for me to stay afloat."

Nick winced. "I'm sorry it's been so rough."

"Not your fault. And I appreciate the offer of help. I'll let Hunter know."

I started out of the barn to figure out what all of the noise was about. As Nick matched my pace, I paused and then turned. "Did Hunter ask you to keep an eye on me?"

Nick flushed. "He, uh, was a little concerned after everything that happened—"

"I am going to kick his butt, I swear."

"Cut the guy some slack. He was really worried."

I stomped off towards the sounds of voices. I didn't care if Hunter was worried. He didn't get to put a guard on me without my permission. As I headed out of the forest and onto the gravel road, I froze. Dozens of people milled about, and most of them weren't on Hunter's crew.

"What in the world?"

Hunter caught sight of me and started in my direction. When he reached me, I held up a hand. "I'm pissed as hell at you, but we're going to have to put a pin in that for a minute. What's going on?"

Hunter's mouth quirked. "And what did I do to earn that?"

"You sicced Nick on me without asking."

Nick gave a sheepish shrug and kept walking towards the group of people. "Sorry, man. She figured you out. You're on your own."

"Chicken," Hunter muttered.

"Will you answer me already? What's going on?"

Hunter moved in close and laced his fingers with mine. "Come on. I want you to meet everyone who'll be helping out for the next couple of days."

He kept moving, but I stayed firmly planted. "Helping out?"

"Friends. People in the community. They heard what happened and wanted to help make things right."

"What?" I whispered.

Hunter released my hand and framed my face. "No one wants you to lose your dream. Not because one person was an asshole or for any other reason."

My first instinct was to push it all away and refuse every last piece of help that would only further cement my growing relationships. It would bind the ties tighter and make it that much harder if any broke away. But then I met the gaze of the beautiful man standing before me, the one who had called in favors and gathered a group of people that I never would've had access to. "You did this."

Redness crept up the back of his neck. "I put out the call. That's all."

I grasped Hunter's t-shirt and pulled him to me so I could take his mouth in a long, hard kiss. The hollers and whistles barely registered. "You're pretty amazing. You know that?"

"If that's my thank you, I'll have these people here every day."

"I'll let you in on a secret," I whispered in his ear. "I'll do that even if you don't."

"I'm a lucky man." He took my hand and led me towards the group. "Come on."

A woman in her mid-fifties hurried towards us, her hands clasped in front of her chest. "Piper. It's so wonderful to meet you. I'm Kara, Hunter's mom. I'm so sorry about everything that's happened, but I'm glad I finally get to introduce myself."

I quickly glanced down at what I was wearing. Denim shorts and a ratty t-shirt. Great. "It's nice to meet you, too. I'm currently trying to restrain myself from murdering your son for not warning me that I would have to meet a whole bunch of people for the first time, wearing my junior year theatre club t-shirt."

Kara barked out a laugh and pulled me into a hug. "Oh, honey, I like you." She arched an eye at her son. "This one is going to keep you honest."

"She's going to keep me something," he muttered.

"You should know better than to spring this on a girl. Especially after all she's been through." Kara kept an arm around my shoulders and ushered me forward. "You come with me. I'll take better care of you."

I stuck my tongue out at Hunter over my shoulder, and he just shook his head and followed. I met person after person. Griffin's adorable wife, Caelyn, who'd prepared enough food for an army. Hunter's friends, Kenna and Crosby, and their precious baby, Harriet, and adopted daughter, Zoe. Bell and Ford were here. And dozens more people I'd never be able to repay.

As Hunter separated the assembled crowd into groups and gave them instructions, an SUV rounded the curve in the gravel road—one that was familiar. As it pulled to a stop and two men climbed out, the tears I'd been fighting to hold back fell. I was running before I could even think about how silly it would look.

Nathan and Vic caught me on the fly, bringing me into one of those group hugs I hadn't had in far too long. "Oh, Munchkin," Vic said as he ran a hand over my hair.

"You should've called," Nathan complained.

I lifted my tear-streaked face. "How did you know?"

"A young man named Hunter gave us a call and said our girl needed us," Vic explained. "We left an hour later."

"Thank you." I hadn't realized how much I needed them. Just one hug had me feeling more centered and hopeful.

"Quite a crowd he's put together," Nathan said.

"I know." I wiped under my eyes. "He's pretty amazing."

"Is that him?" Vic asked in a hushed tone.

I glanced over my shoulder to see Hunter striding towards us. "Yup."

Vic let out a low whistle. "I might have to try and convince him to join our crew."

Nathan elbowed his husband. "Don't you dare."

Hunter slowed as he approached. "I can't tell if you're happy or about to punch me in the face."

"Happy." I threw my arms around him. "Thank you. I don't know how you did it but thank you."

"I got Nathan's number out of your phone when you were in the shower this morning."

I leaned back in his hold. "I should be mad at you for that."

"But you're not going to be because you've got your uncles here."

"That's right," Vic interrupted. "I'm Victor, but everyone calls me Vic. Thank you for calling and letting us know what's been going on."

Nathan stepped forward and held out a hand. "Nathan. It's nice to meet you."

Hunter gave a slight wince as he shook Nathan's hand. "You, too."

"Nathan," I warned.

He gave me an innocent look. "What?"

"Don't try to break Hunter's hand."

Vic smacked Nathan's shoulder. "You promised me you'd behave."

"I am."

Hunter chuckled. "Thank you both for coming. Come on. I'll show you what we're working on."

I'd wanted to carry this all on my own, but now that I saw how everyone pitched in, I wondered why I'd been so set on doing everything alone. I wanted a place that would strengthen the bonds of family and friends, but I'd been reluctant to let it do that. Hunter had unknowingly given me the push I hadn't known I needed. And for the first time, I could truly see all that the Falls could be.

Chapter Thirty

Hunter

THE FLAMES FROM THE BONFIRE CRACKLED, THIS TIME safely away from any of the buildings. Most of the crew had left, but friends and family had stayed. Someone had brought out ingredients for s'mores. The kids were all roasting marshmallows, and more than a few adults had joined in.

I pulled Piper back against me as I leaned into one of the picnic chairs someone had brought. She seemed to melt, her head falling against my chest. I knew she had to be exhausted, but I loved that she didn't want to miss a moment of this.

We'd made incredible progress today, and with all the help we'd have tomorrow, we'd likely end up ahead of schedule. I never would've thought it was possible until I saw everyone in action. They'd come together in the best way imaginable.

"Hey, man."

I looked up to see Brody, his arm around Shay.

"You got room for two more?"

I inclined my head towards the two empty picnic chairs. "Of course. Brody, Shay, have you met Piper yet?"

The set of Piper's shoulders changed at the mention of their names, and I knew she realized this was the person I'd been shot trying to save.

Shay smiled at her. "There were so many people here today, we haven't had the chance. I'm sorry you've had so much trouble, but I'm glad to meet you."

Shay didn't show any sign that being back in the place she'd almost lost her life bothered her, but I could tell that her husband was sticking close.

"It's nice to meet you, too. Thank you both for coming to help out. I know it's probably not easy—" Piper stopped talking mid-sentence. "Oh, God, I'm sorry. I shouldn't have brought that up."

Shay reached out and squeezed Piper's arm. "Don't apologize. It's actually been really good being back here. To see all the changes you've made. Help with some of those things. Cathartic, somehow."

Her gaze met mine, and I gave her a gentle smile. "I think it's been that way for a lot of us. Me. Nick. Celeste. Piper."

I looked around the fire and saw Celeste chatting up Piper's uncles, and Nick showing Crosby's daughter, Zoe, the best way to roast a marshmallow. I felt Piper relax against me again. She squeezed my arms. "I'm so glad it's been that for more than just me."

"Me, too," Brody echoed, pressing a kiss to Shay's temple.

Shay sent Piper a searching look. "You've been here before?"

"Growing up, I came here every summer with my uncles and my best friend and her family. But Jenn went missing from here ten years ago."

"Oh, Piper. I'm so sorry. I'm putting my nose where it doesn't belong."

She shook her head. "No. I don't want to hide her in the shadows. Buying this place helped me remember her. I want to bring her out into the light. And to do that, I need to talk about her."

I pulled Piper tighter against me, so damn proud of how she was handling all of this. If the roles had been reversed, I knew I wouldn't have dealt with it nearly as well. "There have to be more ways we can do that. Maybe have some of her favorite books in the library, some of her favorite games."

"If she had a favorite spot here, you could put a bench there with a memorial plaque," Shay offered.

Piper wiped under her eyes. "Those are great ideas. I don't know why it makes me so emotional, but that's exactly what I should do. It's not just the big things I've been so caught up in. It's the little ones, too."

Shay reached into her bag, pulled out a tissue, and handed it to Piper. "Sometimes, it's hard to see the full picture when you're in the middle of it."

"I've been hesitant to let anyone in. But today showed me how wrong that is." Piper tipped her head back so she could press a kiss to the underside of my jaw. "Thank you."

"I'm just glad you didn't deck me for doing it without your permission."

Brody chuckled. "Shay definitely would've if I'd done something similar."

"Hey," Shay protested.

"You know it's true."

"Fair enough."

Brody turned his gaze to Piper. "Do you have a photo of your friend that you could email me?"

"Sure, but why?"

"I'm an artist. I'd love to do a piece of her if that's okay. Tomorrow, you can show me where it might make sense to put it, and then we can decide on size."

Shay's eyes lit with excitement. "He'll make you something really special."

"That is incredibly kind of you." Piper's voice cracked as she spoke. "You really found yourself some amazing friends, Hunter. If you're not careful, I'm going to steal them."

"Steal away." I wanted these kinds of friendships for Piper. It was something I'd realized since I'd met her. She was friendly with everyone but let few people past that surface level—to the truth of who she was and what she struggled with. Even now, she let people help, make conversation, but no one knew how she truly felt about Jenn and what had happened here. I hoped that would come with time.

Piper shivered, and I pressed a kiss to the top of her head. "How about I get us some sweatshirts?" Even though we had made it to the thick of summer, the nights were still chilly.

"I can get them." She started to get up.

"No, you stay here. I'll be back in a few. Need anything else?"

"Maybe a water?"

"You got it." I pushed to my feet, leaving Piper to settle back in the chair.

I rounded the lodge and made my way to my cabin. Jogging up the steps, I unlocked the door and headed for the bedroom. Something about picturing Piper in one of my sweatshirts had my blood heating. I found one from high school football that she hopefully wouldn't drown in and then pulled a Hardy Construction one over my head.

As I made my way outside, I stopped when I heard two voices.

"I don't know what you think you saw, but you're wrong. And bringing that shit up now isn't cool," Cal said.

"I was just trying to piece that night together," Nick argued.

"It was a decade ago. Let it be."

I stepped into the light of my front porch, and both their gazes swung my way. "What's going on?"

Cal's jaw worked back and forth. "Nick's sticking his nose where it doesn't belong."

Nick held up both hands. "That wasn't my intention. Truly. It's just that being back here, seeing Piper again, it's bringing up a lot of unanswered questions."

"Well, whether or not I hooked up with someone at that party isn't a question you get an answer to," Cal barked.

"Fine," Nick muttered and took off towards his cabin.

"Trying to create nothing but drama."

I studied my foreman. "What's going on?"

Cal ran a hand over his head. "I hooked up with someone who wasn't Ashley that night. I was pissed as hell and did something stupid. We were on a break, but Ash won't see it that way. The last thing I need is that chump bringing shit up when Ashley's here."

"With who?" It shocked the hell out of me. Those two had been full of drama during most of high school, but I didn't think either of them had ever been with someone else.

Cal shook his head. "It doesn't matter. I fucked up, and I know it. I got my life together after that night and stopped messing around."

"Okay." I didn't have the right to demand answers, even if Cal was one of my closest friends. "But I don't think Nick was trying to be an ass. That night changed a lot of people's lives. I'm sure he's just trying to find closure."

"Digging that shit up will only cause more pain. The more people focus on it, the worse it'll be."

"Everyone deals with trauma in different ways. Some people need to find the truth. That's the only way they'll be able to let it all go."

"Maybe," he muttered. "I gotta find Ash and get her home. I'll see you tomorrow."

I waved him off and headed for the lodge to grab water for Piper. I'd have a word with Nick tomorrow, too. He needed to understand that Cal was feeling extra-protective of Ashley now that she was pregnant.

As I reached the kitchen, I came up short. Nathan stood in front of the open refrigerator. "Want a beer?"

"I'm actually just gonna get Piper a water." I pulled open a cabinet and grabbed one of her bottles.

Nathan held the fridge open as I grabbed the pitcher of water. "How long have you two been dating? She neglected to fill us in about that little detail."

I hid my chuckle with a cough as I filled the water bottle. "It's been a few weeks but feels a hell of a lot longer." It felt as if she'd always been with me. There was a level of comfort and ease that I'd never had before and doubted I'd ever find again. Something about all the hardships we'd faced made us into people who were just right for each other.

"She's special."

I looked up as I closed the bottle. "I know that. She's amazing. This incredible combination of strength and empathy. Fierce and gentle all at the same time. I've never met anyone like her."

The corners of Nathan's mouth curved up, and he slapped me on the shoulder. "Glad you know that."

As we headed out the back door, we ran into Vic, who panicked when he saw us. "Oh, no. Did he threaten your life?" he asked me.

I barked out a laugh. "I don't think life threatening was necessary."

"I like him," Nathan offered.

Vic's mouth fell open. "You *like* him?"

"I take it this is a first?"

Vic looked at me. "It's definitely a first. I've been trying to keep an eye on him so he doesn't ruin this for Piper by telling you he's going to chop you into little bits if you hurt her. But I guess that wasn't necessary."

Nathan gave his husband a quick kiss. "I like to keep you on your toes."

"You certainly do that."

I watched as they headed back to their spots at the bonfire and grinned. I officially had the uncles' seal of approval.

Chapter Thirty-One

Piper

I WATCHED AS HUNTER WALKED AWAY FROM MY UNCLES AND rounded the bonfire. There was something about the way he moved—both commanding and carefree. His strides ate up the space, knowing exactly where he was headed.

He eased down next to me, handing me a sweatshirt and setting down my water bottle. I unfurled the sweatshirt and arched a brow in his direction. "Football, huh?"

"Varsity, all four years."

I tugged it over my head. "Such a bragger."

He moved in closer, nuzzling my neck. "Am not."

"You most certainly are. But I like it." I tangled my hand in his hair. "If your lips are on my neck, that must mean Nathan didn't scare you off."

Hunter chuckled against my skin. "I like your uncles."

Something in me released at his words. Nathan had freaked out more than one boyfriend in the past. "I'm glad."

"Bet they kept your high school boyfriends on their toes."

"You have no idea."

He wrapped an arm around me, pulling me close. "I'm glad you have them."

"They're the best." Even if I tried, I couldn't imagine growing up with my mom. Nathan and Vic had given me everything I needed and more. They'd helped me find my path. Encouraged any interests. And most of all, they always made sure I knew just how loved I was.

"Vic was telling me about the house they're working on in Seattle. We should take a trip to the mainland and see it."

I couldn't imagine stepping away from the Falls for even a minute. Not with so much going on. But I also wanted to see the changes Vic and Nathan were making as they happened. "Maybe once we finish this first set of cabins."

"Sounds good to me."

I leaned a little more heavily on Hunter.

"You tired?"

I nodded against his chest. "Good but long day."

"Let's go to bed."

"There are still a lot of people here."

Hunter stood, pulling me to my feet. "They're all family. They don't need us to babysit them." He waved to the crowd. "We're hitting the hay. Last person to leave makes sure the fire's out."

There were words of agreement and shouts of goodnight from everyone. Vic sent me a wink from across the flames, and I blushed. God, I didn't need my uncles knowing I was going to bed *with* Hunter. "Did you have to announce that to everyone?"

Hunter laughed and tugged me towards the back door. "I hate to break it to you, but they know we're sleeping together."

"No, they don't. They know we're seeing each other."

"*Sure.*"

I smacked Hunter's stomach. "Stop it."

Bruno greeted us when we entered the lodge. He'd worn himself out playing with the kids all day and had been napping in his bed for the past few hours. I bent and rubbed his ears. "You ready for bed?" He nosed my hand in answer.

I opened the front door so he could run out and do his business, and then we headed upstairs. "Maybe I should make you sleep in your cabin tonight."

Hunter froze on the stairs. "You wouldn't."

"It would serve you right."

He moved in a flash, picking me up and running up the stairs. "Not happening, Casper. I've gotten used to sleeping with your body wrapped around mine."

Everything in me heated at his words, a mixture of comfort and desire. Because he was right. In a matter of weeks, I'd grown accustomed to his warmth, the sound of his breathing, the feel of his heartbeat against my cheek. The thought had everything in me tightening, a flash of panic setting in.

Hunter lowered me to the floor and framed my face in his hands. "Hey, what's wrong?"

Of course, he knew that something was wrong. Hunter read me like a book. The set of my body. The expressions flashing across my face. Some days, I swore he could read my mind. "Every time I think about getting used to this…fear sets in."

The words tumbled out of me without thought, the truth setting itself free. I didn't want to lose him. The more time we spent together, the harder I fell, and the worse it would hurt if he left someday. And I knew better than most that people sometimes disappeared from your life. By choice or mistake or violent tearing. The reason didn't matter when they were simply gone.

Hunter's thumb traced circles on my cheek. "What are you scared of?"

"Losing you." I was bold in my truths tonight, letting him in even further. But it wasn't fair to hold something like that back. It had been eating away at my mind without me even realizing it.

"I'm not going anywhere."

"You don't know that." My hands fisted in his sweatshirt. "No one does. Anything could happen. Things that are your choice and aren't."

"Casper—"

I placed a finger over his lips. "Don't promise something that's not yours to promise." Jenn and I had made a million different oaths to each other. To go to college together. Find an apartment together when we graduated. To buy the Falls one day and make it ours. And each vow gone unfulfilled had left a scar.

"The more I care. The harder this will be if something goes wrong." My voice cracked on the second sentence.

Hunter pulled me tighter against him. "Life is full of un-knowns. But that doesn't mean you can't take risks. Make that jump. Because as many things that can go wrong, a million more can go right."

"I know that in my head. But my heart…it's another story." As he held me, I realized just how safe I'd played it over the years. I had friends. Dated. Even had some relationships. But I'd always held myself back just a bit. Some part of my brain told me that if I just held that little piece back, I wouldn't get hurt the way I had when I lost Jenn.

"It tells you to run."

He understood without me having to spell it out. I burrowed deeper into his hold. "But I don't want to run from you." He was the first person I'd truly wanted to fight for. To resist that urge to pull away.

"Then you won't. I'll help you stay."

I tipped my face up to Hunter's, and his lips met mine in a slow kiss. The easy movement turned hungry. A bit desperate. As though he were already losing me and would do anything to hold on.

Hunter's movements turned frantic, his hands pulling me out of my sweatshirt and top, then focusing on his. His desperation fueled mine. I quickly slipped out of my shoes and shorts, my hands going to my panties, but Hunter stilled my movements. "No. I want to do that."

He dropped to his knees, his fingers curling around the sides of my thong. I sucked in a sharp breath as he slowly slid them down my legs. As his knuckles dragged across my skin, pinpricks of delicious sensation peppered my flesh, making me squirm.

He lifted one leg and then the other, the scrap of material falling to the floor. "Can you stay still for me?"

"Depends what you have in mind."

Hunter chuckled, the sound darker than normal. "I think you'll like it."

He trailed a finger up the inside of my thigh until he reached my center. His touch turned feather-light, teasing and toying but not anywhere near what I needed. I dug my fingers into his shoulders, and Hunter looked up at me. "Did you need something?"

I let out some sort of strangled growl. "You know what I need."

"I do." His eyes blazed, the green seeming to spark. "And you're not going to get it by bolting."

My mouth fell open. "Is this sexual extortion?"

"Just a reminder that there are benefits to staying put." Without warning, he darted forward, his tongue flicking across my core.

I let out a muffled curse as I struggled to keep my balance. I sure as hell wouldn't forget any of these benefits. Hunter's mouth explored every part of me except the one bundle of nerves where I needed him the most. My nails dug into the skin of his shoulders, a silent plea.

His tongue circled my clit, and with one single flick, he stood, seeming to know I was a breath away from fracturing. Hunter kicked off his boots and shucked his jeans and boxer briefs. He bent to pick up his wallet, but I stopped him.

"I'm on the pill." It was a gift, those words. An expression of just how much I trusted him.

Hunter's eyes blazed. "Are you sure? I got tested before my accident. And there hasn't been anyone—"

I cut him off with a kiss. "I want to feel all of you."

He lifted me with one arm, carefully laying me on the bed. His hands ghosted over my skin, teasing each dip and curve—no inch left unexplored. As a thumb circled my nipple, he slowly slid inside.

My eyes closed for a moment as I felt him everywhere. I'd never had sex without a condom, and it was different. More, somehow. Having that skin-to-skin contact everywhere gave the deepest intimacy.

As my eyes opened, Hunter began to move. His strokes built on each other as his thumb and finger toyed with the peak of my breast. My hips rose to meet his, my hands grasping onto his biceps. I needed something, anything to tether me to the here and now.

My legs hooked around Hunter's hips, and he was so much deeper. I let out a strangled sound as Hunter muttered a curse. Everything in me spun tighter as I reached for more.

My body moved without thought. Instinctively, I followed everything Hunter had to give. But I didn't lose sight of his eyes. I could drown in those depths. They made every promise I'd told him not to say aloud. Vowed that he'd stay when that was never guaranteed.

I lost myself in those eyes. And as I tipped over the edge and went spiraling down, my eyes returned that promise—even though they shouldn't have.

Chapter Thirty-Two

Piper

I WOKE COCOONED IN WARMTH. HUNTER'S BODY SURROUNDED mine, his comfort and strength seeping into me. The flash of panic came on swift and fierce, but I did my best to force it down. Taking a slow, steadying breath, I willed my muscles to relax.

"How are you thinking so hard so early?" Hunter muttered against my neck.

"It's a gift."

"Well, stop it. I'm trying to sleep, and you're disturbing me."

I grinned and pressed a kiss to one of the arms wrapped around me. "I didn't realize my thoughts were so loud. Excuse me."

"I can hear them like they're mine." Hunter pulled me tighter against him. "We're gonna be okay. Just take things one step at a time."

The therapist I'd seen after Jenn's disappearance had said the same thing. To take things one day at a time. One hour at a time, if needed. But it was easier said than done for a planner like me. "I'll try."

The smell of bacon and coffee wafted into the room, and Hunter perked right up. "I smell food."

"It's probably Nathan. He's an amazing cook."

Hunter started to get up, and I tugged on his arm.

"I thought you needed your sleep."

He pressed a quick kiss to my lips. "I need to get fed more. I'm a growing boy."

I let out a snorted laugh. "Sure, you are." But my stomach rumbled as I swung my legs over the side of the bed. I could only hope that Nathan had made my favorite.

Hunter and I made quick work of brushing our teeth and getting ready. More and more of his belongings had made their way from his cabin to my room. Our worlds were weaving together in a way that I loved, but it was also terrifying. I pushed down the flash of anxiety that rose and headed for the door. "I'm going to beat you to the food."

"Oh, no, you don't," Hunter called after me, but I was already racing down the stairs.

Our footsteps thundered, and I skidded to a halt in front of an amused-looking Vic.

"You would've thought we were expecting a herd of elephants for breakfast."

"Just like the old days," Nathan said. "The smell of quiche always could get her out of bed."

"Because I'm smart." I slid onto one of the stools at the industrial island.

Vic handed me a cup of coffee and passed another to Hunter. "There's sugar over there. And half and half in the fridge."

"Black is perfect. Thank you," Hunter said.

Vic leaned a hip against the counter and turned his gaze on me. "You've landed yourself a pretty amazing group of friends."

"They're Hunter's friends. He's the one who sent up the rally cry."

Hunter eased onto the stool next to mine. "They're your friends now, too."

It was that easy for him. And maybe it should be for me, too. But I still felt a little rusty with deep friendship—the kind you had when someone took a day off work to help you out of a jam.

Hunter chuckled at my silence and pressed a kiss to my head. "You'll get used to them."

I hoped I'd get the chance.

৩

"I wish we could stay longer," Vic said, pulling me into his hundredth hug.

"I wish you could, too. But you have to go make that giant house beautiful. Hunter and I will be checking on your progress soon."

He kissed the top of my head. "We'd love that."

Nathan pulled me from Vic's arms and gripped my shoulders. "You're going to be safe, right?"

"I've only got a bazillion people looking out for me." As much as I loved having my uncles here, I hated that I'd worried them. I knew it was likely killing them to leave me alone while they headed home. "I promise, I'll be fine."

"I'm going to hold you to that."

"I don't doubt it." I watched as they climbed into Nathan's SUV and headed down the gravel road. My chest tightened as they disappeared around the curve.

"You're gonna miss them."

I turned at the sound of Hunter's voice. "I'm used to seeing them at least once a week. I hadn't realized how much I missed that until they showed up."

"Come here." Hunter opened his arms, and I went into them without a thought. "We can go see them anytime you want."

"I know," I muttered into his chest. "But things around here are so crazy, I know it won't be anytime soon."

"But once the renovation is done, it'll be easier. You'll start bringing on more staff, and Nathan and Vic told me they're planning to take a month off every summer to spend it here."

I tipped my head back so I could see Hunter's face. "Really?"

He nodded. "Maybe you can convince them to retire out here."

A smile stretched across my face as I thought of all the trouble we could get into if they moved out to Anchor. "You'd probably have two extra crew members hanging around."

"I'd love it. Their work is grade-A."

"They certainly don't mess around."

Hunter brushed his lips against mine. "You going to be okay?"

"Yes." I let out a long breath, attempting to center myself and shrug off the pang of homesickness. "I need to run into town before things close. Do you need anything?"

"I think I'm good. We've got the world of leftovers, and our supplies have already been delivered."

I pressed a kiss to Hunter's jaw and stepped out of his hold. "Make sure you offer the crew dinner to take home so we can get rid of some of that food. There's still enough to feed a dozen armies."

"You got it, general. Want me to throw the ball for Bruno while you're gone?"

"That would be great," I said as I headed towards the barn. Hunter and I had moved our vehicles there to create more parking space for everyone who'd helped out yesterday and today. It was amazing what we'd accomplished, but I felt the price every time I moved. After I picked up my mail, I was coming home for a hot shower and bed. I didn't think I even cared about eating.

Following the gravel road around a bend, a bird called out from above as the late-afternoon sun filtered through the trees. I needed that pristine silence; nothing but the sounds of nature and the crunch of my sneakers against the gravel. And the Falls would always give that to me. In sound and scent and views. Everything I needed to recharge.

I pulled my keys out of my pocket and beeped my locks. As I moved to open my door, I froze. As my brain took in the image in front of me, bile crept up my throat. A rat lay on the hood of my SUV, its throat slit and blood dripping over the surface. It was on top of the corner of a piece of paper. In red letters, it said: *You're next.*

I waited for fear to set in. But it didn't. Instead, hot anger pooled in my limbs. I'd had enough of this asshole trying to scare me, whoever it was. I wouldn't give them what they wanted. I stomped into the barn and headed to my workshop, going straight for the box of latex gloves I used when staining furniture. Then I searched for the box of Ziploc bags I'd brought out here to organize my hardware pieces.

I snapped on gloves and then pulled out two bags. Heading back to the SUV, I tugged my phone from my back pocket. As I took pictures, I tried to let my gaze go unfocused, not to see the details of the gruesome scene. When I was done, I typed out a text.

Me: *Do you have a few minutes for me to show you something?*

A few seconds later, I had a response.

Parker: *Just finishing up an early dinner at The Catch. I can head to the Falls when I'm done.*

Me: *I'm actually headed into town. Meet you in The Catch parking lot in twenty?*

There was another pause, one I was sure was full of questions, before he answered.

Parker: *I'll be the one in the sheriff's department SUV.*
Me: *Thank you.*

I slid my phone back into my pocket. Steeling my stomach, I reached for the rat with my gloved hand as I held the Ziploc open with the other. I quickly sealed the bag and repeated the process with the note. I stowed both items in the back of my vehicle and then snapped off my gloves. Rounding the barn's corner, I got the hose and sprayed down the hood of my SUV.

My anger heated more as I watched the streams of red flow, my grip on the spray nozzle tightening. It took me a moment to realize that the water was running clear. I turned off the hose and put it away. Climbing into my SUV, I started it up and headed through the resort and towards the main road.

As I drove, I began going over everything in my head. All the people who'd had access to the resort over the past couple of days. But I stopped myself. It had to have happened today. The blood had started to dry, but no other critters had been at the rat. That cut down the list of suspects, but not by many.

One other thing to consider was that someone could've accessed the property through the forest instead of the resort. They could've parked and hiked in. Or they could've come by one of the beaches. There were plenty of stairs for someone to take up the cliffs.

The resort being the size it was made it incredibly hard to keep eyes on anything. Griffin had finally gotten the cameras up and running on the cabins now that we had better internet. But they only covered the front entrances for most of the buildings. I hadn't wanted to invade my guests' privacy.

It made Hunter feel better to have them, but I knew the truth. There was far too much land to cover, as evidenced by what had happened today. There were no cameras at the barn. And there wouldn't be. Our internet didn't reach that far. And I certainly wouldn't pay the astronomical fee required to get it there.

I pulled into the lot at The Catch, and after a quick scan, spotted Parker's SUV in the back corner. I headed in that direction and pulled into the space next to his. As I shut off my vehicle and climbed out, Parker pushed off his back bumper.

"I'll be honest. You've got me real curious. I feel like we're secret agents, meeting for a drop."

I laughed, but I knew it didn't ring true. Moving around my SUV, I opened my back hatch. "I wish we were doing that." I inclined my head to the trunk space, and Parker leaned in.

"What the hell?"

"It was on the hood of my SUV when I went to get in it thirty minutes ago."

Parker's eyes narrowed. "Why didn't you call me? You shouldn't have touched any of this. I can't run tests if the evidence is contaminated."

I held up a hand to stop his diatribe. "I know. But I can't keep having cops at the resort. You're going to scare off the few guests I have. I took pictures, wore gloves, and these Ziploc bags are brand new."

Parker muttered something under his breath and then went back to his SUV. When he returned, he'd donned gloves and carried two evidence bags. "I'll do my best to see what our techs can find, but I'm not sure anything we uncover will hold up in court."

I bit the inside of my cheek. Maybe it'd been dumb to try and play crime scene tech. But I hadn't been able to stomach the idea of more officers combing the property when we'd spent the past few days rebuilding the space. We'd cleared out the bad, and I didn't want a reminder that it was still lurking around. "I don't want this jerk to win. If I look scared and have the sheriff come running, he wins."

"I get that. I really do. But we need to do things by the book. It would be a real pisser if we caught this bastard and couldn't prosecute."

He was right. I knew he was. Yet I couldn't regret not calling in the cavalry. I was tired of everyone being worried about me.

Parker surveyed my face. "You don't look overly concerned."

"I'm concerned that a crazy person's running around, wreaking havoc on my resort. But I've found my mad. If they really wanted to hurt me, they would've done it by now."

"Piper. I don't want you being reckless. Just because they haven't lashed out at you physically yet doesn't mean they won't. You need to take precautions. Not work alone. Be aware of your surroundings. Be smart."

The concern in Parker's gaze softened something inside me. He was one of the good ones—the people who worked a mostly thankless job with the goal of keeping others safe. "I promise I'll be careful. It means a lot that you're looking out for me and the Falls."

He peeled off his gloves. "I'm trying. But I can't figure out a damn thing that would have someone so angry they'd tear up a bunch of buildings."

"And no prints have come back so far?"

"Plenty have, but nothing that's popped as someone in the system."

I leaned against the side of my SUV. "I'll just have to hope they mess up, and we catch a break."

Parker inclined his head towards the note. "Maybe we'll find something on the paper that will give us a clue."

I hoped he was right. But, somehow, I doubted that whoever this was would suddenly forget to wear gloves. Even if they kept playing it smart, they wouldn't chase me away. I'd found my home, and I wasn't giving it up for anyone.

Hunter

"TAKE HOME SOME OF THE LEFTOVERS FOR DINNER so you and Ash don't have to worry about cooking."

Cal's head snapped up from looking at his phone. "What?"

"We've got a ton of food left over from yesterday. You should take some of it home." I spoke slowly, studying my foreman and friend. "Are you okay?"

He ran his hand over his head. "Ash and I got into a fight last night, and I slept like shit."

"I'm sorry. Everything okay?"

"It'll be fine. But leftovers might help win her over."

I motioned him towards the lodge. "Growing a kid has to take a toll."

"It's no joke. She's feeling sick and not like herself."

I clapped him on the shoulder. "You guys will get through this."

Cal let out a sigh. "You're right. I know you are. But it's a hell of a rollercoaster at the moment."

As I pulled open the front door, Bruno bounded up to greet us. "Hey, buddy. You wanna go play some fetch?"

Bruno jumped and twirled. Cal chuckled. "I'd take that as a yes. You go on and take that beast out. I know where the kitchen is."

"Call me if you need anything. And if you need to take a day off to spend with Ash, you know you can."

"Thanks, man. I appreciate it."

"Anytime." I snapped my fingers, and Bruno was by my side in a flash. Leading him out the back door, I looked out at the view. The sun was heading towards the sea and casting an amber glow along the coastline.

Something in my chest loosened as I took it all in. The Falls no longer held a trigger for a downward spiral of memory. Not even when I'd worked on the same cabin I'd been shot in. Somewhere along the line, I'd replaced those bad memories with good. And in doing so, I could finally take in everything this spot had to offer.

I could see the potential that Piper saw. All the ways the Falls could grow. I knew she could pull it off. And I loved that I'd get to watch it happen. Be a part of it all.

Bruno barked in my direction. I shook myself from the trance the view had put me in. "Sorry, buddy. Got distracted. Let's go."

Bruno made quick work of the stairs leading down to the beach while I took them at less of a breakneck speed. By the time I reached the sand, Bruno had found a stick and was waiting. I took it from his mouth and lobbed it into the sea. He let out a happy bark and took off.

Taking in the space around me, I tensed. Two figures strolled down the sand. This little cove was mostly protected. While the dock with the small sailboat was private property, the rest of the beach was public. But you'd have to climb over some pretty gnarly jetties to reach it. I'd yet to see a single person who wasn't a guest down here. Until now.

Jasper Leclair and his friend, Aaron, walked towards me. Jasper wore what seemed to be his signature smirk, while Aaron looked more uneasy. Bruno bounded out of the surf, shaking the water from his coat before racing to me and dropping the stick at my feet. As soon as he saw the teens, he lost all interest in the stick and took up a protective stance in front of me.

"What are you guys doing here?"

"In case you didn't know, this is a public beach. I checked," Jasper said.

"Didn't say it wasn't. Still want to know what you're doing here."

"Come on, Jas," Aaron whispered. "Let's just get out of here."

Jasper turned his glare on Aaron. "He doesn't own this fucking island. He doesn't get to say where we go."

"My parents are going to ground me for life if we get into trouble again."

"Don't be such a pussy."

I arched a brow. "You guys need privacy for your little tiff? If you leave the cove, you'll have it."

"Fuck you," Jasper spat.

Bruno let out a low growl and moved a step closer to the boys. "I'd tread very carefully if I were you. Charges are already pending for both of you. And you showing up here, saying the things you are…that could be construed as a threat."

"Shit, Jas. I told you this was a bad idea."

Jasper ignored his friend and kept his gaze locked on me. "Heard your girlfriend had some trouble around here. That's a real shame."

My jaw worked back and forth as I tried to keep my temper in check. Parker had said that Jasper's parents had alibied the boys, but it was clear they'd do anything to protect them. The destruction of the cabins had seemed too intense for two teen-agers, but maybe I'd been wrong. Jasper had more than enough anger and darkness in him to leave three destroyed cabins in his wake.

He grinned at my silence. "It'd be real unfortunate if something like that happened to her."

Bruno lunged. He didn't bite, but he snapped his jaws at Jasper. The move had the kid stumbling back and falling on his ass. He scrambled to his feet. "Call off your fucking dog."

"You know…I can't seem to remember that command."

Bruno kept moving the teens back, a growl low in his throat.

"I'm going to fucking sue you," Jasper sputtered.

"Good luck with that."

Once Bruno had moved them back at least twenty feet, I snapped my fingers, and he returned to my side. "I'd get lost if I were you. When I start playing fetch with him, he might mistake one of your legs for a chew toy."

Aaron took off without looking back, but Jasper glared in my direction. I didn't look away. The look in his eyes spoke of rage and hatred. Bruno barked, and Jasper finally turned, following his friend to the jetty.

I crouched and rubbed behind Bruno's ears. "You're a damn good dog, you know that?" He licked my face. "Gross, man. That's crossing a line."

I picked up the stick and hurled it into the water. Bruno ran after it. I needed to call Parker and fill him in on this latest run-in, but I couldn't find it in me to do it tonight. I wanted to soak in the setting sun. The beauty of this place. And watch a dog experience sheer joy. I wouldn't let some pissant teenager ruin it.

Chapter Thirty-four

Piper

I RESTED BACK ON MY HEELS, SURVEYING THE NEWLY PLANTED beds outside the finished cabins. There was a good chance I could open them for rental in the next few weeks. I'd offer them at a discounted rate since construction was still ongoing around them during the day. But when the rest of the rental market was booked because of the height of tourist season, I guessed I'd have more than a few takers.

Celeste waved as she walked towards the cabin next door for a thorough post-construction cleaning. "That looks beautiful."

"Thank you. I'm moving on to that one next." I pointed.

"No, you're not."

I squealed as strong arms went around my waist, lifting me into the air. "Hunter, your shoulder—"

"Is fine," he said, setting me on my feet.

"It won't be if you keep doing things like that."

He pressed a quick kiss to my mouth. "I'm in perfect working order. I promise. But I am kidnapping you…"

"Are you, now?"

He laced his fingers with mine, tugging on my hand. "Come on."

I looked back at the other cabin and Celeste, who had an amused smile on her face. "I need to plant the other beds and—"

"You need to take a lunch break." Hunter opened the passenger-side door of his truck and ushered me in. I gave him a mock glare but hopped in. He quickly rounded the front of the vehicle and climbed behind the wheel.

"What is the destination of this kidnapping?"

"You'll just have to wait and see."

I grumbled something about ruining my schedule for the day, and Hunter chuckled.

"You know. It's good to take a break now and then. Enjoy the fruits of your labor."

"Easy for you to say. You aren't running the numbers every week." I wasn't close to bankruptcy or anything, but the figures made me sweat a bit.

The grin fell from Hunter's face. "Do you need an infusion? I'd be happy to loan you—"

"No." The single word came out harsher than intended. "Thank you. I really appreciate the offer, but I can manage it. And I've pitched the restoration of the Falls to several travel magazines and blogs. I'm hoping one or two of them might do a feature. That would help a ton."

"Is getting you to accept help always like pulling teeth?"

"It's not like pulling teeth."

He gave me a sidelong glance. "I was pretty sure you were going to shank me in my sleep when all of those people showed up to help the other day."

"I might've thought about it. But if you remember, I thanked you. I liked having them here." It was probably the greatest gift anyone had ever given me. Having dozens of strangers put in back-breaking work. I'd remember it forever. But that was very different than Hunter cutting me a check.

I couldn't let go of my need for the Falls to be *mine*. Not just mine, though. In my mind, it was Jenn's and mine. Letting someone into the running of it, the funding would seem like I was somehow replacing her. I simply couldn't do that.

"Okay. I promise not to give you a cent."

"Thank you."

Hunter chuckled. "Never thought a promise like that would make someone so happy."

"What can I say? I'm unique."

"Understatement of the century."

Hunter guided his truck away from the resort and towards the barn, but just as we were about to reach it, he took another road that looked as if it hadn't been used in a decade. Branches haphazardly littered the lane, and the potholes were the size of craters. But it was all achingly familiar. A path that Jenn and I had taken countless times.

I stayed silent as we made the journey towards the back of the resort property. But within five minutes, Hunter pulled to a stop. "This is my favorite spot here."

"Mine, too." My voice had gone hoarse. "Jenn and I used to get popsicles from the kitchen and walk out here."

Hunter turned in his seat, his hand grabbing mine. "Is it okay that we're here?"

I nodded. "I hadn't realized I'd been putting off coming here. And it helps to have you with me."

"Sometimes, making new memories, good ones, helps to take the sting out of the old."

He was right. All sorts of beautiful memories were filling up my bucket when it came to the Falls. But I didn't want them to cast out my memories of Jenn, either. It was always a delicate balance, remembering but not becoming stuck in the past.

Hunter squeezed my hand and then released it. "Come on."

We climbed out of the truck, and Hunter went around to the bed, pulling out a cooler and a blanket. My mouth curved. "Did you make me a picnic?"

Redness crept up the back of his neck. "I might've."

"You're a romantic at heart."

"For the right woman, maybe I am."

Something about his words had a mixture of warmth and anxiety stirring to life within me. I did my best to shove down the panic and hold onto the heat. Hunter crossed to an open spot about thirty yards back from the cliff's edge and spread out the blanket.

I stared out at the sea, looking at the small islands poking up. Something about the view was comforting in its vastness. It reminded me what a small part of the world I truly was. As big as my pain might seem at times, it was only a drop in the bucket.

I eased down onto the blanket. "It really is the best view in the entire place."

"I agree. And I think it's where you should build your house one day."

My eyes widened. "What?"

Hunter unloaded sandwiches, fruit, and chips from the cooler. "It's the perfect place to build. I'd make the back of the house all windows with a massive deck, a hot tub built into it. Two stories. I think Craftsman as opposed to log cabin. It's close enough to the rest of the resort that you can be there in minutes if you're needed, but far enough away that you'd have your privacy."

"You've really thought about this, haven't you?"

He shrugged. "I'm always thinking about what would make the perfect spot for a house."

His analysis had my head spinning. "It's going to be a nice long while before I'm thinking about building anything else on the property."

He popped a grape into his mouth. "Might not be as long as you think."

For as much as Hunter had been through in the past few years, he'd seemed to have held onto his eternal belief in all the possibilities of life. I wanted to tap into that. "Have I told you what else I want to do with the resort?"

"You mean besides hot tubs for every cabin?"

I grinned. "Besides the hot tubs."

"Lay it out for me."

"I want to build a few larger cabins that people can rent out for large groups. Weddings, family reunions, maybe retreats. I've been thinking a lot about doing some sort of glamping. Platformed tents and yurts wouldn't be as expensive to build as more cabins, but it would increase income."

"That whole thing is super on-trend now, too."

I'd spent hours last week pricing out what it would all cost, and I might be able to make it happen next year. "I also want to get the barn up and running again so that guests can take trail rides. I might even be able to open it up to people who aren't staying here."

Hunter leaned on his elbow. "You know much about horses?"

"Haven't ridden one since the last time I came to stay at the Falls."

"You might want to hire some help in that arena. Otherwise, you could end up drowning in horse shit."

I picked up a potato chip and took a bite. "The horses are a long way off. Those buggers are expensive."

"You could always use Bruno to give pony rides."

"He'd probably love it."

Our lunch hour slipped by quicker than I could've imagined. We lost ourselves in the food, dreams for the resort, and just being together. Hunter made for a great sounding board. While he'd never run anything in the hospitality world, he was an expert in all things construction. And he already had me rethinking where I would put the glamping area.

I glanced at my watch. "We really should get back."

His hand curved around the back of my neck, and he pulled me to him. His lips brushed mine, his tongue diving in. "I'd like to spend this afternoon another way."

A small moan escaped me, but I pulled back. "You, sir, are a bad influence. We have a resort to get up and running."

Hunter pushed to his feet. "Fine, fine. Be a spoilsport."

"Careful, or I'll kick you out and give Bruno your spot in bed. You'll never get it back."

"You wouldn't dare."

"Just try me."

He wrapped an arm around my waist. "I promise never to call you a spoilsport again. Am I forgiven?"

"Your spot in bed is safe…for now."

"Thank God." He bent and put all of our trash into the cooler, and I folded up the blanket.

"Thanks for kidnapping me. I think I needed this more than I thought."

Hunter pressed a kiss to my temple. "Gotta make sure you're taking care of yourself, not just the resort. This whole process is a marathon, not a sprint. Don't burn yourself out."

"I'm not."

He arched a brow. "Really?"

My fingers dug into the blanket as we headed back to his truck. "I'm working hard, but I'm not burning out." I was pushing myself but not over any edge.

"All right."

We climbed into the truck, and I looked at Hunter. "Why does that 'all right' sound more like *bullshit*?"

Hunter started up the engine. "I don't think there's any good way for me to answer that one."

"I know my limits."

He guided us down the gravel road, trying to avoid the worst of the potholes. "I know you do. I just worry about you."

The honesty in that sentence took the wind out of my sails. "I'm fine. I promise. And you're clearly going to make sure I take plenty of breaks."

He sent me a mischievous grin. "Next time, I vote for a naked one."

"Men," I huffed.

Hunter pulled into the parking spot next to the cabin that he was no longer using since he spent every night with me. "Aw, shit."

"What?" I looked around but didn't see anything alarming.

"That's Courtney's car."

"The ex-girlfriend, Courtney?"

"That's the one."

"Did you ever call her and have that talk?"

Hunter sighed and scrubbed his jaw. "Things have been more than a little hectic around here. I just haven't had time."

Things had been crazy. But a phone call like that took a half-hour, tops. Everyone had thirty minutes in their day if something was important enough.

"Don't give me that look."

"What look? And I was looking out the window, not at you."

"The look that says you think I want her. I don't."

"Okay." I wasn't sure what else to say. We hadn't made any promises for the future. And I didn't want that. Those kinds of commitments made that invisible vise around my chest crank up its tightness. But I did want Hunter. And I wasn't quite sure how to reconcile the two.

"Why does that 'okay' sound more like *bullshit*?"

My lips twitched. "Don't go stealing my lines."

Hunter wrapped his hand around the back of my neck and

tugged me towards him. "There's only one woman I want, and she's sitting in the passenger seat of my truck, giving me shit while barely saying a word."

"Sounds like a good choice to me."

"She's a force of nature. I'm just along for the ride."

I brushed my mouth against his. "At least you know you won't be bored."

"Never. Come on, let's go see what's going on."

I wanted to stay in the truck. Or better yet, run and take cover in the lodge. But instead, I was an adult and climbed out of the vehicle. Hunter met me at the back bumper and laced his fingers with mine. The heat of his palm, the roughness of his skin, were always a balm. Something about it eased whatever happened to be raging inside me at the time. Worries about the Falls, memories of Jenn, missing my uncles. That simple touch grounded me in the here and now.

Hunter tugged me towards the cabins where his crew now worked. I could see the men gathered around a couple of picnic tables nearby. Two women were in their midst. I recognized Courtney from our brief meeting outside Goodwill. She looked effortlessly gorgeous in her pale pink sundress. I felt instantly frumpy in my cutoff shorts and dirt-streaked tank top.

The second woman I'd met briefly at the cookout the other day. It was Cal's wife, Ashley. She caught sight of us first. "Hunter, you missed all the fun. Court and I made you guys lunch."

"That was kind of you, but I needed to steal my girl away for a picnic."

Courtney's gaze zeroed in on our joined hands, and her face paled. I tried to slip my hand from Hunter's grasp, but he held firm. I dug my nails into his skin, trying to send the message that I didn't want to rub this in Courtney's face. No one deserved that. But Hunter didn't budge.

"That's a shame," Ashley said, her eyes roaming over my mess of a form.

"Not for me, it wasn't. Hope you guys had fun, but it's time for us to get back to work."

Ashley wasn't giving up without a fight. "Why don't you come over for dinner tonight? You and Court, me and Cal, just like old times."

The crew traded glances and began getting up from the table, sensing the ensuing drama. "Ash," Cal warned, his voice low.

"What? Four old friends can have dinner, can't they?"

I gave my hand a swift tug and broke free of Hunter's hold. "I think what your husband's getting at is that it's pretty rude to invite Hunter on a double date when the person he's with is standing right there."

Ashley's mouth fell open. "That's not what I meant at all. We've been friends for forever. Surely, you wouldn't stand in the way of friends spending time together."

"She wouldn't. But I would," Hunter interrupted before I could respond. "I don't spend time with people who go out of their way to hurt those I care about. And that's what you just did, Ash."

"Hunter, I never—Cal, say something. Are you just going to let him talk to me that way?"

Cal shook his head. "Take it easy on her, Hunt."

Hunter moved his gaze to Cal. "Your wife's stirring up drama about something that is none of her concern. She's got her own relationship. She needs to stay out of mine."

"Ashley," Courtney said quietly. "Let's go."

Ashley straightened. "You have every right to be here. Everyone knows you and Hunter are going to end up together. And then things will be just as they should be. This one is going to end up back in Seattle in a few months."

"Actually, this is private property, so…" I began and then

turned to Courtney. "You're welcome here anytime. I'm sorry this turned into such an awkward cluster. You seem really kind, and like you didn't want to get roped into all of this—"

"I didn't," Courtney cut in. She turned to Hunter. "I'm sorry about all this. Both of you. I'll see you around."

She started for her car, and Ashley whirled on Hunter. "That girl loves you, and you're making a huge mistake." She stormed after her friend.

"On that note, I'm going back to my gardening. Much less drama there."

Hunter stepped towards me. "Piper—"

I waved him off. "I'm fine. I just need my hands in the dirt for a while."

Over the past week, I'd learned that small-town life had plenty of perks. I guessed there had to be some downsides, too.

Hunter

"WHAT THE HELL, MAN?"

Cal winced. "I'm sorry. I'll have a word with her. She just loves you and Court and thinks you'll be happiest together."

Ashley had always been a bit nosy, but it was more like a mother hen trying to make sure all her chicks were safe and cared for. She hadn't been happy when I ended things with Courtney and had dropped more than one comment about us getting back together. But I'd never known her to be this rude before.

I glanced towards the flower bed a few hundred yards away, where Piper worked. She turned the soil with a bit more aggression than normal, and I didn't blame her. I just hoped Ashley hadn't gotten into her head.

I turned back to Cal. "It needs to be a strong word. If she pulls that shit again, I'm banning her from the jobsite. This is none of her damn business."

"She didn't mean any harm—"

"The hell, she didn't. She wanted to make Piper feel unwanted and like an outsider. And she succeeded. Piper's been going through hell since she came back. Do you really think she needs Ashley pulling this kind of shit on top of it all?"

Cal's shoulders slumped. "You're right. I'm sorry. I'm sure Ash wasn't thinking about all of that. I'll remind her of everything Piper's dealing with."

"Thank you. Now, can we get back to work? I'm sure the crew is hiding in the windows of the cabin, gossiping."

Cal chuckled. "Of course, they are."

I slapped Cal on the shoulder and steered us towards the cabin in question. "Once we get this cabin wrapped up, I think we need to divide and conquer. You take a couple of the guys and tackle cabin four. I'll do cabin two. And I want to take a look at the barn, too. Piper will eventually want to fix it up."

His steps faltered. "The barn, really?"

"Yeah. Why?"

He gave an exaggerated shiver. "It's always given me the creeps."

"Don't tell me you believe all of these ghost stories."

Cal shot me a grin and shrugged. "Enough people have seen weird stuff up here. You never know what might be true."

"God save me from all the ghost believers," I muttered.

"You won't be saying that after you have a spooky encounter..."

I sent Cal a wave as he headed down the road. It had taken us a minute to find that easy camaraderie after the scene with Ashley, but we'd gotten there. And the crew had slowly relaxed, realizing that we weren't going to take each other's heads off.

I scanned the property, looking for Piper, and saw her headed to the barn. I muttered a curse and followed her. Even though we hadn't had any other issues over the past couple of days, I still didn't want her working alone.

As I walked, I pulled out my phone and hit Parker's contact. With everything that had been going on, I'd never filled him in on my run-in with Jasper and Aaron on the beach. He needed a full picture of what was happening.

Parker answered on the second ring. "Please tell me you haven't had another break-in."

"No break-ins."

"Thank God. I just cracked a beer and am sitting on my back deck, enjoying the view. I did not want to have to head over to Anchor."

"Understandable. I wanted to fill you in on a little run-in I had."

The sound of a bottle being set down came across the line. "Hit me with it."

I walked Parker through my encounter with Jasper and Aaron, sparing no details. "I've got a bad feeling about that Jasper kid."

Parker muttered a curse. "I wonder if they were the ones who left the rat on Piper's car."

I stilled. "The what?"

He was silent for a moment before speaking. "Did Piper not tell you that someone left a dead rat and note on the hood of her SUV?"

"No, she didn't," I growled. "When?"

"The day you guys wrapped up your construction party."

"What did the note say?"

Parker cleared his throat. "'You're next.'"

I let out a slew of curses and picked up my pace towards the barn. "Why didn't you tell me?"

"I assumed Piper had."

I would've assumed the same. But everyone knew what they said about assumptions. "Do you have any leads?"

"Not until you told me about the troublesome twosome. I'll

question them tomorrow. But I need to tread carefully there. The Leclairs won't hesitate to level a harassment charge on the department."

I kicked at a pinecone, sending it flying. "Do you have any idea how long they're staying on the island?" As much as I wanted to see those kids sitting in a cell if they were the ones behind everything we'd been dealing with, I cared more about keeping Piper safe. I doubted that Jasper would find his way back to the island once he and his parents returned to the mainland.

"They're here for the duration. Won't be leaving until September."

"Shit."

"You got that one right. But with all this trouble, I can only hope the parents will get a clue and go home early."

"I wouldn't hold my breath." I'd seen the outrage on the Leclairs' faces when the police accused their son and his friend of setting the bonfire. They'd finish their stay on principle.

"Hunt, you need to give them a wide berth."

"I'm trying. They're the ones who showed up here. I'd like nothing more than to never see their faces again."

"I get it. Just be careful."

"I will. I need to go. I have to talk to Piper."

Parker sighed. "Go easy on her. She's dealing with a lot right now."

I swallowed back the retort I wanted to level at the sheriff, knowing he didn't deserve me biting his head off. "She also needs to realize that she's not in this alone."

"Good luck with that."

"Thanks." I hit end on my screen and finished the rest of the trek to the barn.

The soft sounds of music came from the workshop— not eighties power ballads this time but some sort of folky composition. Piper didn't hear me approach—another reason she shouldn't be out here alone. Especially not when someone clearly wanted to do her harm.

I watched in silence as she worked. Piper rolled her lips together when she needed to focus, two little lines appearing between her brows. I wanted to rub them away with my thumb.

"Are we together?" The words escaped before I'd even thought about what to say.

Piper startled and reached out to the wall to steady herself. "Geez. It's not nice to sneak up on a girl like that."

No smile reached my lips. "Are we?"

She straightened from her crouch. "I'd like to think so. What brought this on?"

"The fact that I had to learn from Parker that someone threatened you. Left a fucking dead rat on your car. If we're in a relationship, why am I learning that little fact from the sheriff instead of my girlfriend?"

Piper flushed. "I had it handled."

"It doesn't matter if you had it handled or not. That's something you share." I tried my best to keep my voice even, not to lash out, but every word seemed to vibrate in the small space.

"I have to fight some of my battles. You can't fix everything for me."

"This isn't about fighting. It's about you hiding something from me. I asked you how your trip to town was. You didn't share a damn thing about meeting up with Parker to give him a dead rat."

Piper stiffened. "I don't answer to you, Hunter. Just because we're seeing each other doesn't mean you have a right to everything in my life."

I fought the urge to throw something against the wall. "I have the right to know if your life's in danger. Flip that little scenario around. How would you feel if I'd done that?"

All the anger vibrating through Piper seemed to defuse with that one question. Her shoulders slumped, and she eased into the chair behind her. "I didn't mean to hurt you. I didn't want you to worry, and…"

Her words fell away as she struggled to voice whatever was running around in that beautiful brain of hers. I moved in closer and leaned against the dresser she'd been sanding. "And what?"

Her eyes met mine, and I saw such turmoil in those dark orbs that I wanted to take back every word I'd said. Her fingers dug into her knees. "I don't know how to do this. How to remain my own person and be self-reliant yet let you in at the same time."

It was more than that, though. Over the past couple of months, I'd seen that Piper only let people in so far. She had erected this invisible barrier that no one but her uncles crossed. And they'd only made it behind that line because they'd raised her from birth. The problem was, I'd crashed through that wall without even knowing it. And some instinct in Piper told her to push me out.

I bent forward and framed her face in my hands. "Loving me doesn't mean you have to lose yourself."

Panic flared to life in her eyes. "I—I don't—I don't—"

I wanted to laugh. She couldn't even get the words out. "I'm pretty sure you do. I've fallen head over heels for you, even though I promised myself I wouldn't. But there's no rush. I don't need the words yet. I see it in other ways."

She scowled at me. "You're very sure of yourself."

I shrugged. "I know what I've got, and I'm not gonna lose it. Even if it scares the hell out of you."

"It does. Scare me, I mean."

I brushed my lips across hers. "I know it does. But I'll be here to scare away the bogeymen every time."

"Sometimes, the bogeymen are real, and there's nothing you can do to scare them away."

My chest constricted. I wasn't sure Piper realized how much Jenn's disappearance had colored her life. Her choices. The relationships she chose. But right now, knowing how easy it was to lose someone kept her from jumping in with both feet.

"They might be real, but they're still afraid of the light. And what we have has a whole lot of light in it, Casper."

Chapter
Thirty-Six

Piper

I WANTED TO SINK INTO HUNTER'S WORDS. TO TRUST THAT the light we created when we came together was enough to scare any monsters away. But I knew that hope didn't always come to fruition. That knowledge didn't change how much I wanted Hunter. This thing between us only seemed to grow each day. And with it, my need for him.

I moved without thinking, pushing out of my chair and fisting my hands in his t-shirt. I pulled him to me with a force that surprised even me. But Hunter was more than up for meeting my challenge. He stood, his hands cupping my ass as I hopped up and wrapped my legs around his waist.

Our mouths met in a duel for dominance, pouring every ounce of frustration from our earlier fight into the action. Each stroke of tongue or nip of lip was a silent plea for understanding. And the feral nature of it all spoke to the desperation we both felt. As if the other might slip through our fingers whether by choice or outside force.

Hunter turned, seating me on the dresser, his hands going

straight for the button on my shorts. He slid them down my legs in a few quick movements and let them fall to the floor. Before I had a chance to say a word, he sank to his knees and pushed my thighs apart.

There was none of the teasing Hunter was typically so fond of. I gasped as his tongue drove inside me and grabbed hold of the back of the dresser to steady myself. "Give a girl a little warning, would you?"

He chuckled against my core, sending a cascading wave of sensation through me. "Where would the fun be in that?"

Hunter's tongue moved to my clit, flicking as two fingers entered me, stroking that perfect spot deep inside. I shuddered, and his movements halted. "Don't come," he ordered.

His tone sent a shiver across my skin as my nipples hardened. "Why the hell not?"

"I want you to come while I'm inside you. Not before. Haven't you heard of delayed gratification?"

My hands fisted in his hair. "I'm really more of the instant gratification type."

Hunter's tongue circled that bundle of nerves. "Let's see if I can get you singing a different tune."

I spit out a slew of curses, most of them ones that would make a sailor blush. None of them affected the man between my legs. His fingers stroked and twisted while his tongue drove me impossibly higher.

My thighs began to tremble and shake. "If you don't get inside me soon, I'm going to leave you behind."

All touching ceased immediately, and Hunter was suddenly on his feet, his hands on the button of his jeans. The sound of his zipper seemed to echo off the walls and was the only thing I could hear beyond the beating of my heart and the blood roaring in my ears.

Hunter lifted me from the dresser and spun me around. "I want you like this."

"Take me," I whispered.

He entered me in one swift stroke, my hands going to the dresser top for balance. Hunter's hips thrust forward again. "Hell, so much deeper."

My hips arched back to meet him. I could feel him everywhere as if he'd invaded my very marrow. But I still wanted more. Our movements became desperate. Frenetic.

Hunter drove himself deeper inside me. A bite of pain punctuated each thrust, the edge sending me to a place I'd never gone before—one where I finally let go. I realized amidst the haze of sensation that I'd always held onto at least a bit of control in my previous relationships. But in this moment, I couldn't hold onto anything but Hunter and sensation. Soaking up every nuance running through my body.

Hunter's hand wound around my waist, his finger finding my clit. I couldn't take any more. The world closed in, the edges of my vision going dark before everything exploded in a shower of light. White dots danced as Hunter called out my name.

I lost all sense of time as we came back to ourselves, then collapsed against the dresser, our chests heaving. Hunter brushed my hair away from my neck and pressed a soft kiss to the skin there. The gesture was so tender, I felt tears stinging the corners of my eyes.

"I'm going to have to buy this dresser from you," he mumbled.

"What?"

"No one gets this dresser in their bedroom but me."

I laughed, and Hunter groaned as he pulled out of me. I winced at the movement. Hunter's arms were around me in a flash, turning me to face him. "Too much?"

I shook my head. "Just tender."

"We need to get you in a bath."

I arched a brow at him. "Only if you join me."

He pressed a kiss to my temple. "I think that can be arranged."

As he pulled back, I couldn't hold in my laugh. We were both standing there naked from the waist down but with our shirts on. I grinned up at him. "This would make a hell of a picture."

"For my eyes only," Hunter growled.

I patted his chest. "Sure, sure." I wrapped my arms around his neck. "Take me to that bath, would you?"

"You only have to ask."

⌒◯

"Piper."

I stopped at the sound of Cal's voice and turned. I did my best to keep a smile on my face, but I simply didn't have it in me for drama this morning. The few gulps of coffee I'd managed to get down hadn't made their way to my bloodstream yet. Bruno leaned into my side as if sensing that I needed his support. "Morning, Cal."

He shuffled from foot to foot. "Do you have a second?"

"Sure." I needed to get a jump on the day. Four more furniture pieces needed to be finished before I could begin booking out the three cabins Hunter and his team had redone, but it would be better to get this over with now.

"I'm really sorry about yesterday. Sometimes, Ash gets it in her head that she knows what's best for the people she loves. She's had it in her head that Hunter and Courtney should end up together and…she just doesn't know you yet."

After the run-in yesterday, I had zero desire to get to know her. "Look, if she doesn't come around starting trouble again, then we'll be fine. But this is my place of business. I can't have another scene like yesterday's."

Cal nodded woodenly. "I get it. We talked last night, and it won't happen again."

Yet Cal was the one apologizing to me, not his wife. I had a feeling she wasn't quite as on board with the plan as her husband.

But I didn't have people in my life that I'd known forever as they did. I was supposed to, but that had been stolen away. Maybe I needed to have a bit more empathy for Ashley.

I sighed. "I'm not trying to be a bitch. I honestly don't know what it's like to share the kind of friendship you guys have. The only person I had like that…"

Cal's jaw worked back and forth. "You lost."

"Yeah. I miss her every single day. And I'm sure if she were still here, and some guy was stealing her away from all the plans I had for us, I wouldn't be too happy about it." I tried to envision what it might be like to have Jenn at the Falls with me, some new guy taking her in a different direction. I knew it would hurt.

"I'm sorry you lost her," Cal said softly.

When I met his gaze, I saw so much grief there. As if he could see all the hurt and fear and questions that had piled up in me over the years. Everything in that look told me that Cal had an empathetic side that made him a good man. "Thank you. Me, too."

"We all think about it. Especially those of us who were there that night. No one's forgotten her."

Yet they'd all let her walk off alone, never to be seen again. I shoved down the anger. Because if I let it fly, it would hit one target above all others. Me. I had let her walk away first. I was the one who'd known she was going to a party she had no business being at. And still, I'd let her go. I swallowed against the burn in my throat. "You met her that night?"

"Yeah. She seemed nice. A little wild. Like she wanted every experience life had to offer."

My mouth curved. "She was always ready for that next step, while I constantly wanted to hang back and play it safe."

Cal studied me for a moment. "Why didn't you go with her to the party?"

It was the question I'd asked myself a million times. "Truth?"

He nodded. "I was scared. We hadn't even started high school. I knew there'd be drinking and older boys. I wasn't ready for it. I used the excuse that we might get into trouble. But really, I was just scared."

"Being scared and needing to go at your own pace doesn't make you a bad person."

That burn crept up my throat again. "I needed to hear that. Every time I think I've let go of the guilt, it comes back around again."

Cal rubbed a hand over his head, staring out at the water. "I think guilt comes in cycles. It'll keep coming around, but it gets less and less intense with each pass."

I thought about his words, how I'd felt since arriving at the Falls. It had awoken every memory. But over time, the pain of those recollections had eased. Just the other day, one hit and had me laughing out loud as I watched the Gragert family out on a couple of paddleboards. Mrs. Gragert had fallen off and into the chilly water. It had sent a memory into my mind that might as well have been a movie.

Jenn had dragged me down to the beach, determined to take the paddleboards out. Never mind that we'd never had even one lesson. She'd said it would be easy. But as soon as we made it out a bit, Jenn had started to waver. She'd tipped into the water, sputtering and flailing. When I laughed, she'd tugged me in with her.

As I'd stood on the beach remembering it all the other day, I hadn't been sad or guilty or angry. I'd been grateful. Felt grateful that I had memories like that to hold onto and that I had a place that would always remind me of her.

I looked up at Cal. "I think you're right about that. Hunter says he gets his wisdom from working on houses."

He chuckled. "Don't listen to that nonsense. I taught Hunter everything he knows."

I barked out a laugh. "I'll make sure to correct him next time."

"You do that."

With a wave, Cal took off, and Bruno and I headed for the barn. "You can't use the furniture pieces in the shop as your personal chew toys," I warned. Bruno seemed to deflate as if he understood every word.

"But I brought you this." I pulled a rawhide bone out of my back pocket, and Bruno danced and leapt into the air, letting out a happy bark. I handed it over with a smile.

As we rounded the bend in the road to the barn, my steps faltered. A figure was bent over and looked to be digging. My hand went for the personal alarm in my pocket that Hunter had made me carry as part of our agreement for him to let me work alone. No music, Bruno, this alarm, and my pepper spray.

As the figure straightened a bit, the tension in my muscles eased a little, and my lips twitched. "Good morning, Mr. Simpson. Are you digging for treasure?"

He whirled, his scowl firmly in place. "It's rude to sneak up on someone."

"I wasn't sneaking. I was walking."

He eyed Bruno. "Is that beast going to attack me?"

"Not unless he's provoked."

His scowl deepened. "Well, tell him I'm just digging for worms for my fishing today."

I sighed as I took in the several holes near the barn. "You know there's a bait shop in town, right?"

"Why would I spend money on something I can get for free?"

"Fair enough. Just make sure you fill in those holes, so no one trips."

"Yeah, yeah," he muttered and went back to work.

I headed inside the barn, shaking my head. I needed to start keeping a journal of guest encounters. I had a feeling I would have some doozies to record.

Hunter

I LEANED BACK IN THE CHAIR ON THE BALCONY OUTSIDE
Piper's room. The sliding door was open, and I heard her
muttering to herself as she got ready. My gaze shifted back
to the sketchpad in my lap. Bringing the side of the pencil down
to the thick paper, I shaded the slope of the roof.

Drawing houses had become a hobby since the moment I
started working construction in high school and began seeing
what was possible. I was good enough now that I could create
full plans on a computer and simply have an architect sign off
on them. But this initial stage of the dream, when my pencil
scratched against paper, was my favorite.

The creation coming to life in front of me was a mixture I
didn't want to think about too deeply. A blending of things Piper
had mentioned loving, and everything I'd planned to do whenever I finally built. And the setting was the bluff where Piper and
I had picnicked.

The Craftsman exterior was full of character, taking the history of that type of construction and bringing it into the present.

There was a wall of glass at the back as I'd described. The massive deck. A library Piper could fill with all the books she wanted. A bedroom suite on the second floor that would feel as if you were floating over the water. It was perfect.

And I could see myself there. With Piper. Making a life together. But she wasn't anywhere near ready to make that kind of leap. At least if tonight was anything to go by. When I'd asked her to come to dinner at my parents', she'd come up with every excuse in the book not to go. But I'd shot down every single one.

"Does this look okay?" she mumbled.

I turned to take in Piper. She wore a casual sundress but somehow made it look as if she were ready to attend a Hollywood premiere. Her hair hung in loose waves around her face, and she'd lined her eyes with a pop of color that seemed to make them glow.

I stood, striding towards her. "I changed my mind. We'll stay here, and I'll have you for dinner."

She held up a hand to stop me. "Oh, no, you don't. I'm not going to be that rude person who doesn't show up to your mother's house after you told her that we were coming."

I ducked around her arm and buried my face against her neck. "Trust me. She'll understand."

Piper pinched my side. "She will not."

"Ow. That was uncalled for."

She scowled at me. "We need to go if we don't want to be late. I want to stop at the florist and pick up some flowers."

"We don't need—"

She skewered me with a look. "It's polite to bring something. If you'd warned me you made plans for us, I wouldn't be so rushed."

I pulled her into my body. "So you could come up with a dozen more reasons not to go? Run away and hide, maybe?"

Her mouth opened and then closed, but she stayed silent. I pressed a kiss to her temple. "I promise they won't bite."

"I know that."

Her voice was quiet, almost timid. I straightened and brushed the hair away from her face. "What's so scary about going to dinner with my family? You've met them all before."

"I don't know. I just—I'm nervous, I guess."

"They already love you." My mom was practically planning our wedding in her mind. She'd called me almost daily to see how Piper was doing after the vandalism.

She took a long breath. "Okay, let's go."

I grinned down at the floor. She sounded as if she were marching to her death, not headed to a casual family dinner. "You never know, you might even have a little fun."

Piper huffed, mumbled something about interfering men under her breath, and took off for the stairs.

I should've known there'd be payback for springing a family dinner on Piper without warning. But as nervous as she'd been, she fit right into our tight-knit little crew, befriending my mom and charming my dad. She and Bell got along great, and she loved helping Ford give me shit.

My parents had made a feast, and we were now lounging around the living room with coffee and dessert. "So," Piper said to my mom, "I heard you might have some entertaining photos of Hunter growing up."

Ford nearly choked on his coffee. "I love this girl."

"Piper," I warned in a low tone, squeezing her shoulder.

"You were the one who said your mom had incriminating photos. You can't honestly think I wouldn't ask to see them."

My mom stood from the chair next to Dad's and went to a bookcase lined with albums. "This is one of the true pleasures in a mom's life. Getting a little revenge for all the trouble your sons caused you."

"It didn't work so well with Ford because Bell was there for half the photos," my dad said.

Bell grinned. "I think there were still a couple of doozies in there that I hadn't seen before. And your little butt cheeks running through the sprinkler were pretty dang cute."

Ford grimaced and took another sip of coffee. "We don't need to go there."

My mom sat on the other side of Piper, opening a photo album. "I think this is a good one. It was during his Batman phase."

"Batman phase?"

Mom nodded. "He refused to wear anything but his Batman costume for almost a year. But it was getting too small for him already…"

Her words trailed off as the pictures began. The costume had been from the Halloween before, and the pants looked like highwaters that left me with a permanent wedgie. Piper leaned over the album. "I'm gonna need a copy of one of these. Maybe I can blow it up and put it in the resort somewhere."

"You aren't funny," I grumbled.

Ford grinned at me. "I think she's hilarious."

My mom continued taking Piper down memory lane, one embarrassing story after another. I did my best to be a good sport and avoid looking at any of the photos that Ethan was in. I wished my mom had simply gotten rid of those. But she never would. Mom always said that one needed the whole picture. The good and the bad. You couldn't rewrite history.

Piper's hands stilled as she flipped the page. This one was full of summer shots. The beach my family had always frequented growing up. She sucked in a sharp breath.

"What's wrong?" I asked, searching her face.

She pointed to a picture. One of me building a sandcastle with a little girl I didn't recognize. "That's me."

"What?" My mom gasped. She leaned forward to examine

the photo. "I always wondered what happened to that little girl." She straightened, the light in her eyes dancing. "You were with another family at the beach, but the other little girl wanted to play in the water, while you were more interested in building sandcastles. You and Hunter spent hours constructing your masterpiece. It was adorable."

Piper's gaze lifted, meeting mine. "I remember it. You showed me just how wet the sand needed to be."

"And you made me build a moat to protect the princess that would live inside."

"It's a hell of a small world," Ford muttered.

Bell swatted at her fiancé. "It's so sweet. Like it was meant to be."

As I stared at Piper, the room faded out around us, and I could almost see the invisible tethers that tied us together. They'd taken hold before we had any idea they even existed. "That's the picture that should go up at the Falls."

Her mouth curved. "I don't know. I'm still partial to Batman."

The spell broke, and we returned to our stroll down memory lane at my expense. When we finished, the girls tackled the dessert dishes, while Ford, my dad, and I went outside to clean the grill and pick up any straggling dishes from dinner.

Dad brushed down the grill. "You're serious about her."

I froze while stacking napkins. "I can see a future there." It was more than that, though. After feeling as if I'd never find the person who *got me*, who made me *better*, I couldn't imagine my life without Piper.

"She's a good fit for you. I like her."

"But she's also gun-shy," my brother interjected.

I eased down into one of the chairs. "She is. But I'm not in any rush. I've got all the time in the world."

Ford tossed me another of my mother's cloth napkins. "Bad breakup or something?"

"Not that I know of. I think it's more about her friend."

"The one who went missing?" Dad asked.

"Yeah. She lost someone who might as well have been her sister. Something like that makes a person scared to really let someone in."

Ford leaned a hip against the table. "That kind of thing can really mess with your head."

My brother knew that better than most, having lost his first love in a car accident when they were just eighteen, and he was behind the wheel. I studied him, not for the first time amazed at how he'd turned things around and found the happiness always meant for him. "How'd you finally let go of the guilt?"

He sat down in the chair opposite mine. "It wasn't some magic moment. It took time. I had to work through a lot of it myself. But Bell was the final piece. She's who helped me see another way to look at it all."

My dad came around and squeezed Ford's shoulder. "And we're more than grateful for it."

Piper wasn't running from her feelings the way my brother had. She had faced them head-on since Jenn disappeared. But while she was dealing with them, she was also holding herself back from other people in her life. "It's going to take time." That was the magic ingredient in it all.

Ford met my gaze. "But at some point, she'll have to make that jump."

And all I could hope was that she felt the pull enough to leap.

Chapter Thirty-Eight

Piper

FOOTSTEPS SOUNDED ON THE CEMENT FLOOR OF THE HALL outside my workshop, and I stilled in my painting. "It's just me," Nick called.

"It's a good thing you told me because I might've pepper sprayed you in the face."

He chuckled as he appeared in the doorframe. "That would not be a good start to my day."

"No, it would not. Everything okay with your cabin?"

"It's great. Just going a little stir crazy. Yesterday was a rough day with Dad, and I can't seem to focus on programming today."

I leaned back in the chair I was perched on, taking in Nick's face. Dark circles rimmed red eyes, and lines had appeared where I hadn't noticed any before. "What's going on?"

"More of the same. He has these episodes where his mind plays tricks on him, and he can get really agitated. Yesterday, he was determined to get to the resort. It kills me to tell him that he has to stay there."

My heart ached for them both. I couldn't imagine watching

one of my uncles go through something like that. "Is there any-thing I can do?"

"Put me to work."

"Work?"

"I need something to keep my hands busy."

I glanced at the kitchen table waiting to be touched up. "How are you with sanding?"

"I got a brush-up course during our group construction project."

"Then that puppy is yours." I inclined my head to the table. "I need it sanded down so I can paint it." I was going with a teal gray on that piece, and I had a feeling it would be stunning.

"You got it." Nick stopped to scratch Bruno's head before turning his attention to the table. "How is everything coming along? Were you able to make up the time you lost?"

"We were. Thanks to everyone who stepped up. It was really amazing for them to do that."

Nick ran the sanding block along the top of the table. "This island is good for that kind of thing."

"Do you miss it? Living here, I mean."

"Yes, and no. I needed a fresh start. It felt like I'd lost so much of my life to this place. The Falls especially. It just sucks all the energy out of you. I always had to help out here, never had a real chance to explore what I was interested in. College gave me that. And when I got a dream job offer after that, I took it. Maybe it was selfish…"

"It's not selfish to follow your dreams. If you're only living for other people, you'll never be happy."

His hold on the sanding block tightened. "There had to be a way to balance it better. I didn't realize how bad things were until it was too late."

I stilled in my painting. "Did you want to take over the Falls for your dad?"

"God, no. I just wished I knew what was going on earlier, so I could've helped him sell before the bank foreclosed. But Dad never looped me in on all of the goings-on behind the scenes. We were always so close when I was growing up, always working on projects together. But he wanted to shield me from the tough stuff."

"I think that's just part of being a parent. They want to protect us no matter how old we get."

"I guess you're right about that. But it didn't make it any easier when everything started to fall apart."

I slid my paintbrush along the grain of the wood. "I'm really sorry that you had to pick up the pieces of something you didn't know was broken."

"I think part of me was in denial. The resort was struggling long before I went away to school. Not a ton of people want to stay where a girl disappeared."

I stiffened, and Nick muttered a curse. "I'm sorry, I shouldn't have said it like that."

"It's okay. It's not like I don't know what happened here. And I'm sorry it hurt the resort so much. It affected so many people's lives…"

"Sometimes, I feel like it marked the whole island."

"There's something about that…it's comforting. I've always known it scarred me but knowing I'm not the only one who remembers helps somehow. Maybe that's weird."

Nick looked up from his sanding. "I don't think it's weird."

I focused back on my painting. We'd had more than a little trouble since I'd come back. And the work was exhausting, but I'd also never felt prouder of anything I'd done. I'd come alive in a whole new way here.

My phone rang on the counter. The little cell signal booster I'd bought for the barn gave me just enough service to make and receive calls. The area code was unfamiliar, but I hit accept. "Hello, this is Piper."

"Hello, this is Judy Dexter with *Travel Magazine*. Your pitch came across my desk, and I'd love to do a piece on the restoration of Whispering Falls."

Air caught in my throat. *Travel Magazine* was my reach. The pipe dream of all my pitches. "I would love that," I managed to get out.

"Do you have more of these *before* shots you included with the pitch?"

"I do. And some additional historical shots, as well."

"That's perfect. Do you think you'll have the lodge and the majority of the cabins done in say…two months?"

My mind whirled as I tried to think about Hunter's last estimation. "I would say we're on track for phase one to be finished by then."

"Wonderful. I'll plan to come out with a photographer then. There might even be the chance for a follow-up piece when all the work is finished. But I think readers will enjoy being looped in on the process."

"Thank you so much, Ms. Dexter."

"Please, call me Judy. I'll email all the details. Talk soon."

She hung up before I had a chance to utter another word. Slowly, I pulled the phone away from my face and stared at the screen.

"Are you okay?"

I turned to Nick. "That was *Travel Magazine*. They want to do a piece on the restoration of Whispering Falls."

His jaw fell open. "What?"

I leapt up and threw my arms around him. "This is amazing."

He patted my back. "Unbelievable. Dad was never able to get anything like that."

"We'll have to show him the magazine whenever it comes out."

Nick pulled back, a small smile on his face. "He'd like that."

"Crud. I have to go tell Hunter because we will be on the tightest deadline known to man now. I really hope he doesn't murder me for agreeing to this."

Nick grinned. "I'm sure he won't."

"We'll find out soon enough."

Hunter

I LOOKED UP FROM THE STACK OF LUMBER THAT HAD JUST been delivered to see Piper flying down the hill. Panic flooded my veins, only halting when I saw the wide smile on her face. Bruno bounded after her, thinking it was some sort of game. When she was three feet away, she launched herself at me.

I caught Piper as her legs wrapped around my waist. She pressed her mouth to mine in a hot, hungry kiss. When I pulled back, I staggered a step, and the guys whistled. "Not that I don't love an enthusiastic greeting, but what was that all about?"

"Best news ever."

"I love best news." Or I loved how it made Piper's eyes glow and her cheeks turn pink.

"*Travel Magazine* is going to do a feature article on the Falls!"

"Seriously?" They were the top travel publication in the country. A feature from them could be a game-changer for Piper.

"I just got off the phone with one of the editors. I'm still shaking."

I could feel the slight tremble of her hands against my

shoulders. "When are they coming?" She bit her bottom lip and looked away. "Piper…"

"Two months," she whispered.

I set her down. "What do they expect to be done in two months?"

"Phase one…"

"Hell," I muttered. "That doesn't give us any room for setbacks. And there are always setbacks."

"I can help, though. And if I tell my uncles, they might be able to steal away for the weekend and give us some extra hands."

I knew she wanted this, and it was a great opportunity, but I didn't want Piper to work herself into an early grave to achieve it. "You have to make sure you don't forget to take care of yourself along the way."

She made a face at me. "I'm fine. Never felt better. But I do think I'm going to take Bell up on her offer to help me finish a couple of the furniture pieces this weekend. That will get us three cabins completely finished, and that's a great place to start."

I wrapped an arm around Piper and pulled her against me. "You're right. It is." I brushed my lips against hers. "Proud of you, Casper."

"I'm proud of me, too." Her gaze drifted off to the sea. "And I can't help but think of how excited Jenn would be."

"She would. She's a part of this. You've made her a part of it. No one's going to forget."

Piper looked back at me, eyes glistening. "You always know the perfect thing to say. How'd you learn to be so charming?"

My lips twitched. "Just born that way."

She rolled her eyes. "Sure…"

I kissed her again, deeper this time. "Gonna argue my charm now?"

"I guess not." She stepped out of my hold. "Those lips are dangerous."

"Lethal, Casper."

Piper shook her head. "Can you lend me a couple of pairs of strong arms to help me get some furniture down here? I have a few finished pieces."

"You got it. We can use my truck." I whistled and motioned for Cal to come over.

"I'm going to put Bruno in the lodge so he doesn't trip us."

"Sounds like a good plan."

She started towards the lodge with Bruno in tow.

"Hey, Piper."

"Yeah."

"You're making that dream come true."

She grinned back at me. "Thanks for helping me do it."

Cal and I leaned against the kitchen counter in the final cabin as Piper surveyed the layout. "Do you think she's finally done?" Cal whispered.

"I heard that," Piper called from the living room.

I chuckled. Other than a break for lunch, Piper had put Cal and me to work, lifting furniture and helping her arrange it so it was up to her perfect specifications. "I think we're on the home stretch now."

"Don't jinx us."

Piper strode towards us. "Who knew you'd be such babies about a little furniture?"

"A little?" Cal's brows rose. "You had a dozen different pieces in…I don't know how many different places."

She took Cal by the shoulders and guided him to the entry-way so that he could take in the whole place. "And now it's perfect. Worth it, don't you think?"

"Might not be worth my hernia," he mumbled but then looked around the space. "But it'll look damn good on the pages of a magazine."

"Thank you. Now, we just have to get the rest of the cabins down here looking the same way."

Cal groaned. "I'm making Manny help you next time."

I crossed to Piper and tugged her to me. "If you want those cabins done, you gotta let us work."

"Okay, okay. I'll ask Celeste if her grandsons want to earn a little extra cash. They can help me."

I brushed my lips against hers. "Good plan."

Cal gave us a salute. "On that note, I'm headed home. See you guys tomorrow."

We waved to him, and then I pulled Piper down onto the couch with me. "It does look amazing in here."

"I still need to add the little decorative details, but I'm going to ask Bell for some help with that this weekend. I feel like she might have some good ideas."

"I'm sure she will." The fact that Piper was asking for that help without someone demanding that they let her give it had me smiling into her hair.

She turned her head to face me. "Thank you."

"For?"

"Everything you've done to make this a reality. For the first time, I feel like I have a real shot at making a go of this place."

I tucked a strand of hair behind her ear. "You've always had a shot. Because you work harder than anyone I know, and you don't let anyone or anything sideline you."

"I might've given up after the cabins were destroyed. But you had a plan before I could even wrap my head around what'd happened."

"You wouldn't have given up." Nothing could keep Piper from bringing the Falls back to life, from honoring her friend the best way she knew how.

Her fingers found the necklace at her throat, and she began tracing circles on the metal. "I hope not. Given everything Nick has said about growing up here, it won't be an easy road."

"Nothing worth having is ever easy. But it's also about enjoying the journey along the way. Even when it's hard."

"More contractor wisdom?"

I brushed my lips against hers. "Always." Piper's stomach rumbled, and I laughed, picking her up as I stood. "Time to feed you."

"I'm never going to argue with that."

Setting Piper on her feet, we headed out the door and towards the lodge. "What are you in the mood for?" I asked.

"Hmm. You know what sounds good?"

"What?"

"Grilled cheese. I need some classic comfort food."

"I'd say you earned it."

Piper pulled open the door to the lodge, and we stepped through. Bruno raised his head from his bed in the corner, but when he went to stand to greet us, he wobbled on his feet. Piper rushed forward. "What's going on, buddy?"

Instead of the trembling easing, it got worse, and he fell back onto his bed. Piper ran her hands over his body. "What's wrong with him?"

I crouched beside them as Bruno laid his head in her lap. "I don't know. Has anything like this ever happened before?"

"Never."

I pulled out my phone. "I'm going to get my truck, and we'll get him to the vet."

"Hurry," she whispered.

I jogged to my vehicle as I searched for the name of the island vet. I tapped the number, and a man answered after three rings. "Anchor Veterinary, this is Josh."

"Are you guys still open?"

"For another fifteen minutes, but the doc doesn't have any openings until tomorrow."

"My girlfriend's dog is really sick. Shaky. Can't stand. We're bringing him in."

The man's voice completely changed. "Of course. Bring him straight here. That can be a symptom of stroke or ingesting some kind of poison."

My steps faltered at the word *poison*. So much damage had been done at the Falls. By someone doing everything they could to hurt and scare Piper. Why wouldn't they strike at the creature she loved the most? "We're on our way." I just hoped we got there in time.

Chapter Forty

Piper

I HELD BRUNO THE BEST I COULD IN THE CAB OF HUNTER'S truck. Just as we reached the outer town limits, Bruno started trembling and shaking. "Oh God, Hunter, I think he's having a seizure."

Hunter pressed down on the accelerator, screaming past the twenty-mile-an-hour speed limit. "Just hold on. We're almost there."

I held Bruno tighter and sent up a silent prayer. He had been with me through so much over the past seven years: the end of college, my first real job and apartment, my first true breakup. And every time I missed Jenn so much, it felt like my heart had been ripped from my chest. He was the best cuddler and the most loyal companion. I couldn't lose him.

Hunter flew into the parking lot of a small cottage with a sign that read *Anchor Veterinary*. He was out of the truck and pulling open the door nearest Bruno before I could even adjust my hold on my dog. He'd stopped convulsing, but his breathing was shallow.

Hunter slipped his hands under Bruno's body and lifted. I jumped out after them, slamming the door. I ran ahead to open the door to the vet's office, holding it so Hunter could get past. He rushed into the waiting room. "I called about the dog a few minutes ago. This is Bruno. He just had a seizure on the way here."

"Right this way," a man said, ushering us into an exam room.

Hunter laid Bruno on the table just as a woman who looked to be in her late twenties bustled in. She immediately went to work checking his gums and listening to his heart. "You said he had a seizure and was trembling earlier?"

"Yes." My voice cracked as I said the single word.

"Do you have any insect or rodent killers at your home? A slug repellent, perhaps?"

"I'm honestly not sure. I own Whispering Falls. That's where we live. There's an old storage shed with those kinds of things that I haven't gone through yet."

"Could Bruno have gotten into that?"

I glanced at Hunter and then back to the vet. "I don't know. Maybe." But it didn't seem possible. The door to that shed was always closed, and I'd left Bruno in the lodge for most of the day.

The vet nodded. "Let me run some tests and do a more thorough exam. Josh, can you show them to the waiting room?"

I pressed my lips to Bruno's head. "You got this, buddy. Fight." Tears filled my eyes as I forced myself back so the vet could do her job. The space around me went blurry as Hunter guided me out of the exam room and down the hall. I barely noticed when he pulled me down onto his lap and wrapped his arms around me.

But when his lips brushed my temple, and he told me that Bruno was strong and that the vet would do everything she could, I lost it. Heaving sobs wracked my body. I shook from the force of them, but Hunter simply held on. Never once letting go.

I didn't know how long I cried, but as I slowly came back to myself, I saw that the receptionist was gone, and just Hunter and I remained in the waiting room. He was rocking me slowly back and forth, keeping me tucked tightly against his body.

"I'm sorry," I whispered.

"Don't you dare apologize. That dog is your family. Of course, you're upset."

My ribs gave a painful squeeze. I couldn't lose Bruno. Everything about the thought felt like too much to bear. A brutal reminder that those closest to you could disappear without warning. My fingers dug into Hunter's arms as if he might slip away, too. The desperate need I had to hold onto him scared the hell out of me.

Hunter held me even tighter, just shy of the point of pain. But I wanted those arms tighter. Needed him to crush me to him. "I love you," he whispered.

My heart spasmed, taking up a rhythm that had me wondering if I was having a heart attack. I opened my mouth to give him the words back, but I couldn't. Not because I didn't feel them. I felt it so deeply, I knew I'd never dig it out. But because saying it made it real for the world around me. And I'd learned one thing; it was that sometimes the Universe tried to steal away what you loved most.

"You don't have to say it back. I just needed you to know it. You're loved. And I'm not going anywhere."

I stayed silent but nodded against his chest. Fire lit my sternum, a delicate dance between pleasure and pain. The knowledge that I was loved but that, one day, I would lose that love. I didn't know how. By choice or force. But I *would* lose it.

I remained tangled in Hunter's arms for at least an hour before the vet emerged. We both stood immediately. I rushed forward. "How is he? Is he okay?"

The woman gave me a gentle smile. "I think he'll make a full recovery. We had to put him under anesthesia so we could get a dose of charcoal into his stomach. Once we did that, his vitals improved. I need to keep him here—at least overnight. Maybe longer. But I can take you back to see him."

Tears slid down my face. "Thank you…" I suddenly realized I hadn't even gotten her name.

"I'm Dr. Wells. And I'm so sorry you had this scare. I will tell you that he definitely had poison in his system. I would do a thorough accounting of what Bruno might have had access to."

"We will," Hunter interjected.

She nodded and led us to a back room where Bruno was sleeping. He had an IV in his arm, and for the first time since he was a puppy, he looked so damn small to me. I hurried over to him and bent over the table. "I'm right here, buddy. You're going to be just fine. They're taking great care of you."

His eyes opened the barest amount at the sound of my voice. "That's my boy. Love you." He licked my cheek, and my tears fell faster.

Dr. Wells moved into my view. "We'll have a vet tech with him all night, so he'll be monitored, but everything is looking good."

"I can't thank you enough. I don't know what I would've done…" I couldn't finish the sentence.

She gave me a kind smile as she tucked her jet-black hair behind her ear. "I completely understand. They hold our hearts, these creatures."

"They do."

Hunter squeezed my shoulders from behind. "We should let Bruno rest so he can heal."

I knew he was right, but all I wanted to do was throw a sleeping bag on the floor so I could be with Bruno all night. Dr. Wells seemed to understand my predicament and pulled out a pad of paper. "Give me your cell phone number. I promise to have the vet tech call you if there are any changes."

"That would be great. Thank you."

Dr. Wells jotted down both my number and Hunter's, just in case. But even with that reassurance, walking away nearly crushed me. I gave Bruno one more kiss. "I'll be back tomorrow."

"You can come in first thing," Dr. Wells said. "We open at eight."

"I'll be here at eight, then. When do you think I can take him home?"

"Maybe tomorrow afternoon. Day after, at the latest, if there are no complications."

I sent up another of those silent prayers for no complications. "I'll see you tomorrow."

Dr. Wells nodded, and Hunter led me out of the room, down the hallway, and out the front door. The sky was beautiful at twilight, but none of it truly sank in. I moved like a robot as Hunter helped me into the truck. I barely took in my surroundings as he drove us home. The only thing I could think about was how fragile life was. And how easily you could lose it all.

Chapter Forty-One

Hunter

PIPER WAS QUIET AS I NAVIGATED THE DARK ROADS BACK to the Falls. I wished for the right words, ones that would bring comfort, but everything seemed so damn lacking. She'd almost lost the dog she'd raised since he was a pup. One of the few beings she'd let through the stone fortress around her heart.

Neither of us had said anything about the possibility that Bruno's poisoning had been more than an accident, but I couldn't imagine the thought wasn't also on Piper's mind. My only hope was that whoever it was hadn't left a note. With the rat and the destruction of the cabins, there had been messages.

The image of the anger flashing in Jasper's eyes when Bruno had lunged at him filled my mind, and my hold on the steering wheel tightened. If that kid had hurt Bruno… I should be ashamed of the thoughts going through my head. But I wasn't. Because at least the things I was thinking were actions. Things that might make me feel a little less powerless.

I glanced over at Piper as we drove past the welcome sign. She stared out the window as if she didn't see anything we passed. Instead of words, I opted for touch. Slipping her hand in mine, I curled my fingers around hers.

Her body shuddered. "He's going to be okay, right?"

"Dr. Wells gave us every reason to believe that. We got him there fast."

"Thank you for that. I don't know what I would've done if I was alone…"

I squeezed her hand. "Well, you're not. And it doesn't make you weak to lean on someone for help."

Her mouth curved the barest bit as if she were trying to smile but couldn't quite finish the action. "Sometimes, I swear you can read my mind. It's creepy."

"I thought every woman wanted a man who could read her mind?"

"No, thank you." Piper looked over at me. "But in this case, I appreciate it. I don't know why I feel like such a failure, not being able to do things on my own. I had these grand plans of coming here and getting everything up and running in weeks. Instead, I've had one setback after another."

I rubbed my thumb back and forth across her hand. "You put too much pressure on yourself. Trying to race a ghost."

She gave a small jerk. "I'm not…" Her words fell away, and she went quiet for a moment. "I want to make her proud. And I want to cement her memory. It feels like if I can just bring this place back, I'll get that."

"Makes sense. But it doesn't mean you have to do it alone. It doesn't make it any less powerful to have people helping you along the way. It might make it *more* powerful. A community coming together to restore the Falls and remember the girl who was lost here."

Piper nodded slowly. "I know you're right, but it's still hard for me to release it."

"One step at a time."

"You're great at that. I feel like you've handled working at the Falls better than I could've imagined."

I pulled my truck in next to Piper's SUV in front of the lodge. She was right that things had felt easier. I turned in my seat to face her. "That's in large part because of you."

"Why me?"

"I hadn't realized how much I needed someone who understood. Who didn't placate but actually got it. I'll probably always struggle with the guilt, but it gets easier every time I see Bell and Shay happy and breathing, living their lives to the fullest."

"I'm glad you're not hiding how you feel anymore."

I leaned forward and brushed my mouth against Piper's. "Thanks for giving me a place to be." With Piper, I could let my guard down. I didn't have to think about keeping up a façade or worry about what nightmares might come. Whatever I was going through, I knew she could handle it.

She deepened the kiss before pulling away. "Let's go to bed."

"Sounds like a great plan to me."

We climbed out of the truck and started for the front porch, but my steps faltered. I grabbed Piper's hand and pulled her behind me. Her gaze snapped to me. "What is it?"

"It's too dark." I scanned the area and saw that the lodge's lights were out, and so were the ones on the cabin across the road.

"Maybe something just burned out."

Not likely since we put in the LED bulbs less than a month ago. "Stay here." I started as quietly as possible towards the lodge's front door, listening for any sounds and watching for any flickers of movement.

There was nothing. I eased up the front steps, straining to make out the light fixture we'd installed not that long ago. Footsteps sounded, and I turned in a flash. Piper skidded back on her heels. "I didn't want you going in alone."

I shook my head and looked back at the light. "Stay behind me."

"That's spray paint."

I narrowed my eyes, stepping closer. It certainly was. I pulled out my phone and hit Parker's contact. It rang three times before he answered. "Please tell me you're calling me away from the nightmare in front of me right now."

I could hear people yelling and music playing in the background. And I was pretty sure someone was yelling for someone named Joey to kick someone's ass. "Where are you?"

"Maverick's, where else?"

It was a bar where the rougher crowd tended to congregate, and it wasn't unusual for the owners or patrons to call the sheriff or his deputies out there. "We've got a situation at the Falls."

All humor fled Parker's voice, and the sounds of the bar faded away. "What's going on?"

"Lights knocked out. Covered in black spray paint."

"Get Piper in your truck and wait for me. I'm on my way." He hung up without another word.

"Come on." I wrapped an arm around Piper and guided her away from the front door and down the stairs. I wanted to go inside and check the place, but my gun was in my lockbox in Piper's bedroom. I was beginning to think I might need to start carrying the thing on me at all times.

"Parker?" Piper asked as I helped her into the truck.

I nodded and closed her in, rounding the bed. My head stayed on a swivel as I climbed into the driver's seat. But I didn't see any movement anywhere.

"When is this going to end?"

I turned to Piper and took in her exhausted expression. This was all too much for anyone to take. So much had been leveled on her since returning to Anchor. I framed her face in my hands. "Whatever this is, we'll deal with it."

"I'm so tired. To my bones."

"I know." I brushed my lips against hers as if I could give her some of my energy. "I promise it'll all look better in the morning."

Piper let her head fall to my chest. "I want to junk-punch whoever's doing this."

I couldn't hold in my chuckle. "Maybe you should put up posters threatening as much. Might make someone think twice."

"I'd do it if I thought it'd do any good."

I massaged Piper's shoulders, trying to relieve some of the tension that had settled there. "I know you would."

Lights flashed as an SUV tore up the drive, but Parker thankfully kept his sirens off. They pulled to a stop behind my truck and cut the lights. We all climbed out of our vehicles at the same time.

"Seen any signs of life?" Parker asked, one of his deputies following behind.

"Nothing. Just the lack of lights gave me pause."

"Smart. We'll clear the lodge and the surrounding buildings."

"Thanks." I pulled Piper to my side and leaned back against my truck. We watched as, one by one, lights flicked on in each room of the lodge. Not more than ten minutes later, the two officers exited the building and headed across the road to check the cabin. That one took even less time. Soon, they were crossing the road back towards us.

"He looks pissed," Piper whispered.

Parker was indeed radiating a healthy dose of rage. I squeezed her shoulder. "Just remember, whatever it is, we'll deal."

"I know."

Parker came to a stop in front of us. "Someone's been inside."

Piper straightened. "How bad?"

"It's centralized to your bedroom, but it's wrecked. And there's more paint on the walls."

"What does it say?" I gritted out. I knew there had to be a message.

"First your dog. Then, you."

Chapter Forty-Two

Piper

I TOSSED A PIECE OF A BROKEN PICTURE FRAME INTO THE trash bag.

"Are you sure you don't want me to stay and help you this morning?" Hunter asked.

"I'm fine, really. And we need to keep making progress on the cabins."

"Okay…"

Hunter hovered in the doorway, but I couldn't find it in me to look up and meet his gaze. To thank him for everything he'd done for me over the past twelve hours. "I'll come and get you when it's time to pick up Bruno."

At seven this morning, Dr. Wells had called to tell me that Bruno would be ready to go home this afternoon. But there was no way Hunter would let me go anywhere alone now. And Parker had ordered a deputy to remain at the resort, as well. He'd had enough of people messing around.

My thoughts swirled as Hunter's footsteps faded down the hall. I should've been grateful, and in some ways, I was. But more than anything, it all fueled my anger. Stoked the flames higher and higher. Why couldn't I have this one thing to remember my dearest friend by? Why was someone so set on destroying it all? Just out of spite? For some transgression I hadn't even realized I committed.

The only thing I wanted was to bring the property back to life. To be a part of the history here. To give others the kind of precious memories I had of this place. To honor the sister of my heart.

The pressure behind my eyes built until tears trailed down my cheeks and fell off my chin and onto my shirt. I missed her so damn much. And even ten years later, I would give anything to see her again. To have one more conversation. To take back that fight we'd had. To tell her that I loved her.

But I would never get that. Some part of me knew it in my bones. All that was left was a pile of questions. Unknowns that would bury me if I let them. Had someone taken Jenn? How had they hurt her? Had we come close to finding her? Or had we always been a million miles away?

I wasn't sure how someone lost a person on a thirty-acre island. The sheriff at the time hadn't understood either. It was why he'd settled on an accident being the likely outcome for her disappearance. Sure, he'd kept the case open, but how hard had he actually looked?

"Oh, Piper."

I looked up to see Celeste in the doorway. She moved into the room and sank to the floor, wrapping an arm around me. "I know it's awful, but it can all be fixed. We'll get everything cleaned up and right as rain."

"It's not that. I just… I was thinking about Jenn, and it all kind of caught up with me."

She began rocking me slightly, a steady back and forth motion. "It's natural to miss her."

"I know." I inhaled a shaky breath, trying to get myself under control. "I'm sorry you walked in on me losing it."

"I'm not. No one should lose it alone. And, trust me, I've had more than a few of these moments here myself."

I glanced up at Celeste. "Is it hard for you being back here because of Mr. and Mrs. Crowley?" I kept getting these reminders that I wasn't the only one lost in memories here. So many others had been marked by this place and their experiences here.

"It's a mixed bag for sure. Harder than I thought it'd be, but good, too."

"Have you been able to spend much time with Nick?" I had to think it would be good for him to have someone to remember his mom with when his dad's memory was failing.

Celeste leaned back against the wall. "Some. I think it's hard for him. He wants to see this place brought back to life, but it has a lot of reminders, too. We talked about his parents, some memories of the good ol' days. It's good to remember those. But I bet you feel the same way about your Jenn."

"I do. Why is it that it always seems to be the good ones who go before their time?"

"It does seem that way." She turned to face me, her expression serious. "I don't want you doing the same. If it's too hard being here, let this place go. It's not worth running yourself into the ground or tearing your heart apart to bring it back. Some might say the signs are telling you to let it go."

I stiffened at Celeste's words. I knew she meant well, that it was merely her mother-bear protective instincts coming out, but it didn't sit right, just the same. "I can handle this. I had a weak moment, but the Falls is important to me. It's worth some hard work and heartache."

She eyed me skeptically and then let her gaze travel around the room. "This looks like a little more than that. And Sheriff Raines still has no idea who's responsible."

I pushed to my feet and picked up my trash bag. "But he will." My words had more resolve than I truly felt. After half a dozen conversations with the Leclairs and searching for any possible suspects, Parker had come up empty so far.

Celeste got to work picking up ripped clothing and other broken odds and ends. "I just don't want to see you get hurt. That's all. I know your uncles would be heartbroken if something happened to you."

I scowled in her direction. "That's playing dirty."

She shrugged and handed me a photo of my uncles and me that had come loose from its frame. "It's worth it if it means you'll be careful. Think long and hard about whether this mission of yours is worth it."

It was. I looked down at the photo. It had been taken on the beach right here. And in the corner of the frame was the hint of a figure. It was blurry, but I knew it was Jenn, the hot pink coverup she'd scrimped and saved for fluttering in the wind. It was exactly how she always was to me: ever-present but out of focus. But with each piece of the Falls I put back together, I got a little more of Jenn, too. And I wouldn't give that up for anyone.

Hunter

"THAT'S LUNCH," I CALLED TO THE GUYS AS CAL AND I finished installing the new countertop.

He brushed his hands off on his jeans. "You going to find Piper?"

"Yeah, but I'll be back in an hour."

"Take all the time you need. She holding up okay?"

She'd been doing better since we got Bruno home yesterday. He was moving slowly but already remarkably better. And it seemed this latest incident had lit a fire under Piper, the likes of which I'd never seen. She'd been a hard worker from day one, but the past two days, she'd looked more like that cartoon Tasmanian devil.

I scrubbed a hand over my jaw. "She's handling it the way she likes to handle everything—by staying busy."

Cal glanced towards the parking area in front of the lodge. "How long is Parker keeping a deputy on the place?"

"As long as it takes, he says." But I knew that could change the moment a big case hit his desk, or an emergency came in. I'd take what we could get, though. I stayed with Piper in the evenings with a deputy downstairs or out in their SUV. During the days, she had to have the deputy or me with her. Piper hadn't been pleased with the dictate, but I didn't give a damn. Someone out there was pissed as hell at her for some reason, and I wasn't taking any chances. I'd taken to carrying my Glock when we were alone, just in case.

Cal let out a low whistle. "He's not messing around."

"Thankfully, he's not."

Cal's gaze shifted back to me. "You still think it's those kids?"

"I have no idea. It's what makes the most sense, but I just can't wrap my head around a teenager being so vicious."

"Teenagers can be just as messed up as adults. Look at what happened with Shay's brother and Sam—they both hurt people before they turned thirteen—" Cal's words cut off. "Shit. I didn't mean to bring up bad memories."

I waved him off, but the guilt still caught hold. I'd underestimated people close to me before, ignored what they were capable of, and it had nearly gotten people I cared about—and me— killed. I wouldn't do that again. And if that meant Piper biting my head off because I was with her twenty-four-seven, so be it.

Cal started towards the open door of the cabin. "You think she's gonna sell?"

"Who? Piper?"

"Yeah. A lot of shit has gone down around here. No one would blame her."

"That's not how she rolls." If someone challenged Piper, it only made her dig her heels in more.

Cal's jaw worked back and forth. "I just hope that's the smart play. Someone is seriously messed up in the head, and they're gunning for her."

"I know that," I gritted out.

Cal came to a stop at the base of the cabin's steps and clapped a hand on my shoulder. "I'm not trying to piss you off. I just want her to be careful."

"Well, thinking about this shit pisses me off."

"Understandable." He released his hold. "Go see your girl. Maybe she'll make your ass less cranky."

"Let's hope," Manny called from the picnic table.

I sent them both middle fingers and started towards the lodge. As I walked inside, Deputy Hughes looked up from her coffee. She inclined her head towards the open doors of the library. "She's in there."

"Thanks. Any trouble this morning?"

"Everything's been quiet as a mouse."

As long as they stayed quiet, Piper would be safe. But we also wouldn't catch whoever was behind this. "Any updates from Parker?"

"Not really. He talked to the Leclairs' lawyer again, but it's the same runaround."

Of course, it was. I gave Deputy Hughes a nod and headed for the library. As I walked in, Bruno lifted his head from his bed in the corner, but Piper was oblivious to my entrance. She was bent over a pad of paper and a laptop. I cleared my throat, and she jumped.

"It's polite to knock, you know."

I bent and took her mouth in a hungry kiss. "Don't be grumpy with me."

"You'd be grumpy too if someone had basically put you on a leash."

"You're not on a leash, don't be overdramatic."

"Okay, under guard."

I tucked a strand of hair that had fallen out of her bun behind her ear and then squeezed the back of her neck. "You're important to me. I need you safe."

The set of her shoulders softened a bit. "I am safe."

"And we're going to keep you that way. Come on. There's something I want to show you."

"I really don't have time. I'm trying to get the reservation software up and running, and I'm working on a website that's making me want to throw my computer against a wall—"

I took Piper's hand and tugged her to her feet. "All the more reason to take a break."

"Hunter…"

"Come on, Casper. Give me one hour. Then I'll let you return to the salt mines."

"Fine," she huffed. "But we have to bring Bruno. I'm not leaving him alone."

"Of course." I snapped my fingers, and Bruno got to his feet, looking steadier than he had this morning.

We made our way out to the main room of the lodge. I nodded at Hughes. "I'll have her back in an hour."

"You armed?"

"In my truck."

"I feel like I'm a kid being babysat," Piper mumbled.

"You're certainly pouting like one."

She elbowed me in the stomach and headed for my truck.

"Have fun?" Hughes said, but it was more of a question.

"If I get murdered, you know who the culprit is."

She chuckled and waved me off. By the time I made it to my truck, Piper already had Bruno in the cab and was settled in the passenger seat, arms crossed.

I climbed behind the wheel and started the engine. I'd put a cooler in the back this morning, knowing I planned to steal Piper away. It wasn't a gourmet feast, but it would fill our bellies. Piper was silent until we reached our spot. "You've already shown me this spot."

"Patience," I urged as I got out of the truck and picked up the cooler and my sketchbook from the bed. Piper helped Bruno down and grabbed the blanket for us to sit on. She laid it out just where I had told her a house should sit one day, and Bruno instantly made himself at home.

I set the cooler beside me and eased onto the ground next to Piper. She perked up as I opened my sketchbook to a page midway through. "That's beautiful."

"It's your house."

"M-my house?"

"The one you'll build right here when you're ready." I handed her the book. "Flip through."

Slowly, she turned from one page to the next, taking her time with each one. They were filled with sketches of her home and the vision she had for the Falls. The glamping section, the larger cabins, everything.

A tear slipped down Piper's cheek. "It's just like I described, only better. You thought of things I never would have."

I wiped the tear away with my thumb. "It wasn't supposed to make you cry."

"They're good tears. I promise."

"Thank God for that. Deputy Hughes might shoot me if I bring you back tear-stained."

Piper chuckled. "I think you're safe there." Her fingers traced across the page. "You think I can make this happen?"

"I know you can. It's gonna take time, and we've had our fair share of setbacks, but even with everything we've had to deal with, we're still on schedule. You might not see it, but things are changing around here."

Piper looked out at the water. "I see it. But, sometimes, I don't take it in enough."

"That's why these breaks are important. Gives you some perspective."

She leaned into my side. "Sorry I was a bitch earlier."

"Not a bitch. Testy."

Piper buried her face against my chest. "Whatever it was, it wasn't pretty. And I shouldn't have taken my frustrations out on you." She looked down at the book in her lap. "Can I frame these? It will remind me of what I'm working towards."

My chest tightened. No one I'd ever been with had cared enough about my work or how I brought things to life to ever even think of framing something like this. "Of course."

"Thank you." She tilted her face up to mine so that our eyes met. I could almost see the words on the tip of her tongue. That "*I love you*" she was so desperately trying to hold back. When it didn't come, I simply kissed her, knowing it was enough for now that I was hers, and she was mine.

Chapter Forty-Four

Piper

"THIS WAS A GENIUS IDEA."

I rolled into Hunter's side as we lay on the blanket under the stars. "I'm going to have to agree with you on that one." Bruno let out a grumble from his spot on the blanket as if agreeing.

Hunter had given me a good reminder yesterday. I needed to slow down and remember to enjoy the place I was pouring so much of my lifeblood into. "There's the Big Dipper." I traced the constellation with my finger in the sky.

"I think I see it. Looks like a big ladle or something."

"Yup. I wish I could remember more of them. Vic used to take Jenn and me out here at least a few times when we visited to show us different ones. You can see so much more here than in the city."

Hunter toyed with a strand of my hair, wrapping it and unwrapping it from around a finger. "I'm glad you have those memories."

"Me, too. And the more I work on this place, the clearer they get. It's like she's coming back to me in a way."

His lips ghosted across my temple. "Love that for you."

"Thanks for helping me find it."

"Always."

We lay there quietly for a while, soaking in the sounds of the sea, the smell of the salt air, and the feel of Hunter's strong body pressed against mine. I could've stayed forever.

"Bell and Ford's wedding is a week from Saturday. Feel like being my date?"

I tipped my head back so I could take in Hunter's face. "Isn't it a little late to be telling them you're bringing a plus one?"

He brushed the hair away from my face. "You're more than a plus one. And they already said they'd love to have you."

"Okay."

"That simple?"

"That simple." But it wasn't. I could feel the weight of attending a wedding where Hunter would be the best man. The weight of becoming a part of his family. The more deeply woven I became in the fiber of who they were, the harder it would be if I lost any of them.

"Sounds like you're thinking pretty hard."

"Is that so?" I casually tossed the words out, but my heart hammered against my ribs. I knew it was a little bit crazy to see each tightening tether of our relationship as the potential for harm. But I couldn't seem to let go of the fear.

Hunter cupped my cheek, running the rough pad of his thumb across the bone there. "It's just a wedding. A small one. Family, good friends, great food, and music. If we're lucky, Shay will get up with the band and play her violin. You won't want to miss that."

"She plays the violin?"

"Better than anyone I've ever seen or heard. It's like her fingers fly across the strings."

"Well, I can't miss that."

"No, you can't. So, just stop freaking out and enjoy the ride."

I pinched his side. "That's like telling someone to stop thinking about pink elephants. Then the only thing they can think about is—"

"—pink elephants. I know. But try to let go if you can."

"I'm trying," I said quietly. "It isn't always easy for me. I'm used to my uncles, a small group of friends, of—"

"Not truly letting anyone in."

I stilled, my hand tightening in Hunter's t-shirt. "I let people in."

"But only so far."

I opened my mouth to argue and then stopped. He was right. Since I'd lost Jenn, almost all my connections had stayed at that outer layer. I had friends I went to dinner with. Boyfriends for months at a time. They weren't shallow relationships, exactly, but I never let them see my pain. The truth of what losing Jenn had done to me.

But something about Hunter had called to me from the first day. A kindred spirit, I realized. Someone who knew what it was to struggle with guilt and ghosts. Someone who I knew wouldn't judge me for the mess that was my heart and soul. But that kind of vulnerability carried risk. And it felt like I was walking around with an open chest cavity.

Hunter's lips ghosted over my ear. "I'm not going to hurt you."

"You will. You won't mean to, but you will. That's life. I'm just trying to keep going, knowing that truth."

"Casper—"

A loud crack and pop cut off Hunter's words. He moved before I even realized what was happening and covered my body with his. "What the hell?" I mumbled into his chest.

Deputy Hughes raced from around the front of the lodge. "Gunshots?"

Hunter lifted his head. "Not sure."

Another crack sounded, and Bruno launched himself off the

blanket and away from the noise. "Get off me. I have to get Bruno. He's scared of loud noises."

Hughes moved towards the edge of the cliff, peering down in the direction of the noise. "Dammit. It looks like those two kids."

Hunter was off me in a flash. "I'm going to kill them."

"No, *I'm* going to arrest them. But I wouldn't mind some backup in case one tries to run."

"Happy to help," Hunter gritted out.

I climbed to my feet and started after my dog. "You help her. I have to get Bruno."

"Be careful," Hunter ordered. "It's dark."

I stuck out my tongue and then picked up my pace to a jog. "Bruno! Come. It's okay. No one's going to hurt you." But he was already on a tear. Instead of heading to the lodge as I'd hoped, he took off for the forest. "Crap."

I picked up my pace and followed his trail the best I could, weaving through the trees towards the barn. Hopefully, he'd go straight for the workshop and stay there. If he didn't, he could get lost and not stop running for hours.

A bark sounded, and then a hushed yell. "Get out of here, you damn mutt."

I pushed my muscles harder until I came to a skidding stop in front of a large hole to the side of the barn. "What the hell?"

Mr. Simpson whirled around in the same spot I'd seen him digging for worms a few weeks ago, a flashlight in one hand and a shovel in the other. Only this shovel was much larger than the hand trowel I'd seen him with before. "W-w-what are you doing here?"

"What am *I* doing? You're digging up my property. Don't tell me you're digging for worms."

A flash of anger lit in his eyes, and then he moved quicker than I'd ever seen before. The large flashlight swung out. There was a brief flash of pain before the whole world faded away.

Chapter Forty-Five

Hunter

THE BOYS RAN AS SOON AS THEY HEARD OUR FOOTSTEPS on the stairs, but apparently, neither of them had invested their time and energy into a sport in high school because they were slow. Not even the dump of adrenaline gave them an edge. We caught up with them in a matter of seconds.

Hughes went for Jasper, taking him to the sand in a clean tackle. I simply reached for Aaron's shirt and gave it a swift tug. He stumbled and landed on his ass. "Shouldn't have run," I quipped.

"W-we didn't mean any trouble. I swear," he said.

"You keep saying that, but I don't believe you."

Jasper writhed on the ground. "My dad will have your badge. Then he'll sue."

"Somehow, I don't think Daddy is going to save you from this one," I cut in.

Hughes shot me a glare. "You're not helping."

I snapped my mouth shut. The last thing I needed was for these two to get off because of something I did.

Hughes lifted Jasper to his feet and began reading him his rights. "Don't move." She did the same with Aaron, who looked as if he might start crying at any second. But I'd lost all sympathy for the boy who blindly followed his idiot friend around. "We're walking up those stairs, and then I'm taking you in. If you cause any trouble, it'll just mean more pain for you."

"Setting off firecrackers isn't against the law," Jasper griped.

"But harassment is. And I'd say Piper has a pretty strong case for that," Hughes said as she urged Jasper along.

I took up the rear of the group, making sure neither kid decided to make a run for it. "Looks like you might be kissing senior year goodbye, boys."

"Hunter…" Hughes warned.

"Yeah, yeah, I know." I quieted down again, only to hear Aaron sniffling.

Jasper cut his friend a glance. "Are you seriously crying right now?"

"My parents are going to kill me. They said one more strike, and they'd send me to boarding school."

I fought the urge to roll my eyes. They had bigger problems than parents and boarding school. They were looking at actual jail time. Especially if Parker found a link to the damage at the Falls.

Deputy Hughes put the two teens in the back of her SUV. My eyes narrowed on Jasper, who didn't seem cowed at all while sitting in cuffs in a police vehicle. Hughes stepped into my line of vision. "Come on now. Go help Piper find that dog. I've got these two. I'm hoping this is enough to revoke their bail. They set those firecrackers off on the dock, and that's Piper's private property, even though the beach is public."

"Tell Parker to call me once he gets them booked." I wanted an update, and I wasn't waiting until tomorrow.

"Will do." Hughes gave me a wave and climbed behind the wheel.

I scanned the area around the lodge and cabins but didn't see any signs of Piper or Bruno. I started in the direction of the forest where I'd seen Bruno run. I was about to call out but then thought better of it, remembering the sleeping guests.

Pulling out my phone, I turned on my flashlight app to guide my way. I froze when I heard a bark and a low growl. I went from a walk to a run, shutting off the light.

"You damn dog. This is all your fault. I didn't want to hurt her. Just stay back. I've almost got it."

I stopped just shy of the clearing in front of the barn. A flashlight lay on the ground, illuminating a hole and Mr. Simpson standing in it. He muttered a curse. "I know it's here."

As I shifted to get a better look, everything in me locked. This wasn't happening. A crumpled form lay on the ground, and I recognized the blue sneakers. They were the same ones Piper had been wearing earlier. Bruno stood guard over her.

She let out a mumbled groan, and Mr. Simpson's head shot up. Bruno bared his teeth. "Don't think about it, you damn dog. I'll kill you both if I have to. Just let me get my money, and I'll be gone."

I didn't think, I simply moved, more like I charged out of the trees. I tackled the man who was a little less elderly than I'd originally thought. We landed with a thud, and Mr. Simpson tried to elbow me in the jaw. I caught his arm and twisted it behind his back. "Don't move."

"I don't think so." With his free hand, Simpson lashed out. I saw the glint of metal and then felt a burn across my chest.

I let a slew of curses fly as I dug a knee into the man's back. He cried out in pain and dropped the knife, letting me get a hold of his free hand. I grabbed the blade and dug the tip into his back. "I said, don't fucking move."

Simpson froze. "I'm not."

I kept the knife in one hand and slipped my other out of the flannel shirt I had on. Switching hands, I repeated the motion.

My knee remained firmly on the man's spine as I used my shirt to restrain his wrists. "Piper," I called. She let out another moan, and Bruno barked. "Piper, I need you to answer me."

"Hunter?"

"It's me. You okay?"

She slowly sat up, holding her head. "What happen—?" Her eyes widened as she took in the sight of Mr. Simpson and me. "You hit me with your flashlight."

Simpson was conveniently quiet. I tossed Piper my phone. "Call Parker. Tell him we need a deputy."

She moved to pick up the phone but wavered slightly. I started towards her, but she held up a hand. "I'm okay. Just a little woozy."

"You sure?" Hell, I wanted to go to her, but I also didn't trust the man under my knee not to have another weapon hidden somewhere.

"I'm sure." She tapped the screen and held the phone to her ear.

"Let me up. You're hurting my back. I'll sue."

I dug my knee in harder. "You could've killed her. And for what? What the hell are you even doing out here?"

"Digging for worms."

I took in the hole we were in as Piper spoke with Parker. "Doesn't look like worms to me." My gaze caught on something in the light—a flash of pink. I leaned over to tug the piece of fabric from the ground. It was covered in dirt.

Simpson cursed as I shook it out, and the dirt landed on his head. "Quit it, man."

"Shut up." It was a woman's sweater, maybe a girl's, and it was unraveling. But it was also stained with blood—too much to mean anything good.

"What is—?" Piper's words cut off as she took in the garment in my hand. All the blood drained from her face, and she said one word.

"Jenn."

Chapter Forty-Six

Piper

NOTHING CUT THROUGH THE NUMBNESS. NOT THE HARD tree stump I was sitting on. The bite of the midnight air cutting through my t-shirt and into my skin. The harsh glare of the crime scene lights on the hole twenty feet in front of me.

I knew that sweater. I'd committed everything Jenn had been wearing the last time I saw her to memory. Buried it so deep, I'd never get it out.

Little rhinestone buttons in the shape of flowers. A phantom pang shot along my sternum. The pink sweater. The one we'd bought together right before our trip. We had thought it the height of sophistication. Perfect for our new life in high school.

But that sweater had never made it to high school. It was buried beneath the wreckage of ten years of a life lived without her. My dearest friend. The sister of my heart.

I'd give anything to unsee it. To pretend that it didn't exist. Because as much as I'd thought I knew that Jenn was gone, I hadn't. Not for sure. And as that proof began to bear down on me, I didn't think I could take it.

I jolted as a blanket dropped around my shoulders. Hunter carefully wrapped it around me, making sure all my exposed skin was covered. "Are you sure you don't want to go back to the lodge?"

I shook my head and immediately regretted the action. The EMTs said I had a mild concussion. Hunter had wanted me to go to the emergency room on the mainland, but I'd refused. I wasn't moving from this spot. Not until I had answers. "I'm good."

"You're not."

I couldn't tear my eyes away from the careful excavation taking place in front of me—crime scene techs in full body suits slowly carving out the earth. My stomach cramped. Would there be bones there? The last bits of the friend who had been my other half? "I'm not leaving her."

Hunter muttered a curse and then bent to lift me. Before I could let out even a word of protest, he sat back on the stump with me in his lap. He pressed his lips to my hair. "I want to say the right thing, but I don't know what the hell that is."

"There's nothing you can say. I just need to know."

"I know you do. But we might not have answers tonight."

As soon as we'd found the sweater, Simpson had clammed right up, going silent. Parker had arrived on the scene in record time with a trail of deputies and crime scene techs. Simpson had taken one look at all of them and said one word. Lawyer. Parker had sent him back to the station in a deputy's custody.

"They have to find *something*." I couldn't go on not knowing. Not when I'd seen the blood staining that sweater. It would eat me alive from the inside out.

"Parker said they're bringing out some dogs in the morning to help with the search."

Cadaver dogs was the term he wouldn't say. Because they weren't looking for someone who was still alive. "That's good."

278 | CATHERINE COWLES

Parker crossed from the makeshift headquarters that he and his team had set up. "How are you holding up?"

"I'm holding." It was all I could give him. The knowledge that I wasn't falling apart. Not yet.

"How does your head feel?"

"The Tylenol helped." It had barely touched the pain thrumming through my skull. And nothing would touch the agony ripping through my heart.

He nodded slowly as if reading my lie. "We're going to need to put a timeline together. See if Mr. Simpson has stayed here before. Were any old records left behind when Albert Crowley went into assisted living?"

"No—" I started to shake my head and then stopped. "Wait. I found some old registers in the attic. I planned to put them on display in the lobby, but the table I need for it isn't done yet. They're in the library. I'll go—"

"I can get them," Hunter cut me off. "Just tell me where."

I stood, my legs a little wobbly. "They're in the bottom right cabinet. There's a whole stack of them."

"I'll be right back." He gave me a quick kiss and then took off at a jog towards the lodge.

"He's crazy about you."

My ribs tightened around my lungs at Parker's words. "He's a good man."

"The best."

Parker wasn't wrong. But he was more than the best. Not even everything I wanted in a partner. He was everything I *needed*. And now that I knew what it felt like to be loved by him, I was ruined. "Have you found anything?"

Parker looked back at the crime scene techs. "Not yet. They have to move slow, so they don't ruin any evidence."

I tugged the blanket tighter around me. "But you think they will."

"I've learned by now that you can never predict this kind of thing. But we won't stop until we have answers. I promise you that."

"Thank you." My voice cracked on the second word, finally giving way just a bit.

Hunter appeared on the road, jogging back towards us. "Got 'em."

Parker took one half of the stack, and I took the other. I flipped open the first page, checking dates. This one was from before I was even born, so it was of no help. But the next was the summer before Jenn had gone missing. I held it out to Parker. "How about this one?"

He took it and whistled for a deputy. "Anything that's from when Jenn was alive, I want." He turned to the deputy. "Bag and tag this. We'll have more."

I opened the next register, only to find it wasn't a register at all but a journal. My heart squeezed at the name scrawled on the first page. Albert Crowley. I looked up at Parker. "This is Mr. C.'s journal. If you don't need it, I'd like to give it to Nick. He's been looking for it."

Parker carefully took the notebook and flipped through the pages, checking for any guest information. "That's fine. He needs something to remember his dad by. The good times."

"Here, I'll put it in my pocket." Hunter reached for the journal and put it carefully inside his jacket.

"Sheriff," one of the crime scene techs called.

I stiffened as Parker handed the set of registers to the deputy and headed towards the tech. My gaze stayed glued to him as the deputy took the registers out of my hands, as well. Didn't look away when Hunter wrapped an arm around me. I couldn't. "What did they find?"

He tugged me closer against him. "I don't know, but I think we'll find out soon enough."

The tech handed a small bag to Parker, and he glanced back at me before continuing the conversation. My breaths seemed to rattle in my chest with the force I needed to get them out. My fingers instinctively went to the metal at my neck—the last tie I had to Jenn. As if that might help me keep her.

Parker nodded at the tech and then started towards us. Hunter slipped behind me as if he were worried I might fall. My hand tightened around the metal, the jagged edges of the half heart digging into my flesh, the bite of pain keeping me from floating away. "What is it?"

Parker wore the mask of experience well. You could rarely read anything in his expression that he didn't want you to see. But now, I saw nothing but sympathy lining his face. "I need you to look at something for me. Tell me if it looks familiar."

"Okay." The world around me seemed to hollow out. Everything became a tunnel, echoey and far away, my focus solely on the small bag in Parker's hand. He laid the item in the evidence bag flat on his palm.

It only took a single heartbeat for me to recognize it. The reciprocating jagged metal. The other half of my grade-school charm. My legs wanted to give way, but I simply gripped my necklace harder, letting the pain hold me up. "Can you turn it over, please?"

Parker did as I asked. Dirt covered the back. I reached out and rubbed it through the plastic, and some of it fell away. But it left only devastation in its wake. Most of the etching had faded, but there was still a capital *J* carved in cursive in the metal. I couldn't step back or look away. "Was it with anything?"

"Skeletal remains."

"She was right here. All along. Just steps away, and I never knew."

Hunter cursed and swept me up in his arms as my legs started to wobble. "I'm taking her back to the lodge. Call me if you need me."

"I will. I'm sorry, Piper."

I could barely hear Parker's words. And I didn't argue when Hunter started walking with me in his arms back to the lodge. The only thing I saw was how clear the stars were. The same ones that Jenn and I had stared at as we talked about our hopes and dreams. The boys we would one day marry. The Falls that would eventually be ours. Someone had stolen that from her. From me.

Only the disappearance of the stars made me realize that Hunter and I had made it inside. He gave Bruno an order to go back to his bed as he climbed the stairs, me still in his arms. He gently set me down on the edge of the bed, turning on only a side lamp.

"Shit, Piper. You're bleeding."

I looked down, expecting to see a gaping hole in my chest that I'd somehow not been able to feel. But it was only a small trickle of blood escaping from between my fingers. Hunter slowly pried my hand open, and my necklace fell free, streaked with blood.

"I'm going to get something to clean this. Sit tight."

Where would I go? There was nowhere. Nothing. None of it mattered anymore, did it?

Hunter returned with a damp cloth and a bandage. He carefully dabbed at the punctures in my palm and then wrapped it with gauze. It almost broke me when he cleaned my broken heart necklace, too.

When he was done, he framed my face in his hands. "What can I do?"

"I'm so cold. I can't feel anything." I looked up into Hunter's eyes, barely being able to take them in. "Make me feel."

"Piper…I don't know if that's such a good idea—"

"Please, I need to feel warm again."

Hunter bent and took my mouth in a slow kiss, full of tenderness and care. But it wasn't what I needed.

"More," I pleaded.

He deepened the kiss, chasing away the edges of the cold that had invaded, the nothingness. That hint of warmth flipped a switch in me. My hands tugged at his t-shirt, the button of his jeans. My shirt and pants. I wanted nothing between us, only skin and feeling, and everything that was breathing and alive.

Hunter hissed out a breath as my fingers wrapped around his shaft. "Piper, are you sure?"

My eyes locked with his. "I need you."

It was all the convincing he needed. Hunter's hand ran up the inside of my thigh, teasing and toying, then circling the bundle of nerves. But he never once looked away from my face, taking everything he needed to know from my expression.

I lost myself in the feel of his fingers. In the heat of his gaze. In the sounds he made as I stroked him.

"You keep doing that, and I'm going to lose it."

"Lose it with me," I whispered.

In a flash, his tip bumped my entrance. My legs wrapped around his hips, a silent plea for everything I needed. My eyes fluttered closed for the briefest of moments as he slid inside.

"No. Look at me. I don't want to lose you in this."

There was a guttural edge to Hunter's words that had my eyes flying open and locking with his. He held me captive there. I clung to his shoulder as his thrusts picked up speed, desperate and a touch feral. It was everything I needed.

I met his hips in this new rhythm borne of hurt and love and life. My nails dug into his back as he bottomed out inside me, hitting a spot that had my eyes wanting to close again. I refused to let them. I wouldn't leave Hunter's gaze for a moment.

"Not gonna last. Need you with me," he growled.

I reached for it, that final plateau just out of reach. "I'm with you."

It was all he needed. With one more thrust, I spiraled down in a cascade of sensation, never once doubting that I was here and feeling it all. Hunter arched his back as he came but didn't look away from my eyes for even a moment. His hands found my face. "I love you."

"I love you, too." The statement tore from my throat without my permission. Ragged and rough.

Those three words broke me, and tears spilled down my cheeks. Because they were the truth. I loved this man, and I could lose him. No force of will could stop it.

Hunter

I WATCHED HER FROM MY SPOT IN THE DOORFRAME, HER hands expertly wrapping her hair around a curling iron. Her silk robe fell to the side just a bit, exposing one golden shoulder. To anyone else, she probably seemed fine. But I could see under the façade to the pain that ripped her apart, shred by shred.

It'd been ten days since we'd discovered the remains. One week since we'd received the positive identification. Jenn had been buried on the Falls' property this whole time. What we didn't have were answers. Simpson was locked up tighter than a drum, a lawyer answering all questions for him.

The only information we'd gained was from Nick. When Parker had talked to him about who had been around that summer and shared Simpson's full name, Nick had recognized it. Pulling some records out of a storage unit in town, he'd found the pay stubs. William Simpson had worked for the Crowley family as a groundskeeper and handyman for six months. He'd left one week after Jenn went missing. Nick said he remembered his dad telling him that Simpson had had a family emergency.

How the old sheriff or Mr. Crowley hadn't found that suspicious, I didn't know. And the truth was, it didn't really matter now. The district attorney had enough circumstantial evidence to move ahead with the case.

I had to hope that a trial would bring answers. Closure for Jenn's parents, Nathan, Vic, and most of all, Piper. She released the curl from the iron and unplugged the appliance. Combing her fingers carefully through her hair, she shook out her locks.

I moved in behind her, massaging her shoulders and meeting her gaze through the mirror. "Are you sure you feel up to this?"

"I told Bell and Ford I was coming. I'll be fine. I don't want to sit around here and drown in memories anyway."

That was the understatement of the century. Piper had thrown herself into work the day after our discovery and had only slowed when Jenn's parents arrived from the mainland to see their daughter's remains and speak to Parker. Even when her uncles had come for a few days, they'd simply had to work alongside her if they had any hope of having a conversation. They'd left worried and texted me each day for a report on how she was doing.

"Stop looking at me like that. I'm not going to break."

I kneaded deeper into the tension in her shoulders. "I know you're not. But I also know you're hurting. I'm allowed to hate that."

Piper dipped her head and kissed my knuckles. "You are. But I can hurt and be happy at the same time. I can hold those two things at once. And I am happy for Ford and Bell. They deserve this day and everything that goes along with it. And that means you're going to The Catch now to help your brother get ready. And to make sure he doesn't have too many shots of whiskey before the ceremony."

My lips twitched. "Bell would be pissed as hell if he showed up drunk."

"Rightfully so." She met my eyes in the mirror. "*Go.* I'll see you there."

I bent and took her mouth in a long, deep kiss. I poured everything I didn't have the words for into it. "Love you."

"See you soon."

I released Piper and headed out the door. She hadn't given me the words I wanted since that night—the one where they'd tumbled out, and then she'd dissolved into sobs. It didn't change the fact that I knew what was in her soul. The words would come again when she was ready.

I gave Bruno a rub as I passed through the lobby. "Go look out for your mom."

He seemed to understand me and bounded up the stairs to stand guard. I made my way to my truck and headed for town. The wedding itself would be a small affair, held on the land my brother and Bell had bought together, in front of the house they'd lovingly restored. She was getting ready there, but Ford had chosen The Catch for his spot. We'd closed down for the day, though our cook would be there, making lunch for the guys as we waited for our time.

I pulled into the parking lot and slid into an empty spot. While I was the only groomsman, Ford had wanted his friends around to celebrate. Vehicles dotted the space. My parents' car. Crosby's and Griffin's trucks. A rental that I knew belonged to Ford's friends from LA—Austin and Liam. And I knew Brody would be here, too. So many of this ragtag crew we'd assembled had become family.

I slung my tux over my shoulder and pulled open the door to hear seventies rock drifting through the speakers and laughter filling the space. My brother had a beer in one hand and a BLT in the other.

"You certainly don't look like you're getting married in a couple of hours," I greeted.

Ford raised his glass in my direction. "Finally, the celebration can begin."

"Not too much," my mother chided from behind the bar where she arranged platters of food.

"He'd *never* do anything like that. Never been drunk a day in his life, have you, brother dearest?"

Ford scowled at me. "Don't rat me out to Mom."

She patted his shoulder. "Since it's your wedding, I'll let it slide."

Ford ushered me over to the food. "You're lucky she's feeling generous. Hungry?"

"Sure." I took a sandwich and beer, even though I didn't have much of an appetite. I was still mentally back at the resort, worried about Piper.

"Come on, follow me." Ford inclined his head towards the patio doors.

I traded back slaps and hellos with the rest of the guys. When we made it outside and eased into chairs at one of the tables, I studied my brother. "Not having second thoughts, are you? I'm not taking you to Mexico."

"Hell, no. I wish I could've married Bell months ago."

"Glad to hear it. Everything else okay?"

He took a sip of his beer. "That's what I wanted to ask you. Piper doing okay?"

"Man, it's your wedding. We can talk about that later."

"Just because I'm getting married doesn't mean I don't care what's going on in your life."

I leaned back in the chair and let my gaze drift out to the water. "She's hurting. But she won't talk about anything. All she wants to do is stay busy—inhumanly so."

"That's how some people work through their grief."

"I just wish I could take it all away. It kills me that she's in pain."

"You love her."

I turned back to Ford. "She's it for me."

His eyes widened a fraction. "I didn't realize you were there."

"It's not where I meant to go. Hell, those first weeks on the job, I did everything I could to only see her as a business partner—and maybe a friend. But now I can't imagine my life without her."

"She know that?"

"I think so."

Ford grinned and shook his head. "Think isn't good enough. You have to make sure she knows."

"It might make her run. She's scared right now."

He sobered instantly. "Then you just have to be there. Prove that you're the solid ground for her to stand on when she needs you."

"Is that how you got Bell?"

"Hell, no. I made every mistake in the book with her. Thought I knew what I was doing. But I got it wrong almost every step of the way. It's a miracle we made it work."

I couldn't hold in my chuckle. "I'll never forget when she poured that beer over your head the first day you came back."

Ford rubbed his head as if remnants of beer remained. "I'd take a million more dunkings if I got her in the end."

"That's how you know, isn't it? That you'd walk through fire just for a chance to feel her in your arms."

He let out a low whistle. "You're definitely a goner."

He wasn't wrong. I just hoped Piper didn't take off with my heart in her hands.

Chapter Forty-Eight

Piper

I TOOK ANOTHER SIP OF MY DRINK. I'D SKIPPED THE champagne and went straight for a vodka on the rocks. But it didn't seem to be doing nearly enough to soothe the riot of emotions swirling inside me. The bride and groom moved across the floor, their eyes never straying from each other. You could almost feel the love and devotion pouring off them in waves.

I wanted that. Yet, I didn't. Those two primal reactions warred inside me. Hope and fear. Love and hate. It was a special kind of torture to want something so badly it physically hurt. And to be terrified of it at the same time.

"Dance with me." Hunter's lips teased the edge of my ear.

"Okay." I was powerless to deny him. And no matter what was going on inside me, I wanted his arms around me.

He stood and held out a hand to me. "Have I told you how beautiful you look tonight?"

"You might've said something once or twice."

Hunter pulled me to my feet. "I'm going to keep telling you. You make me forget to breathe."

I shivered as his hand found my bare back, guiding me towards the dance floor. "That doesn't sound healthy."

"Worth it."

We stopped halfway to the crowd when Cal stepped into our path. He nodded and gave me a kind smile, but it seemed almost halfhearted. As if he couldn't form a full grin. "You look beautiful tonight, Piper. Hunter, you're a lucky man."

"Don't I know it."

I looked over Cal's shoulder for Ashley and found her a couple of tables away, scowling in our direction. I wanted to roll my eyes. Didn't she have anything else to worry about but the fact that she wouldn't be able to double date with her best friend and Cal's until the end of time? I shifted my gaze back to Cal. "Are you having a good evening?"

"It's been great." He moved his finger to his collar. "I could lose the tie, though."

My mouth curved. "I bet no one would notice if you stuck it in your wife's purse."

"Good point." His eyes shifted to the side and then back to Hunter and me. "Has the sheriff told you guys anything? Is it for sure Simpson?"

Ice slid through my veins as images I didn't want anything to do with filled my mind. The crew hadn't been around since the event. They were due to start back up on Monday. And I knew it was natural to want to know what had happened. But I didn't need the reminder. Jenn haunted me every moment I was awake or asleep. That sweater covered in blood. All the ways that might have happened.

"Cal," Hunter barked. "Not the place or time."

Cal scrubbed the back of his neck. "Shit, I'm sorry. I didn't mean to—I've just been worried, that's all."

I squeezed Hunter's hand but looked at Cal. "It's okay. We don't know anything. Only as much as has been in the papers."

"I hope they get him," he whispered.

"Me, too."

"Come on." Hunter tugged me to sidestep Cal. "Let's dance."

He navigated us around anyone else who looked as if they might stop us and led me onto the floor. My hands encircled Hunter's neck as his arms wrapped around my waist. "Don't be mad at your friend. He's worried about you. Both of us."

His jaw worked back and forth. "He needs to read a room. This isn't the place to talk about that."

I didn't disagree. But it didn't mean that Hunter should be mad at him. I ran my fingers through the hair at the back of his head. "Then let's switch topics. Ford and Bell look happy."

As if I'd conjured them, they swept past us, still lost in their own world. Hunter grinned at his brother. "I don't think I've ever seen them happier."

"They deserve this."

His gaze came back to my face, the heat of it burning me. "They do." The corners of his mouth tipped up. "You never know, that could be us one day."

The shock of the statement hit my ears and had me missing a step, nearly tripping. Hunter chuckled. "Don't worry. I'm not trying to rope you into heading down the aisle."

"I don't know if I ever want to get married." The words were out before I could stop them.

Hunter's head jerked back slightly. "What? You don't want to get married? Ever?"

"I...I just don't know if it's necessary. People have committed relationships all the time without that piece of paper."

"Sure, but...I want that. Marriage. Children. The whole thing. You don't?"

I swallowed against the burn climbing up my throat. "I don't know what I want."

"I'm not saying you have to decide today."

"But you're pushing."

A muscle in his cheek ticked. "I'm saying it would be good to have a heads-up if you know you don't want to make a family with me, ever."

The tent felt like it was closing in around me. Suddenly, I couldn't breathe. I dropped my hands from around Hunter's neck and started towards the field behind the party. I needed air. I picked up my pace as I made it through the gauntlet of tables. By the time I reached the edge of the tent, I was running.

My heels sank into the soft earth, but I didn't care. I didn't stop until I hit the edge of the woods. I gasped, trying to fill my lungs. It felt like it barely worked, only a bit of air getting in.

"Piper."

I didn't turn at Hunter's voice. Couldn't. I could only focus on breathing. Slowly, a little more oxygen seemed to make its way into my system.

Hands landed on my shoulders and turned me around. Concern filled Hunter's features. "Just breathe. You're okay."

Tears leaked out of the corners of my eyes. I was the furthest thing from okay. "I'm sorry. I can't—I think I need to go."

"You're not driving anywhere right now. It's not safe."

I closed my eyes for a moment, willing my body to calm down. When I opened them, I'd stopped trembling. "Coming tonight was a mistake. You were right. I wasn't ready."

Hunter framed my face in his rough hands. "That's okay. I'll take you home."

I shook my head. "No. This is your brother's wedding. You need to stay. And, honestly, I think I need a night alone. To…process."

Hunter's hands fell away as he took a step back. "You don't want me to come home to you tonight?"

The look of betrayal might as well have been an ice pick to the heart. "Just for tonight. I need to get my head on straight. You don't need to be wrapped up in my mess."

"Your mess is exactly where I want to be."

His words burned a trail over my skin; they were so perfect. "I'm sure there will be plenty of mess left tomorrow."

Hunter pulled me into his arms. "I'm not letting you go. Tomorrow, we'll talk this through. I'll be in my cabin if you need me."

"Okay," I whispered.

We were silent as we walked to my SUV. And when Hunter kissed me, it felt a whole lot like a goodbye on my lips. I drove home in a daze, wondering if this was the beginning of the end. And why, after a lifetime of wanting a family, I'd lied to Hunter on that dance floor.

My chest tightened as my headlights swept across the sign for the Whispering Falls Lodge & Resort. All those dreams Jenn and I had made together. It felt like a betrayal to live them without her.

My tears fell hot and fast as I parked my SUV and stepped out into the cool night air. Nothing but the sound of the water, crickets, and my hiccuping sobs sounded as I walked toward the lodge. I fumbled with my keys, and as I stepped inside, I cursed. No lights.

I flipped the switch. Nothing. I shivered, thinking about having to go down into the basement alone. "Suck it up. A lifetime of being alone means fixing your own lightbulbs."

I started towards the basement door. Just a few steps away, an arm jerked around my neck. I thrashed and twisted. Scratched at the arm locked around me. Tried to kick back. A cloth covered my mouth, an almost sweet taste filling my senses.

"Just breathe," a voice whispered. It was familiar. Too much so. But before I could place it, my limbs went limp, and darkness engulfed me.

Hunter

A S Piper's SUV disappeared down the lane, I
whirled, kicking a rock and sending it flying. "Fuck!"

"Hey, now. That's not exactly wedding talk."

I scowled at Brody as he stepped closer.

"What happened?"

I scrubbed a hand along the thick stubble on my jaw. "I
messed up."

"Piper?"

Only one person could have me this tied in knots. I nodded.

Brody rolled his shoulders back. "Been there, man. You can
fix it."

I wasn't so sure. If Piper truly didn't want the same kind of
future that I did, what hope was there for the two of us? "She
said she doesn't want marriage and a family."

"And I take it you do?"

"Not tomorrow. But someday, I do."

Brody toed a piece of gravel with his shoe. "I'm all for whatever makes people happy. Me and Shay, we're good with each

other and our dogs. But are you sure it's not just Piper's fear talking? She lost someone incredibly close to her. She's coming to terms with that right now. It's bound to make her a little gun-shy."

Guilt began gnawing at my gut. Hell. She'd been through so much these past few weeks, and here I was, pushing her about something we didn't even need to be talking about right now. "I don't know what happened. I went a little crazy when I didn't think she wanted what I did."

"You love her. You want forever with her. Cut yourself a little slack. You'll make it right."

"And how the hell am I going to do that?"

"Give her time. Let her know you're here for her and you can go at whatever speed she needs." He arched a brow. "But you have to be ready to move at a snail's pace."

"I am." I'd do whatever I needed to have Piper with me. Even, I realized, standing there in the dark, give up on a dream I'd always had. She was more important than some plan in my mind.

Brody clapped a hand on my shoulder. "Good. But first, we have to get in the tent. They're about to cut the cake."

We made our way inside, and I did my best to relax my expression, even curve my mouth into a smile. I scanned the crowd for Cal, needing to have a more serious discussion with him about what not to say to Piper, but I didn't see him or Ashley anywhere.

"Hunt," my brother called. "Get your ass over here."

Our mom slapped him upside the head. "No cursing at your wedding."

I made my way towards them. I had to stick out the reception for my brother and Bell, but I couldn't give Piper tonight like she wanted. I had to let her know I wasn't going anywhere.

I guided the wheel of my truck with one hand and loosened the bowtie at my neck with the other. I'd pulled off happy and carefree for the rest of the night, so my brother hadn't known what was wrong. My mother, of course, had seen right through it. She'd pulled me aside and asked where Piper was. I'd told her that she wasn't feeling quite up to the crowd and had left. It was true enough.

But it wasn't the whole of it. I didn't want her to know how badly I'd messed things up. I threw my bowtie onto the passenger seat, working out in my head what I might say when I showed up at Piper's door tonight. Whatever was needed to take the pressure off.

All I wanted was to hold her in my arms and assure myself that she was here. Breathing. Safe. Mine. We would figure out the rest as it came.

I pulled into the spot next to Piper's SUV and turned off the engine. There were no lights on in the lodge. I checked my watch. A little after eleven. She might already be asleep. It didn't matter. I needed my body curved around hers, the feel of her heartbeat under my palm.

Climbing out, I shut the door and beeped my locks. The silence around me was deafening. The Gragerts had left after the police activity, and the only guest remaining was Nick, who always kept a low profile.

I jogged up the steps and pulled out my set of keys. Moving to unlock the door, I realized it was already open. I mumbled a curse. Even though Simpson was locked up tight, anyone else could walk through the door.

I felt for the light switch and flicked it on. Nothing happened. I tried again. Still nothing.

The cool sea air and the complete darkness made the hair on my arms rise. I went straight for the stairs, taking them two at a time. I could hear Bruno whining, and I picked up to a run. I didn't bother knocking, I simply burst in.

Bruno leapt all over me, but Piper wasn't in bed. "Piper," I called. Silence but for Bruno's yips. "Where's your mom?"

I led him down the hall, checking every room on our way. She was nowhere. My ribs seemed to close in around my lungs, but I refused to let the panic take hold. I went for my holster and gun in the lockbox in the closet.

"Come on." I motioned for Bruno to follow me downstairs and opened the back door to let him out to do his business. He bounded onto the lawn while I searched the coastline, half expecting to see Piper walking there. But she wasn't.

I pulled out my phone and hit the flashlight app. I scanned the lobby, the library, and finally, the kitchen. Nothing.

I needed to get the lights working again for a more thorough search of everywhere. I made my way towards the basement, but I faltered just steps away, my pace stuttering. Sharp scratches were in the hardwood, along with dents. Marks that certainly hadn't been there before because Piper had refinished these floors herself. I'd admired the work.

I crouched, my fingers ghosting across the grooves. Then, I froze, and my lungs seized. Right there in front of me, were a few drops of blood.

Chapter Fifty

Piper

THE SHIVERING WOKE ME. IT SEEMED TO EMANATE FROM somewhere deep inside. A place where I had no hope of getting warm. My teeth clacked together with an especially vicious bout of it, the jarring motion forcing my eyes to flutter open.

The space around me was blurry as a wave of nausea swept through me. I inhaled through my nose, doing everything I could to stop it as the walls came into focus. The room was familiar yet not. The rough wood of the walls seemed to be falling apart in places. The only thing I could focus on was how the wood seemed to fracture the same way my body was.

I set my teeth, trying to stop the shaking. Slowly, I blinked my eyes, and a little of the fog cleared away. I tried to roll, but my body seized in protest. Catching sight of an old painting on one wall, the pieces came together—the old groundskeeper cabin.

It was the worst of the bunch and not even on my list of buildings to tackle in the near future. But how had I gotten here? I searched my brain, things coming back to me in flashes and half-memories. The wedding. My fight with Hunter. Passing the sign on my way home. Fumbling with my key...

Because it had been so dark, I realized now. The lights had been completely off. And I couldn't get them on. I jerked as the memory of the arm around my neck slammed into me. The feel of the cloth over my mouth. Not being able to breathe.

The trembling in my limbs intensified, whether from fear or whatever I'd been dosed with, I didn't know. I pushed to a sitting position, and my head swam, the room around me dancing in waves. If I could barely sit, how the hell would I run? And running was my only hope—and before whoever had me returned. My legs and arms weren't bound. I just needed my body to stop betraying me.

I struggled to push to my feet but wavered and had to sit again. Counting my breaths, I focused on my hands, trying to get them to stop shaking. Just as I was about to try again, the door flew open.

A figure stood silhouetted in the frame. I squinted, trying to make out who it was. He muttered a curse and stepped into the low light of the cabin. "It was supposed to knock you out for two hours. I didn't want you to have to feel this."

My body locked as I took in the familiar face. The dark hair and eyes. They'd always been so warm and welcoming. "Nick?"

He dumped out a box of rags and crumpled-up newspaper in front of a lamp. "I never wanted to go this route. I'm so sorry, Piper."

"Go what route?"

He crouched in front of the lamp and lifted the cord. Pulling a small item out of his pocket, he flicked open a knife and began peeling at the cord's plastic coating. "You couldn't leave well enough alone."

"The Falls?"

His head snapped up. "Some things need to stay buried."

I watched as Nick's dark eyes blazed. So much heat and anger there. I could feel it coming over me in waves. "Jenn. You—you're the one who killed her?"

He took the words like a physical blow. "Of course not. And my dad didn't mean to hurt her either."

Another vicious wave of nausea slammed into me. "What?"

"She saw something she shouldn't have. She never should've been at that party. And then she went off sulking after Ethan decided he wanted nothing to do with her. Dad was doing everything he could to keep this place afloat…"

His words trailed off, but I needed more. I needed the truth. "I know he was. He always worked so hard."

Nick sent a glare in my direction. "You have no idea. He gave his whole life to this place. But we were drowning. He needed an infusion of cash, or we were going under. Our groundskeeper, Simpson, had a history. He'd gone away before. He talked my dad into one robbery. No one was supposed to get hurt, and the insurance companies would cover the loss for the business."

But it was never that simple. Every action had an equal and opposite reaction. "Jenn did."

Nick launched to his feet, pointing the knife at me. "He panicked. It wasn't his fault. She showed up out of nowhere when he was burying the money. It was just a reaction. He hit her with the shovel, and she just…died. There was nothing he could do."

My stomach cramped viciously. There was always something a person could do. Help to be found. Answers to give a family in agony.

Nick's arm trembled as he held the knife in my direction. "I helped him bury the body before anyone knew that she was missing. I thought we were safe. I couldn't lose my dad." His gaze shifted away from my face. "We'd been working on getting running water from the well to the barn, so no one thought twice about freshly turned earth over there."

But we should've. So many regrets, things that I'd never get to make right.

He tightened his grip on the blade. "I didn't know it, but Dad kept a journal." The notebook I'd meant to give Nick but had forgotten about flashed in my mind. "When the Alzheimer's set in so fast, he lost it. But he remembered enough that he knew it could hurt us. And he knew he'd hidden it somewhere here."

The silver of the knife flashed in the light as Nick moved in closer to me. "No one had shown any interest in this place. Not for years. And then you just had to come along and buy it. I'm sorry, Piper, but this place has to die, and the memories along with it. I tried so many things to get you to leave, but you never took the fucking hint."

"It doesn't have to die." I tried my best to keep my voice from shaking. "I've been over every inch of this place. There's no journal. If you let me go, I promise not to say a word. And even if I do, who's going to believe some crazy story I tell about you kidnapping me? It's insane."

Nick seemed to consider it for a moment and then thought better of it. "I'm sorry. I can't. It all needs to go."

"Y-you can't erase this entire place. It's impossible."

"I can if it burns." He sank his free hand into his pocket and pulled out a lighter. "We're in the dry season now. The trees between here and the cabins and lodge, they may as well be tinder."

I swallowed the bile creeping up my throat. He was right. We were on red alert for forest fires right now. One carefully placed flame, and we were done. "Please…don't."

Nick bent and lit a piece of newspaper on fire. It danced and caught a rag that burst into flame. He straightened and locked eyes with me. "I'll give you a choice. I can knock you out again so you don't feel a thing, or you can die choking on smoke and fire."

I swallowed back a sob. I wasn't going down without a fight. Not when I'd left so many things unsaid with Hunter. It seemed insane now that I'd told him that I wasn't sure I wanted a future with him. A family. It was *all* I wanted. And I wouldn't let regret steal any more of my life.

Without warning, I charged, sidestepping Nick and running for the door. But I wasn't quite fast enough. He caught me around the throat again, this time the blade cutting into my chest. "I guess you're opting for pain."

Hunter

I SNAPPED MY FINGERS AND GAVE BRUNO THE COMMAND TO heel as I jogged down the back steps and pulled out my phone. I kept right on moving, Bruno at my side as the phone rang on the other end.

"Raines," Parker answered.

"Need you at the Falls."

"Just wrapped up another call. I'm about ten minutes out. What's going on?"

"Piper's missing, and there are drops of blood on the floor by the basement." I'd checked the dark, dank underground space to make sure that she wasn't anywhere down there, and she hadn't been. "I don't see any sign of her or anyone else."

I scanned the coastline and the forest as I rounded the lodge. Nothing. Parker started up his SUV. "I'll be there as soon as I can, and I'm calling in backup. Stay put."

"I'm searching the cabins."

"Hunter…"

"I've got my Glock. I'll be fine."

Parker mumbled something under his breath. "You have no idea what you could be walking into."

"I don't care what the hell it is. Piper's missing and—" My words halted as I caught something on the breeze. I inhaled deeply through my nose. "Call fire and rescue, too. I smell smoke. It's coming from over by the barn, I think."

"Wait for backup—"

Parker's words abruptly ended when I hung up and picked up my pace to a run. Bruno matched me, stride for stride. My damn dress shoes slipped on the ground, but I simply pushed harder. The scent of smoke grew stronger as I charged through the woods.

I broke through the trees, expecting to see the barn engulfed in flames, but that wasn't the source. I rounded the old building and caught sight of the culprit. The side of the old groundskeeper cabin danced with flames.

My lungs burned as I strained to go even faster. I skidded to a halt as I heard a scream—Piper's scream. I unholstered my Glock and gave Bruno a silent command to stay. The hair along his spine bristled, but he obeyed.

Slowly, I approached the door, trying to stay as quiet as possible. My palms dampened, and I had to readjust my grip. Visions of Shay being held by her brother and Sam danced in my head. The burn of the bullet as it pierced my shoulder. The moment I thought it was all over.

Memories flashed, taunting me. I gave my head a good shake and pictured Piper's face when she let loose one of those completely uninhibited laughs. She needed me, and I couldn't lose it now.

The door was slightly ajar, so it flew open with one swift kick. The vision in front of me stopped me dead in my tracks. Flames grew on one side of the cabin while Nick had hold of Piper on the other, a knife at her throat. Despite the heat, ice slid through my veins. "Nick, let her go."

His gaze flew to me, his eyes wild as his focus jumped from me to Piper and back again. "No, no, no. You were still at the wedding. You're not supposed to be here."

"Let her go. You don't want to hurt Piper. She's your friend."

Tears leaked from the corners of Piper's eyes, sliding down her cheeks and onto her chest—a chest stained with blood. That beautiful gold dress she'd donned for tonight now bloomed red. My heart pounded in my ears.

Nick shook his head furiously. "You come in here. Or—or I'll slice her throat."

"Don't," Piper called. "This whole place is going up."

"Shut up!" Nick sliced the blade across her chest, and Piper cried out in pain.

I leveled the gun at Nick's head. "I said, let her go." I did my best to keep my voice even, but it shook with fury. I would've shot him dead, but his head was too close to Piper's. I didn't trust myself to make the shot. All the failures leading up to this moment taunted me from the back of my brain.

"Go!" Piper's eyes pleaded with me. "Love you," she whispered. "Forever."

The fire flew higher, catching the ceiling. I took aim, but as I did, fur flew by in my peripheral vision. With a growl, Bruno lunged. His teeth sank into Nick's arm that held the knife. The man cried out as the blade clattered to the floor. Piper fell, and in that moment, I had him. I didn't hesitate. My shot rang true. Right into his shoulder.

I ran forward, hauling Piper into my arms as I called for Bruno. I stumbled out of the cabin, almost running into Parker. "Nick. He's in there. I shot him, but he's alive."

Parker didn't say a word, simply charged in. I lay Piper on the ground as sirens blared through the night. "Casper."

She coughed and sputtered. "I'm okay."

Bruno licked her face as I tore off my jacket and pressed it to the wounds on her chest. "He cut you. You're fucking bleeding. That is *not* okay."

Piper reached a hand up to my face, pressing her palm against my cheek. "I will be."

She seemed pretty damn confident, but I wouldn't be until she was in a hospital, and we'd gotten the all-clear. I pressed harder, trying to slow the bleeding, and she cried out. "I'm sorry. I don't want to hurt you, but you've already lost too much blood."

Firefighters and EMTs rounded the building as Parker emerged, dragging Nick, who was unconscious. One of the medics dropped to the ground next to me. "What happened?"

"She's been cut and likely has smoke inhalation. I'm not sure what else." I didn't even know what had happened or why. Had he hurt her somewhere I couldn't see? My mind locked down those possibilities.

"I've got her. I need you to step away and let me work."

I tried. I really did, but I couldn't remove my hands from Piper's chest. Parker gripped my shoulder. "Let him work, Hunter. He can help her."

Piper's gaze met mine, her eyes trying to reassure me. "I'm right here. I'm not going anywhere."

It had to be true.

Chapter Fifty-Two

Piper

I LET OUT A GROAN AS I ROLLED OVER, THE STITCHES ACROSS my chest pulling with the movement.

"Careful, Casper. You don't want to rip those stitches."

I blinked, my vision filling with Hunter. He was fully dressed and propped against the headboard. "Hi," I whispered.

"Hi." He brushed the hair away from my face. "How are you feeling?"

"Much better having slept in my own bed."

Hunter scowled. He'd wanted me to stay in the hospital last night. But I truly hadn't needed it, and I knew the night of uninterrupted sleep would help. My throat was still raw from the smoke, and Nick choking me. And my chest burned where the stitches were, but I was alive, breathing. And Hunter was here.

I laid a hand on his chest, the beat of his heart a strong reassurance. "Have you heard from Parker?"

"Talked to him first thing."

"And?"

His lips ghosted across the top of my head. "Are you sure

you want to talk about this right now? You're recovering. You will be for a while."

I pressed a kiss to the underside of his jaw. I knew it would take time for Hunter to get past all we'd been through in the past twenty-four hours. The best I could do was reassure him that I was okay, strong and alive. "I can handle it. I promise. I need to know."

Hunter wrapped an arm gently around me. "Nick is still in custody. Bail hearing is tomorrow. Simpson had lots to say once Parker told him they knew Albert was the one who had killed Jenn. He never knew about the murder. And he'd ended up in prison on an unrelated charge a month later. He just got out a few months ago. That's why he just came looking for the money now. Only he couldn't remember exactly where Albert had said he buried it."

"What about Albert?" I couldn't bring myself to use *Mr. C.*, the nickname that had always held such warmth.

"Parker tried to question him, but Albert isn't in his right mind. And the money's gone, whether he already spent it trying to keep the resort afloat, no one knows."

My chest burned, but it wasn't my stitches this time. It was the knowledge that all of this could've been avoided. One bad decision, a robbery where no one was supposed to get hurt, had led to a lifetime of pain for so many. "I'm not sure what the right punishment is for a man who's no longer in his right mind."

Hunter sighed as he leaned back farther against the headboard. "I'm not either. But his son certainly needs to be held accountable for his actions."

I didn't disagree there. "I still can't believe it was Nick. That he was so ready to..." My words trailed off as Hunter's jaw turned to granite. "I'm sorry."

He tipped down his head to meet my gaze. "You don't have

to apologize for anything. I just—I almost lost you. I don't know if I'll ever get over that."

I reached a hand up to brush against his scruff, and Hunter leaned into my palm. "But you didn't. I'm right here, and I'm fine."

His fingers trailed lightly around the edge of the bandage that peeked out of my tank top. "This isn't fine. And everything could've been so much worse."

"I know. But it wasn't."

Hunter tucked my head into his chest. "It's going to take me some time to believe you're here and safe. And I need you to let me have it."

"I love you. You know that, right?" His t-shirt muffled the words.

His voice filled with a mix of love and pain. "I know. But it doesn't hurt to hear it."

I tipped my face up to his. "I've been scared."

"Of what?"

"Losing you. I've never loved someone like I love you. It's terrifying. To know how deep that runs, and that one day it could just be gone."

He took my face in his hands. The roughness of his palms that spoke of the hours we'd spent restoring the Falls, of the effort he poured into everything he did. Of *life*. "You're not going to lose me."

My fingers latched on to his wrists. "One day, one of us will lose the other. It's how it goes. But I'm not letting that stop me anymore. I could've lost you last night, and all I could think about were the last words I gave you...lies. I never want to feel that kind of regret with you."

His eyes searched mine. "Lies?"

"I want a future with you. Building this place together. Marriage. Family."

"Are you sure about that?"

I brushed my lips against his. "I've never wanted anything more."

His mouth quirked. "You know…you're going to have to ask me to marry you. I'm not risking it."

I burst out laughing but immediately regretted it, muttering a curse as my stitches pulled.

"Shit." Hunter helped me sit up. "No laughing for you. I'll just have to be less charming."

"I know it'll be a challenge."

"But for you, I'll try." He pressed a quick kiss to my temple. "What do you think? Ready for some food? It's already eleven."

My stomach rumbled. "I think that means feed me."

Hunter chuckled. "Let's go."

He helped me out of bed, but I stayed in my PJs, opting for just my slippers. I glanced around the room. "Where's Bruno?" My hero dog deserved at least a few slices of bacon. Parker had joked that he would try to hire him for the K-9 unit.

"He's downstairs. I'm sure he'll be happy to see you."

Surprising that he wasn't sticking to my or Hunter's sides, given everything that had happened. We made our way down the stairs. As we did, voices sounded. "Hunter? Who's here?" I asked pointedly.

He sent me a grin. "Come on down and find out."

As I reached the bottom landing, tables crammed with people appeared. In a flash, Nathan and Vic were in front of me, gently pulling me into a group hug.

"What are you guys doing here?"

"Where else would we be?" Vic asked with a sniff.

Nathan kissed the top of my head. "Our girl needed us." He glanced at Hunter. "Thankfully, *someone* let us know what had happened."

I winced. "Sorry."

"You should be," Nathan sniped. "You can make it up to us by eating everything on your plate. We've been cooking up a storm."

"I can see that." I took in all the familiar faces around make-shift tables, and tears burned the backs of my eyes.

Vic shooed us ahead. "Go on, sit. We'll get you everything you need."

As we made our way to a table, Cal and Ashley appeared. Cal wrapped an arm around me carefully. "I'm so glad you're okay. This bastard would've been a shell of a man without you."

Ashley stepped forward. "I'm glad, too. And"—she looked from me to Hunter and back again—"I'm sorry. Maybe we could start fresh?"

I gave her a small smile. "Fresh sounds good to me."

Hunter guided me to the table and pulled out my chair. My mouth fell open as I took in Bell and Ford. "This is your wedding morning. What are you doing here?"

Bell stood and came around to hug me as gently as possible. "We love you guys. There's nowhere else we'd rather be."

"Not exactly the wedding brunch you had in mind, though," Hunter said, shaking his head.

Ford appeared next to his brother. "We're together, and that's what matters."

I looked around the room, taking in everyone who was here. Crosby and Kenna with their two girls. Caelyn and Griffin, trying to referee Mia and Ava while Will just shook his head. Shay and Brody, who were feeding a strip of bacon to Bruno. Celeste and her grandsons. Hunter and Ford's parents.

And even though we'd been through hell, there was so much joy in this room. Love. Family. I felt for the necklace at my throat as warm arms came around me. "She'd love this, Jenn would. She always wanted to be surrounded by life like this."

Hunter pressed his lips to my temple. "You'll honor her every time we come together like this here."

Warmth spread through me at his words. A peace I hadn't known since Jenn had disappeared. "Thank you for giving it to me."

Hunter's lips met mine in a slow kiss. "It's the least I can do. You gave me everything."

Epilogue

Piper

SIX MONTHS LATER

I SLUNG MY BAG OVER MY SHOULDER AS I CLIMBED OUT OF my SUV. Hunter let out a low whistle from where he stood outside what would be our house a few months from now. "You're a sight for sore eyes."

I tore my gaze away from the framing I saw for the first time and took Hunter in. That disheveled brown hair and long scruff. Those eyes that saw everything. I loved him more today, and I hadn't thought that was possible. "Sorry I'm late. I had to get Suzanne set up at the front desk before I left."

Hunter strode forward and wrapped an arm around my waist, pulling me in and kissing me soundly. "You're worth the wait."

"And I brought dinner."

"Even better. We eating up here?"

"I thought it might be nice. And I wanted to really get a chance to see everything you've done."

Hunter released his hold on me so we could both take in the

house—the one he'd dreamt up all those months ago. We'd made some changes along the way as we planned, but it was still mostly the same structure from Hunter's sketchpad. "What do you think?"

My mouth stretched into a smile. "I think it's going to be amazing."

"Come on." Hunter held out a hand and started towards the front steps.

I set my bag down and then went on a Hunter-guided tour as he laid out where the open kitchen and living spaces would be. The library and mudroom. All the bedrooms upstairs. There would even be a gym and a home theater.

I spun around. "I'm really starting to see it. Show me again where the hot tub is going."

"Right over there on the back deck. With a little privacy lattice so I can get you naked in there."

I arched a brow in his direction. "You seem pretty confident."

He made his way back to me again, pulling me into his arms. "I am."

I nipped his bottom lip. "If you want to get me naked, you'll need to feed me first."

"Always want to keep you happy." Hunter released me and crossed to my bag, pulling out the blanket and spreading it across the floor.

I pulled out the two to-go meals I'd snagged from our new chef. "I got you the chicken penne."

"You know I'm a sucker for it."

"I also brought this." I pulled out the copy of *Travel Magazine* and handed it to Hunter.

His eyes widened. "The cover? They gave you the cover?"

I nodded, tears filling my eyes. "When I went to The General Store to get my copy, Caelyn was beaming. She handed over a stack of about twenty of them. The editor didn't even tell me we were on the cover."

Hunter stared down at the glossy photo. It was me, him, and Bruno in front of a newly restored cabin. The photographer had caught us mid-laugh as Bruno jumped and twirled. There was so much life in the image. He looked up and met my gaze, moving in close but not touching me. "I'm so damn proud of you."

"Of *us*." My attack had been the wake-up call I'd needed. I lost my drive to do everything alone and welcomed the help. Over the past six months, the Falls had truly come to be both mine and Hunter's. Honestly, our whole community's in a way.

Brody's painting of Jenn on the cliffs hung in the lodge. Shay and Caelyn had cooked up a feast for our official grand opening. Griffin had become a de facto member of Hunter's crew. Bell had helped me decorate each and every cabin. And Ford had been Hunter's silent support as he worked through what had happened to me. My uncles came out almost every weekend to lend a hand or simply enjoy the peace. And Hunter's parents had brought us more meals than I could count as we worked to get the place going.

Whispering Falls had become all of ours. And in that, I felt like it honored Jenn even more. I found my friend in so many places around the resort. In occasional tears, of course, but so much more in the laughter. In memories that would hit me and remind me that I would always find her there.

I fisted my hands in Hunter's t-shirt and rose on tiptoe to brush my lips across his. "Love you."

His arms encircled me, a hand dipping beneath my hair. "Never get tired of hearing those words."

I tipped my head back so I could see his eyes. "Ask me."

His mouth curved. "Ask you what?"

"To marry you."

He stilled his ministrations on my nape. "What?"

"Ask me to marry you. Or are you going to hold me to asking you?"

Hunter shook his head. "Are you for real right now? I don't have a ring. The house isn't done. I—"

My kiss silenced him. "All I need is you."

His eyes blazed with everything that was beyond words. "Marry me, Casper."

"Yes." It was the only word we needed.

Hunter lifted me in the air, bringing his mouth to mine. "Never been happier than I am in this moment."

Tears spilled over my eyelids. "Thanks for giving me this home. It's what I always dreamed of but was afraid to reach for."

He linked his fingers with mine. "It's yours, forever. Just like I am."

I pulled him in close. "I can't imagine anything better."

THE END

Acknowledgments

I can't believe the final (for now anyway) Wrecked book is here. So many people have supported me as I worked on these books, and I'm grateful for every single one. An extra-special thank you to Laura and Willow for making this solo career a lot less lonely, and a lot more fun. Emma, for being my forever sounding board and listening ear. I can't imagine doing this without you. Grahame, for letting me drone on about every crazy idea I ever have and always being so incredibly supportive. And to the Goldbricker ladies for all of the motivation and encouragement.

To all my family and friends. Thank you for supporting me on this crazy journey, even if you don't read "kissing books."

To my fearless beta readers: Angela, Crystal, and Trisha, thank you for reading this book in its roughest form and helping me to make it the best it could possibly be!

The crew that helps bring my words to life and gets them out into the world is pretty darn epic. Thank you to Susan, Chelle, Janice, Julie, Hang, Stacey, Jenn, and the rest of my team at Social Butterfly. Your hard work is so appreciated!

To all the bloggers who have taken a chance on my words... THANK YOU! Your championing of my stories means more than I can say. To my launch and ARC teams, thank you for your kindness, support, and sharing my books with the world. And an extra special thank you to Crystal for wrangling it all.

Ladies of Catherine Cowles Reader Group, you're my favorite place to hang out on the internet! Thank you for your support, encouragement, and willingness to always dish about your latest book boyfriends. You're the freaking best!

Lastly, thank YOU! Yes, YOU. I'm so grateful you're reading this book and making my author dreams come true. I love you for that. A whole lot!

Also Available from
CATHERINE COWLES

The Wrecked Series
Reckless Memories
Perfect Wreckage
Wrecked Palace
Reckless Refuge
Beneath the Wreckage

The Sutter Lake Series
Beautifully Broken Pieces
Beautifully Broken Life
Beautifully Broken Spirit
Beautifully Broken Control

Stand-alone Novels
Further To Fall

For up-to-date information on all titles, please visit:
www.catherinecowles.com.

About

CATHERINE COWLES

Writer of words. Drinker of Diet Cokes. Lover of all things cute and furry, especially her dog. Catherine has had her nose in a book since the time she could read and finally decided to write down some of her own stories. When she's not writing, she can be found exploring her home state of Oregon, listening to true crime podcasts, or searching for her next book boyfriend.

Stay Connected

You can find Catherine in all the usual bookish places...

Website: catherinecowles.com

Facebook: www.facebook.com/catherinecowlesauthor

Catherine Cowles Facebook Reader Group:
www.facebook.com/groups/CatherineCowlesReaderGroup

Instagram: instagram.com/catherinecowlesauthor

Goodreads: goodreads.com/catherinecowlesauthor

BookBub: bookbub.com/profile/catherine-cowles

Amazon: www.amazon.com/author/catherinecowles

Twitter: twitter.com/catherinecowles

Pinterest: pinterest.com/catherinecowlesauthor

Made in United States
Orlando, FL
18 May 2024

46985203R00200